MALIK'S REVENGE

Alan Brodie Thrillers
Book 1

LES HASWELL

Chapter 1

THE SOLITARY FIGURE RAN AT PACE ALONG THE DESERTED, RAIN soaked beach. Despite the heavy rain and the soft golden sand underfoot, he was breathing comfortably, his feet hitting the ground in time to the music playing through his Bluetooth earbuds, his lips occasionally forming the words of the now familiar songs. This was a man in a world of his own, solitary, relaxed, enjoying life in his new home, despite the best attempts of the weather to dampen his spirits.

It rarely rains in the Almeria Region of Spain the people he had bought his villa from had told him. It rained very infrequently on the Almanzora region of the Costa Almeria, the desert of Europe, where Hollywood had filmed its Spaghetti Westerns. When it did rain, it tended to rain in short sharp torrents.

The man, well over six feet tall, had a muscular, athletic build, accentuated by the wet t-shirt clinging to his upper body. In his late thirties or early forties, his complexion was tanned, as you would expect of someone who lived in that area and spent much of his time outside. His unfashionably long, unruly mop of blond curly hair was tied back with a red headband.

He approached a beach front development of townhouses and apartments which fronted on to an adjoining paseo and small harbour with a number of berths associated with the development. Originally planned as a "Little Venice" style community, the worldwide financial and property market crash had ensured that the canals and bridges had been trimmed back to attractive avenues and small plazas all designed around the centrepiece of a large, Spanish fountain.

Running up the ramp on to the paseo the man passed the new buildings and harbour area without breaking stride. Along the harbour front was a small number of retail units, all displaying their wares in grill protected windows, wares which would later that morning spill out onto the promenade. In the middle of the paseo, a small harbour stretched out into the Mediterranean, one side of the wall had been formed into a small marina with the berths being allocated to the town-houses and apartments which made up the recently completed development. The other side of the wall had been formed into a small harbour for a select number of local fishing boats.

Approaching the end unit, a popular bar/restaurant, El Puerto, which he visited regularly for a light lunch or a few evening drinks, he noticed with more than a passing interest, a "Se Vende" ("For Sale") sign in the window. He ran down the ramp at the other end of the paseo and continued along the beach to his home.

The market crash had allowed him to buy what was now his main home, from a Dutch couple, in severe financial trouble, desperate to offload their Spanish property at around sixty percent of the original purchase price. He was in the right place at the right time and as a cash buyer it was an opportunity not to missed

His was a modern, three bedroom beachfront villa, one of six built as part of a recently constructed development, built in traditional Moorish style, popular along that stretch of the

Spanish coastline. An open plan living and dining area; ensuite bedroom and a kitchen took up most of the ground floor. A stairway in one corner of the living area led to the upper floor. The first floor consisted of two double ensuite bedrooms, the master bedroom had its own private roof terrace which gave uninterrupted views of the beach, the small harbour and across the clear blue waters of the Mediterranean. The front door opened out to a large garden; two sets of French doors led from the lounge onto an extensive full-width wooden terrace over-looking the pool and the beach beyond. The entire footprint of the house was home to a spacious basement which he was considering kitting out as a gym.

As he went upstairs to the shower room, his thoughts turned again to the "Se Vende" sign on El Puerto. He knew the Spanish couple who ran the bar, well enough to help them out on the odd occasion when they were really busy. It seemed strange to him that they had said nothing about leaving. Lunchtime would give him an opportunity to talk to the couple in an effort to satisfy his curiosity.

By the time he had showered, dressed and breakfasted it was almost nine o'clock. The rain had thankfully stopped and the skies were returning to their normal cloudless blue. He wandered around the kitchen, listing things he needed from the supermarket in Garrucha and set off to do his shopping. His car was parked in a garage at the side of the house. Stopping only to power down the roof on the red Ford Mustang, he drove out into bright sunlight.

Supermarket shopping was not an enjoyable experience for the man, more a necessary evil. He grabbed a trolley, strode round the aisles, ticked off the items on his list and hit the checkout all within twenty minutes. He made his way down to the supermarket's underground car park, dropped his supplies onto the passenger seat of the car, and headed for home.

Chapter 2

DRESSED IN A PAIR OF DENIM SHORTS AND A WHITE LINEN SHIRT, he strolled from his beach house to El Puerto, grabbed a stool at the bar, swivelling round to watch the activity around the small marina and paseo. He watched two men in a small fishing boat lift their catch onto the quayside, then into a little white SEAT van. He smiled and waved as one of his neighbours walked past the bar with his wife. At long last, he had found somewhere which he was happy to call home. He loved the pace of life, the social lifestyle that the climate afforded and although sometimes irritating, the "manana" attitude to life. He had a comfortable villa in a small, quiet development, which overlooked the beach and was a two-minute walk from the marina and the welcoming ambiance of El Puerto. His neighbours, mostly Spanish, with a smattering of northern European expats, were friendly without being intrusive. Some, who were not permanent residents, let out their properties from time to time. They all had their own lives and spent little time intruding or enquiring into that of others. No one was interested in his past.

"Hey! Big Al."

A familiar friendly voice broke into his musings. He swivelled round to face the petite figure behind the bar.

"Wee Conchie," he addressed Conchita Gutiérrez, who with Manuel her husband, owned El Puerto. She laughed and came round the bar to get a big friendly hug from her favourite customer.

She looked up at him with a smile, "I swear you get higher every time I see you," she laughed, patting his chest.

"What you want, a beer?

"No, una cerveza, por favor"

"That's what I said, you big lump"

"Oh, sorry. Me being Scottish, my English isn't too good, Conchie."

"You're a bad boy, Alan Brodie," Conchita chided as she opened a bottle of chilled Corona, which she placed on the bar in front of him. "You want some food or just your cerveza?"

"You got any cocido montañés left?" he asked looking at the Menu del Dia.

"Si, plenty left"

"OK, I'll have that, please"

"She disappeared into the kitchen, returning a few minutes later with a large steaming tureen of Cantabrian Mountain Stew and a plentiful supply of fresh crusty bread.

As Brodie ate, he noticed the bar was very quiet and took the opportunity to nod at the "For Sale" sign.

"What's all this Conchie? How do I get fed now?"

"Is too much, this place and the bar in Mojácar, so we sell this and keep the other one we've had for years. We have built a good business here but now we look for someone to buy it from us."

"I might be interested Conchie, that's why I came round today, I saw the sign this morning when I was out running. I've been looking for something to do out here for a while. I've looked at a couple of other bars, one in Mojácar and one in

Villaricos. I've worked in bars before and I live just along the beach. It just kind of appeals to me. What do you think?"

"Maybe too busy for you, am not sure." Conchita shrugged at him. "You should talk with Manuel."

"OK." Brodie said, somewhat deflated by Conchita's lack of enthusiasm for his approach. "Maybe I'll pop into Mojácar tomorrow and have a chat with him."

Having finished his lunch, he said goodbye to Conchita and walked back along the beach, which was now neither rain-soaked nor deserted. This afternoon was all about getting information to his accountant for his UK tax return, so he set about doing that with little enthusiasm. He took his laptop and paperwork out to his roof terrace and sat in a shaded corner where he was able to read the laptop screen, and lost the rest of the afternoon in receipts, accounts and HMRC forms. He only realised how much of the afternoon he had taken up with these when, due to lack of daylight, he found himself unable to read some of the receipts. At that point he cleared up everything, went back down to the living area on the ground floor, and put everything except his laptop into a small safe in the lounge.

He spent the next hour preparing his dinner, which he took out to his terrace with a glass of Rioja Reserva and sat listening to the rhythmic breaking of the waves while enjoying his own recipe, chicken and chorizo paella in the warm evening air. After dinner he returned to the terrace, read some more of a book, pouring a couple more glasses of wine as the evening passed. At around 10.30 he went back inside, set the alarm system then headed to bed.

Chapter 3

THE NEXT DAY, AFTER HIS MORNING RUN, BRODIE HEADED TO THE Parque Comercial shopping centre in Mojácar in search of a couple of new shirts from his favourite clothes shop. He then made his way along the paseo, which ran the full length of Mojácar Playa to talk to Manuel about the bar in Puerto Ricos.

He arrived in Manuel's bar finding himself the only customer as it was still early for lunchtime traffic. There was no sign of Manuel. He picked a few nuts out of a bowl on the bar and was chewing on these when a tall slim man wearing a light grey suit and pale blue open neck shirt walked out of the kitchen followed closely by Manuel. The two men shook hands and as the tall man walked round the bar he pointed at the table closest to the window and asked Manuel for a coffee and a tostada con tomate, a fairly typical Spanish breakfast choice. Manuel waved him to the table and turning to walk back to the kitchen, noticed his other customer.

"*Hola, buenos dias mi amigo.* How are you?"

"I'm fine wee man, just wanted a refreshment and a chat"

"OK, two minutes, my friend," Manuel replied, disappearing into the kitchen. True to his word, Manuel reappeared a couple of minutes later. "Coffee or beer?" he addressed Brodie.

"Cerveza, por favor"

Manuel opened a chilled, dew-coated bottle of Corona and put it on the bar. "So, that's the refreshment you wanted, what you want to talk about?"

"El Puerto, I'm interested in buying it, Manuel. I've looked at a couple of bars before, I need to find something to do out here and that just fits the bill. I have no idea how much you want for it or how to go about getting the licence but I thought if we could talk a deal, you might help me with what I need to do."

Manuel looked over at the man sitting at the table, now with his coffee and tostada con tomate, then back at Brodie.

"If you're serious, we agree a price, and you go to the Town Hall and apply for a licence. If the Mayor's office gives you the licence you can run the bar, but the Mayor's office might not give you the licence because you are an expat"

"There are loads of expats running bars, Manuel."

"Ah, that's the problem, too many." Manuel's eyes again flicked towards the man in the grey suit.

"OK, but surely it's worth a try," Brodie persisted.

"Sure, but don't think it would be easy."

"What about price then?"

"It's on the market for 270,000 euros. For you, I would take 250,000 euros but a mortgage would be difficult for you, after the property crash."

"I wouldn't need a mortgage, Manuel, it would be a cash sale."

"What, you a millionaire?" Manuel joked.

"Strangely enough, yeah. I sold my parents' property in Scotland a wee while back, so I'm not short of a bob or two"

"What is a 'bob or two'?"

Brodie laughed, "Sorry, Manuel, Scottish euphemism. Let's

just say I've got funds to buy the bar if you'll sell it to me. You don't seem keen. Maybe you think I can't run it."

"No, no, I just think it might take up too much of your time. I know you do all kinds of security work."

"I'm getting too old for that. I left the forces to get away from all that. It's about time I settled down, Manuel, found a good woman, bought a pair of slippers, traded the Mustang in and bought myself a little SEAT."

"Hey, I watch you, you have plenty women, some good, some not so good, some bad maybe, you know that better than me," Manuel laughed.

"Sounds as if you have a buyer for your bar in Puerto Ricos, my friend."

The tall man in the grey suit was standing just behind them. "Sorry, I couldn't help overhearing," he said as he placed his empty plate, cup and saucer on the bar. "I should go Manuel. Thank you for breakfast."

He turned to leave just as a group of British holidaymakers came into the bar and Manuel went to greet them.

"Come down to the bar tomorrow night, early, before we get busy; we can talk more."

"OK, I'll do that. See you then."

Chapter 4

THE NEXT DAY WAS VIRTUALLY A REPEAT OF THE DAY BEFORE, except Brodie spent an hour in his basement gym before showering and eating breakfast. His morning run had not been blighted by torrential rain, rather it was blessed by the blue sky and warming sunshine which was the norm for the region. This was followed by more receipts and invoices, lunch and then reading and answering email.

He spent some time on the internet, reading information and guidance on the Spanish licencing laws required to own and run a bar in the Almeria region. It appeared that the licence was attached to the business not the owner, but would normally require to be transferred to the new owner at a cost of around 600 euros. An ex-pat was required to have a Residencia, a Spanish residency permit and a national insurance or NIE number, which Brodie had acquired when buying his house and opening his Spanish bank account. Similarly, he had appointed a local solicitor to facilitate the purchase of the beach house and he had worked well on Brodie's behalf, spoke good English, and had introduced him to a local sports club and golf club.

At four o'clock that afternoon, he headed along the beach paseo to El Puerto for a chat with Manuel.

As he approached the bar, a vaguely familiar, tall, slim figure exited wearing a pale grey suit and an open-neck white shirt. Brodie recognised him from the previous day, sitting in Manuel's bar in Mojácar. The tall figure turned his head and looked in both directions, up and down the paseo; he noticed Brodie, nodded and smiled briefly then made off in the opposite direction.

Brodie walked into the bar, waved to Manuel, and sat at a quiet corner table at the back of the room.

"Your wine?" Manuel enquired.

"Si, gracias," Brodie replied.

Being a regular customer, Brodie had his favourite Rioja Reserva behind the bar. He bought a bottle of the wine, but didn't necessarily finish it the same night, so Manuel or Conchita would replace the cork and bring it out on Brodie's next visit.

Manuel brought his wine over to the table and sat down.

"So, you want to buy El Puerto, do you?"

"Yeah, I would, Manuel. I have been looking at bars in the area for a while now and really wasn't seeing anything that ticked all the boxes. I've always liked the set-up here, the location, atmosphere, the clientele. I see how busy the place is, I know the staff you have, and it ticks all my boxes. The price is about right, in comparison with others that I've looked at. I know and trust you and Conchita, so yeah, all things being equal..."

"OK, if you are certain and you're happy with the price. In Spain we always ask for more than we expect, so as I said, for you, I will reduce the price from 270,000 euros to 250,000 euros."

"What about the flat above? That's yours as well and I see you have a 'For Sale' sign on the window."

"*Si,* yes, it is a three bedroom, two bathroom apartment, with that big balcony at the front. There is an underground carpark with a private space. I can show you if you have time, but you have that beautiful house and it's not too far from here."

"Sure, but I could rent that out in the summer; it would make sense for me to live above the shop."

Manuel took Brodie up to show him the flat.

"This was one of the show apartments when the development was built and it was finished and furnished with no expense spared as you can see. We bought it fully furnished as an investment. Not a good decision, Alan, we will lose about one third of what we paid for it, but sadly, the market crashed just after we bought it. I will leave the keys for you to have a look around and I will see you downstairs when you have seen everything you want to see."

"OK, thanks, Manuel."

Brodie looked round the apartment. It had a large master bedroom and two further bedrooms, both of reasonable size, all with built-in wardrobes and a large family bathroom. The master bedroom had an en-suite shower and access to the balcony, which stretched around two sides of the apartment. A fully fitted kitchen was separated from the dining and lounge area by a marble-topped worktop and breakfast bar. The lounge had bifold doors on one wall, opening out onto the same large balcony which was also accessed from the master bedroom. The balcony here was much wider than at the side of the property and overlooked the beach, the paseo, and the harbour. In contrast to the traditional exterior of the property, the apartment was fully furnished and equipped in a modern, tasteful manner, which, as Manuel has said, gave the impression of being high quality throughout. As Brodie was about to leave the apartment, he opened a door in the square entrance hall at the bottom of the stairs and found a small but adequate utility and cloakroom.

He was impressed and told Manuel so, when he returned to the bar.

"I like it Manuel. How much is the asking price?"

"I have spoken to Conchita and we have agreed that if you are buying the bar and the apartment, we would ask for 400,000 euros for both. 250,000 for the business and 150,000 for the apartment, which is a good deal less than we paid for it, but, that is the market."

"Are you sure? You might get more for the apartment."

"Maybe, but it makes sense, as you say, to sell both together and we are selling to someone we know."

"Fine by me Manuel. Do you want to shake hands on a deal now or do you want to talk with Conchita first?"

"No, I already spoke with Conchita, she is happy for you to buy. Let's shake hands on a deal. We can talk to our solicitors, then when they are happy they can get us some contracts to sign."

The two men shook hands.

"We should celebrate," Manuel said as he rose from his seat. "Conchita? Conchita, bring a bottle of Champagne and three glasses.

Manuel's wife appeared from the kitchen, carrying her husband's order and placed the bottle and glasses on the table. "Congratulations, Big Al. Manuel and I have worked hard to build a good local trade and we know that you will be good for business. People like you and they will still come here to support you."

The three raised their glasses.

"Salud!"

"Cheers!"

"Salud!"

They talked about the business, the transfer of ownership and what it entailed.

"You need insurances and a safety certificate from a man who checks emergency lighting and fire extinguishers," Manuel said.

"And a food safety certificate. You need go to Almeria for training, it takes three hours."

They chatted about other aspects of the business, Manuel agreed to introduce Brodie to his suppliers.

Suddenly, Brodie asked, "Who's the guy with the grey suit, Manuel? He was in the bar in Mojácar the day I came in to see you and he left tonight, just as I was coming in."

Conchita and Manuel looked at him then at each other. "He is a friend of mine. I know him from university in Madrid."

"OK," Brodie replied, somewhat unconvinced.

The bar was starting to get busier with the evening trade, some ordering food, others just happy to relax with a drink, picking at nuts or olives from the bar or table. The bar employed a chef and two others in the kitchen as well as three waiting staff. Conchita and Manuel had asked Brodie not to say anything about him buying the business until the deal was completed and he had agreed.

He decided to eat at the bar, as he was there anyway and ordered a chicken and chorizo pie which he washed down with the rest of his bottle of Rioja. He paid his bill, waved goodnight to Conchita and Manuel and headed home.

He checked his email, answered ones needing a response then poured himself a sparkling water and carried that and his Kindle out to the terrace where he sat overlooking the swimming pool, contemplating the purchase of El Puerto and the apartment above. He would move into the apartment and use the beach house as a rental property in the summer months as he had suggested to Manuel. He then read his Kindle for a while before heading for bed. He lay awake for some time thinking about the bar and the apartment and the changes it would make to his life, eventually falling asleep in the wee small hours.

Chapter 5

IT TOOK BRODIE THREE DAYS TO GET AN APPOINTMENT WITH HIS solicitor and Manuel two days, but both solicitors pulled out all the stops to move the normally slow and convoluted Spanish legal process along as quickly as they could. Fortunately, because El Puerto was part of a recent development and Manuel was well known at the Ayuntamiento or Town Hall, as he was a good friend of the local Mayor, the documentation flew through the approval process and went to Brodie's solicitor in a matter of days rather than weeks.

While all this was happening, Brodie spent 50 euros and three hours in Almeria getting his food safety certificate. The survey for the safety certificate was arranged and Brodie's solicitor paid the 600 euro fee for the transfer of the licence together with his ten percent deposit which was legally required, to secure the purchase of the bar. Brodie also lodged the balance of the funds in his solicitor's client account. All that remained was for the contracts to be signed by both parties and the Ayuntamiento to approve them and transfer the licence. It had taken just over three weeks to get to this stage.

During this period, Manuel had informed the staff that

Brodie was buying El Puerto; all of them were delighted that their new boss was someone they knew and liked and not a stranger, or worse a national chain. Brodie was also taken to meet all the main food and beverage suppliers. Some had asked him to fill in forms to open accounts, others didn't bother and were happy to continue with business as usual. Manuel also allowed him to work behind the bar for a few shifts to acquaint him with the equipment.

One evening, he decided to check out what would become his nearest competition to El Puerto so he walked along the beach to Villaricos, just over a kilometre from Puerto Ricos. This had been a small fishing village whose popularity with tourists had seen a number of, mainly high end developments with a mix of apartments and townhouses spring up over the years. As a result, almost a third of the village's population was expat British.

Brodie had been told that Spain had more bars per capita of population than any other country in the world and walking into Villaricos did nothing to contradict that fact. There was a varied selection of bars and restaurants in the village, from the small and traditional ones which sold no food, to one or two fairly upmarket eating establishments. The one Brodie had chosen to visit was run by a British couple who had lived in Spain for almost twenty years and had run a small pub in London's east end before settling in Spain. Barril Rojo, or Red Barrel, was so named as a reminder to its owner of his favourite pint, Watneys Red Barrel.

This wasn't Brodie's first visit to the Barril Rojo and the owner acknowledged him as he stood at the bar.

"All right, mate, good to see you again. What'll you 'ave?"

"I'll have a nice Rioja, thanks," Brodie replied looking at a blackboard on the wall displaying the menu.

"And a bowl of your chilli," he added.

"No problem," the host said as he handed Brodie a glass of

Rioja. "Grab a table while you got a chance and we'll bring the food over."

"I'll sit outside if that's OK?"

"Yeah, yeah, go for it, mate."

Brodie found a table on the wooden decking at the front of the outside area and sat facing the road, watching people and vehicles as they passed. He loved people-watching.

A few minutes later a young waiter brought his food to his table. Brodie asked him for another glass of Rioja, then attacked his sizable bowl of food with vigour. As he sat, eating what was a very passable chilli, he noticed four people walking toward the bar. Three young men, who looked and sounded as if their next drink would not be their first of the evening but otherwise everything about them was pretty average; height, build, hair, clothes. The woman with them on the other hand, was anything but average; she was absolutely stunning. Taller than two of the men, slim, with dark skin, which suggested a mix of Spanish and African heritage, long black curls fell past her shoulders. She wore white leggings with a tight fitting emerald green top and a heavy multi-coloured necklace with matching large hoop earrings. This was a girl who dressed to be noticed, Brodie mused as they passed him.

The four entered the bar and Brodie heard them order drinks; he was seated looking out to the road rather than into the bar. He continued to watch the comings and goings from the Barril Rojo and was considering leaving to walk home when he became aware of raised voices in the bar and turned to see the young woman's three friends shouting at each other and then at her. The shortest of the three, had obviously had drink spilled on him and was remonstrating with the others. Brodie's Spanish was passable but these people were shouting very quickly and in an extremely agitated manner, in an already noisy environment, making it difficult for him to fully understand what they were saying. It was obvious, however, that they were having a heated argument.

The woman left her empty glass on the bar and turned to leave. As she got to the door the shortest of the three men moved quickly, slapping her on the back of her head. The woman shouted at him and tried to step out of his reach, bumping into Brodie's table, but the man grabbed hold of her arm pulling her back, causing her to knock Brodie's table away from him, tipping over his empty wine glass.

Brodie stood up and stretched his arm across the front of the woman and placed his hand on the man's shoulder.

"Enough, let her go!"

The man looked at Brodie, but kept a grip on the woman.

"Go back to your own country. This has nothing to do with you," the man growled in heavily accented English and pushed Brodie back.

"You just made it my business. Now let go of her arm and if you push me once more, you'll regret it!"

The smaller man stared at Brodie for a second, then placed his free hand on his chest and tried to push him.

"Bad move, pal," Brodie snarled and slammed a sledge-hammer fist into the soft flesh of the man's solar plexus. The unexpected blow sent him flying across the open doorway and he crashed into the upright, hitting the back of his head on the woodwork as he fell over an empty table by the door.

As he lay on the floor, barely conscious, gasping for breath, the man's two friends came running out of the bar. The woman moved onto the road and shouted something that Brodie didn't hear. The first man out looked at his friend sprawled on the floor and turned to aim a punch at Brodie's head but he saw it coming, blocked the punch with his left arm, stepped forward, and delivered a perfectly executed head-butt to the man's nose. The man's nose broke and began to gush blood onto the front of his shirt as he collapsed in a heap on the floor. The woman's third companion was by this time shaping up to deliver a haymaker right hook to the side of Brodie's head, but was halted in his tracks as Brodie stepped inside the well telegraphed blow and brought his knee up viciously into the man's groin. He dropped to the ground, emitting a high pitched moan, holding his damaged genitals with both hands in a vain attempt to ease the excruciating pain.

Just then, someone grabbed Brodie's shoulder roughly from behind. He reacted immediately, swinging his right elbow into the person's midriff and turned to face his new assailant. He was faced with a rather portly police officer holding his belly and became aware of a second officer standing on the road in front of a green and white Nissan Patrol of the Guàrdia Civil, its blue roof lights flashing. This officer was pointing a pistol at him.

Brodie raised his hands and looked at the officer he had hit. He was still obviously in pain but recovering.

"Really sorry, I didn't realise who you were. Having said that, you shouldn't approach someone the way you did, it's asking for trouble, mate."

"Turn around and put your hands behind your back," the police officer with the gun shouted at Brodie.

"Sorry!"

"I said turn around and put your hands behind your back. Do as I say."

"Why, what's your problem?"

"Not my problem, your problem. Now, do as I say." The police officer took a step forward and lowered his pistol to point it at Brodie's leg.

"OK, OK, don't get carried away," Brodie turned round and put his hands behind his back as instructed and immediately felt the, now recovered officer, handcuff his wrists.

Both officers pushed him roughly towards the waiting police vehicle.

"What's all this in aid of? What have I done to warrant being handcuffed?"

"You are under arrest for assaulting three members of the public and a police officer."

Brodie stopped beside the vehicle. "You what? They attacked me, not the other way around, I just defended myself."

"Ask her," Brodie suggested, looking round for the woman who had been with the three men. The woman was nowhere to be seen.

"Get into the car," the first officer demanded, pushing Brodie into the Patrol slamming the door shut.

Chapter 6

BRODIE WAS TAKEN TO A POLICE STATION IN MOJÁCAR, HIS pockets emptied, his belt and watch taken, then he was dumped unceremoniously into a cell, his handcuffs removed and the door slammed shut. He looked around the cell. It was a Tom Jones room, four grey walls now surrounded him. There was a narrow bed against one wall and a small stainless steel toilet and basin in one corner. No windows just one locked door. The main overhead light was switched off and a solitary weak bulb shone from above the door, shedding only enough light into the room to allow someone from outside to see if a prisoner was up to no good.

"Oh great!" Brodie sighed. It was obvious to him that he was there for the night, so he accepted the inevitable and laid down on the thin mattress, which barely covered the bed. He lay awake for a while contemplating his predicament, eventually falling asleep.

He didn't sleep well or for long. He got up, walked over to the sink and splashed his face with cold water. He had no towel so wiped his hands dry on his jeans, then proceeded to do a round of exercises: one hundred sit-ups followed by a similar number of press-ups. He was about to start his squats when the door to his cell opened and two guards appeared.

The older guard, who was very overweight and sweating profusely, stood at the door while the other, a younger, almost skinny officer with a prematurely receding hairline, brought a tray of food and a cup of coffee into the room, laying it carefully on the end of the bed. He kept well out of Brodie's reach and looked extremely apprehensive, never taking his eyes off him.

Brodie stood up quickly and growled at the young guard then laughed as he watched him scuttle quickly into the safety of the corridor. The older guard could not stop himself from smiling at his young colleague's reaction. The door slammed shut again.

Breakfast consisted of bread, two boiled eggs and a polystyrene cup of unexpectedly palatable, hot, black coffee, all of which Brodie ingested hungrily.

Brodie lay back on the bed for a few minutes, his mind straying back to the events of the previous night and wondered what the Spanish police's next move would be. He hadn't assaulted anyone, they had attacked him. All he had done was robustly defend himself, while trying not to cause serious injury to any of the men. He had known that none of them were likely to be capable of hurting him unless he gave them the opportunity. He had simply denied them that opportunity, using what he considered to be reasonable force.

The cell door being opened interrupted his ruminations. He found two police officers standing in the doorway, one of them holding a pistol and the other, a small heavily built man with a receding hairline and, a set of handcuffs.

"Put your hands behind your back," the officer with the handcuffs said in his heavily accented English, holding up the cuffs to show his intent.

Brodie stood up and complied; the officer cuffed his wrists and pulled on his arm.

"Come with me."

The other officer stood back from the door and showed Brodie to the left down the corridor and into the main office area. He led him into a large corner office and instructed him to sit on one of two tubular metal chairs padded at the back and seat. both facing a large dark wooden desk, with two piles of files, two telephones, two large computer monitors and a keyboard. A large, executive office chair sat behind the desk. The room also had the usual array of filing cabinets, with more files stacked on top of them. A large window opened out on to a view of the car park and the gable end of a small supermarket. The two police officers stood in the doorway, hands clasped behind their backs, eyes blankly staring out of the window.

Brodie became aware of movement by the door and turned to see a tall slim figure, still wearing a light grey suit standing in the doorway. He gestured to the two officers at the door, "Please, I see no need for the handcuffs."

One of the officers stepped into the room and deftly removed the handcuffs from Brodie's wrists

"Thank you, that will be all," the man nodded to the two officers. They left the room and stood in the corridor. The new arrival closed the door, walked across the office and sat in the high backed chair behind the desk and leaned back, smiling at Brodie.

"So, we meet again Señor Brodie."

"Are you stalking me?" Brodie enquired.

The man hesitated.

"I suppose in a way I am. I don't think we have been formally introduced, Señor Brodie. I am Comisario Xavier Moreno and yes we have a mutual friend in Manuel Gutiérrez. I met Manuel at university in Madrid, we have kept in touch ever since. He is a good man, successful in business and has a lovely family, as you know. But what you do not know, is that he has a very large problem which is threatening both his business and his family, which I became aware of in the line of my duty."

"What kind of problem?"

"I will get to that, but first, let us talk about your problem. Last night you assaulted a number of men in a bar in Villaricos."

"Eh, no, let's get this straight before we go any further. I assaulted no one. I was attacked by three men in Barril Rojo last night. I defended myself using what I considered to be reasonable force, I could have killed all three of those guys last night, but I chose not to. I used only enough force to discourage them from hurting me. I think I am entitled to do that, Comisario."

Moreno picked up a pale blue file from his desk.

"Ah, I'm afraid that's not how it has been reported by the arresting officers, Señor Brodie. Who do you think the court is going to believe? Two police officers with exemplary records or an expat Englishman?"

"Scottish expat. I'm not English."

"Oh, I do beg your pardon, I should have known better."

"With all due respect, you know nothing about me, Comisario."

"Why do you British always start a sentence by saying 'with all due respect' when you are about to denigrate someone? I find that very odd. But in this case," he smiled, "with all due respect, nothing could be further from the truth Captain Brodie. I know a great deal about you."

He picked up the blue folder again and flicked through a few pages.

"You are Alan Nicolas Brodie, born in Perth Royal Infirmary on 15th of January 1989, father Colonel Nicolas Brodie, mother, Alice Brodie. Educated at Strathallan School and then St Andrews University. You then went to the Royal Military Academy, Sandhurst, graduated as a 2nd Lieutenant and joined The

Royal Regiment of Scotland. You were promoted to Lieutenant and were later, accepted into the 22nd Regiment of the Special Air Service. Much of the action which that Regiment sees is highly classified, but I do know that you have seen action in Iraq and Afghanistan, to name but two of your deployments. You were awarded The Distinguished Service Order for operational gallantry and successful command and leadership during active operations, then merited a second award of the DSO, which was added as a bar. Despite your rank, which by this time was Captain, you had a reputation, as my contact puts it, for 'getting stuck in'. You left the military four years ago and since then have worked as a freelance security advisor. Your parents were killed two years ago in an automobile accident, when their vehicle was in collision with a large, fully grown deer. You bought a house in Playa Marques three years ago. You recently sold your parents' house in Scotland and are in the process of acquiring a bar in Puerto Ricos, although you still require the transfer of the licence."

"Well, well, you really have done your homework. You've gone to a lot of trouble to find all that out and I'm sure you had your reasons. So, do you want to tell me what this is all about?"

Chapter 7

"Very astute. You are correct, of course. Why would I go to all this trouble to find out so much about a man who has just been arrested for assault?

Being arrested for assault in a bar and assaulting a police officer is not a good way to convince the Town Hall that you are the correct person to hold a licence to own and operate licenced premises, so I think that will be a big problem for you, Señor Brodie.

However, perhaps I can make that problem go away"

Brodie leaned forward in his chair. "I'll take my chance in court before I'd give you any money and if it costs me the El Puerto, then so be it. You'd best just take me back to my cell." Brodie stood and turned to the door.

"I don't want your money, Señor Brodie, I want your help." Moreno leant back in his swivel chair once again. "Help to make Manuel Gutiérrez's problem go away."

"Sorry?" Brodie turned and stared at Moreno. "What did you say?"

"I said I want your help to make Manuel Gutiérrez's problem go away. Please sit down. I am not a stupid or impetuous man, nor am I dishonest and your actions have proved to me that you are also a man of integrity. I don't want your money, I want your help, Señor Brodie."

Brodie walked back to his chair. "Help with what? What's this got to do with Manuel?"

"I will explain. First, some coffee." Moreno lifted the phone on his desk and ordered coffee for two.

A few moments later, there was a soft knock on the door.

"Come," Moreno answered. The door opened and a young woman brought a tray with coffees and Amoretti biscuits.

"Thank you Maria."

Moreno poured two coffees and gestured for Brodie to help himself to cream and sugar.

"Manuel has built a good business at El Puerto, in a fairly short time and the clientele is in the main…. affluent, much of it attributable to the proximity of the marina and some fairly high-end property development in that area. But you know all this, because you live not far from the Bar and frequent it regularly.

What you may not know, is that there is a growing problem in the area with the importation and use of drugs, mainly heroin and cocaine. The people who are bringing in the majority of the drugs are from Eastern Europe or Russians, as in this case and they are using North Africa as a route to Spain. A few months ago, one of the cartels announced to Manuel that they intended to use El Puerto as a drop-off point for their dealers and for selling their drugs. If he did not comply, they threatened they would hurt him or even worse, his family. They said if he went to the police, there would be a death in his family. These are not nice people, Señor Brodie."

"OK, so where do I come in?" Brodie leaned back on his seat.

"Manuel has told me as a friend, not as a policeman, that he was being threatened by these people, so I advised him to sell

El Puerto, use the excuse that two bars was too much for him and Conchita. That way he would not have the worry of these people, the person who bought the bar would be the person they would threaten and it would give us time to investigate who they are and how to get to them. Then you came along, wanting to buy the bar. First impressions were that maybe you were someone we could work with to put these people in prison.

Before we could talk I needed to do my homework. I needed to find out more about you, who you were, what you were, could you be trusted." He patted the file on his desk. "After all that I have read in here, I would trust you with my life, Señor Brodie. Still, I needed to know how you would react to physical threat."

Brodie sat upright, "You set up that fight in the Barril Rojo!"

"I said I was not dishonest, Señor Brodie, I did not say I was not devious."

"You bastard, Moreno. I probably broke that guy's nose."

"That was not part of my plan, but I will do anything I can to make sure my old friend comes to no harm and if that includes being slightly devious then so be it."

"Slightly devious, slightly devious. You set me up in a bar fight last night, got a guy's nose broken, and then have the gall to try to blackmail me into helping you, threatening my bar licence by seeing me in court for assault and that's only *slightly* devious. That's not slightly anything; that's breaking the law, Mr Policeman."

"What laws have I broken? You hit the police officers in the bar, not me. I am not blackmailing you. I may have suggested that we might come to an understanding over certain matters, but blackmail is a very strong word. Now that we have spoken, there is no need for us to worry about assault charges, as you seem willing to help Manuel, and that is what this is all about.

Tell me, Señor Brodie, if it was your friend, what would you do?

Brodie leaned forward in his chair, his head in his hands. He sat for a minute then looked up at Moreno.

"He *is* my friend, Comisario Moreno."

"Then you will help?"

"Yes, of course I will, but you only had to ask. You didn't need to go through all this," he gestured to the office.

"I had to be sure of you. Remember, I knew nothing of you except what Manuel told me."

"He knew you were going to have me arrested?"

"No, no. He knew nothing of this; he only knew we were going to speak about the problem that he spoke to me about in complete confidence. But I needed to find out what kind of man you really are. What we are about to do could have been very bad for Manuel if you did not handle it properly, so, I apologise for my actions but, as I say, I needed to be sure that I was not putting my friend's life at risk."

"OK, I understand.... I think!"

"There is one other thing."

"Yes?" Brodie hesitated.

"I need you to employ one of my officers to work behind the bar."

"What? You're joking! These guys would pick out a great, flat footed, hairy arsed policeman in two seconds flat."

"I understand that, Señor Brodie, but let me assure you that the officer in question has got neither flat feet nor a hairy arse."

"You sound very confident of both, Comisario, which I find a bit worrying," Brodie raised an eyebrow.

Moreno laughed. "I can see why that might worry you, but trust me, you will see why I can be so positive." He picked up the telephone on his desk and pressed a button.

"Ask Sergeant Malik to come through now." He hung up.

"I am sure you and Sergeant Malik will work well together

against these drug smugglers. Two heads are better that one. These are no amateurs, they are well organised and resourced."

As Moreno spoke there was a light knock on the office door behind Brodie.

"Ah, Anita, you and Señor Brodie have met, although in somewhat less cordial circumstances, sadly of my making."

Brodie turned in his seat to find a familiar face smiling awkwardly down at him.

"Sergeant Malik? Oh boy, was I ever stitched up." He shook his head at the tall, dark skinned, curly haired beauty he had last seen in the Barril Rojo the previous night.

She was dressed in a pair of loose, camouflage, cargo trousers and a plain white t-shirt, her hair pulled back into a loose ponytail, but still looked as striking as she had done the night before.

"You're right, Comisario, she doesn't have flat feet."

"Please, Señor Brodie, do not be too hard on Sergeant Malik. You must understand, she was acting on my orders last night, as were the other officers, although maybe they suffered a little more for their attention to duty." He gestrured.

"Please, Anita, take a seat, we need to tell Señor Brodie what we require. As I have mentioned, these people want to use El Puerto as a place where they can supply and sell their drugs.
"

"We want you to allow them to do so, watch them, listen to them and find out as much about their organisation as you can, but do not make them suspicious of you. Try if possible to gain their trust and find out who is further up the chain of command in their organisation. I do not know the best way to do this, but you are experienced in these matters, so I will leave it up to your judgement as to the best way to do this and how far you think you can take it without exposing yourself or Sergeant Malik to any unnecessary danger. Manuel does not know we are having these conversations, he does not know the risks you will be taking. He would not allow me to put you in such danger if he knew, because he says you are his friend. He likes you very much, Señor Brodie."

"Sergeant Malik is on secondment from Madrid as part of a group investigating a major international drugs cartel. She is not local and no one in the Almanzora region knows her, so she can work with you in the bar and not be recognised as a police officer."

"Right Comisario, I can't say I'm happy with your Sergeant being involved but I'll agree on one condition; you tell her she does what I tell her, no questions asked, no doing her own thing. An operation like this needs one leader."

"I'm sitting here, Señor Brodie. You can speak directly to me." Malik said curtly.

"Ah, but therein lies the problem, Sergeant Malik. You can hear what I say, but will you do what I say? On the other hand if the Comisario tells you what to do, you are under his orders not mine."

"I understand." Moreno turned to Malik, "Señor Brodie is correct and is very experienced in these matters, Sergeant Malik. You must take instruction from him at all times, as if that instruction were coming from me."

Malik glowered at Brodie, then nodded, "Understood, Comisario."

"Thank you Sergeant Malik. Señor Brodie will take over the bar tomorrow. Can you be there for your interview at eleven o'clock tomorrow morning? You must be seen being hired in the normal way."

"Yes, Sir"

Moreno stood up and picked up his car keys, signalling that the meeting was over. Malik turned and left the office without looking at Brodie.

Chapter 8

MORENO CLEARED THE PAPERWORK THAT BRODIE'S ARREST HAD generated then drove him back to his home at Av de Palomares. On the way, Moreno explained that Brodie's licence transfer only required one more signature which he would ensure was completed that day, allowing Brodie to take over the bar the next day. He would drop the document off at El Puerto by lunchtime.

"Thank you for doing this, Señor Brodie. I appreciate it very much and I must apologise for what I put you through last night, but it was important for me to be sure that you were capable of doing what needs to be done. Manuel is an old friend and I needed to know that his safety and that of his family were in good hands. I will tell Manuel that your licence will be transferred today, but he must not know of our arrangement."

"Understood, Comisario."

"About Sergeant Malik," Moreno began, "as I have said, Manuel is a dear and much revered friend and I would not involve anyone in this who would be a weak link or would let me down. She is one of the best officers I have ever worked with. I know that she has had to endure both racism and sexism in Madrid because many people see only a woman with dark skin colouring; they do not see a police officer who is very good at her job. That is what she is, make no mistake."

Brodie nodded slowly, "I've worked with a good number of female officers and soldiers over the years. I think sometimes it's because they need to continually prove themselves against men that they become such good soldiers, so I won't malign her in any way because she's a woman."

"Thank you. Tomorrow I will ask Manuel to introduce us in case the bar is being watched. We need to be able to have conversations and it would be natural if Manuel had introduced us. He speaks very highly of you, Señor Brodie, and I hope that when this is all over, perhaps you and I might also become friends."

"Never say never, I actually think that underneath Comisario Moreno, Xavier could be a pretty decent guy." Brodie smiled and held out his hand to Moreno. They shook hands and Brodie left a smiling Moreno as he made his way the short distance to his house.

Lunchtime was fast approaching as Brodie walked into the house. He opened a few windows to let the fresh air which was driven by a slight breeze from the perfectly calm sea circulate round the house. He checked his email to see if there was anything pressing then wandered upstairs for a shower and a badly needed change of clothes. He stood in the shower, digesting the events of the last evening as well as his subsequent conversation with Moreno and tried to put it all into perspective. Much as he had been angry over the way he had set him up the previous night at Barill Rojo, Brodie believed that Moreno had been genuinely trying to test how he would react to the potential physical threat the drug smugglers might pose and whether he would help him to take the heat off his old friend and put the perpetrators behind bars. He admired that kind of loyalty in a man and on reflection, Moreno had risen in his estimation.

Just how much danger was Manuel in, and how much of that would transfer over to him as the drug smugglers realised he was the new owner of El Puerto? What pressure would they put on him to sanction their illegal trade in his bar?

Eventually, Brodie stepped out of the shower, towelled himself dry and went in search of clothes. He dressed in his favourite denim shorts, a blue and white striped shirt, slipped on a pair of Havaianas and headed to El Puerto for a bite of lunch and whatever else might transpire.

As he walked, he surreptitiously noted the people around him, who they were, what they were doing. Was anyone watching him? Having spent years leading undercover operations in places where he should not have been, awareness of his surroundings and the people in them came as second nature to Brodie. In the four years since he had left the military, he had gradually relaxed, knowing that he was not living with the constant danger from an active enemy who would torture and kill British Forces personnel at the drop of a hat. However, working in the close protection and security industry, as he had been of late, meant that he still retained the surveillance skills which had served him well in the military. His recent conversations with Xavier Moreno had heightened his awareness of the need to once again be vigilant.

It took him ten minutes to reach El Puerto, a walk which would normally take three.

"Hola, Conchie," he greeted Consuela Gutiérrez, as he approached the bar, *"Buenos dias, que tal?"*

"Hey, Big Al, I'm good. How are you? You look tired. Did you not sleep well last night?"

Brodie smiled, "No. I'm OK, Conchie, slept pretty good, just busy days, that, and I need a coffee."

"OK, coming up, one café solo"

"Can I have a cheeseburger with fries as well?"

"*Si,* of course you can."

Consuela shouted Brodie's order through to the kitchen and set about making his coffee.

"So, tomorrow is the big day! Your licence is transferred and you finally get to own El Puerto."

"Yeah, so it seems, if everything goes to plan."

"It will, Alan. Comisario Moreno called Manuel this morning to say that he has had the licence signed today and he will bring it with him when he comes in for his breakfast tomorrow morning. He and Manuel are old friends, he will not let him down."

"I'm sure he won't, but even if he gets tied up with something, I don't need the licence in my hand, it just needs to have been signed by the Town Hall."

"I am pleased that you are keeping Carlos as chef, he is excellent. He runs the kitchen well and Manolo, his assistant, is also good, Carlos makes sure of that."

"I'm no chef, Consuela, I'm OK behind the bar and meeting customers but happy to let Carlos and Manolo look after the kitchen."

Consuela moved to serve some customers and as she did so, Carlos appeared from the kitchen with Brodie's Cheeseburger.

"Ah, *el nuevo jefe,* the new boss!" he grinned as he laid the plate of food in front of Brodie.

"*Mañana,* Carlos, not until tomorrow," he replied with a laugh, picking up the plate and cutlery Carlos had given him as he moved to a nearby table. He asked a passing waitress for a beer and settled at the table with his lunch.

Many Spanish bars and restaurants, had tables inside, but did much of their trade outside in the area to the front of the building. El Puerto was no different in that respect, but had the additional benefit of a beach front location with spectacular views over the golden white sand, beautiful blue sea and the small harbour with its adjoining marina.

Brodie ate his lunch slowly, ordered another beer and sat watching the flow of people passing up and down the paseo in front of El Puerto. Some were tourists, others locals, going about their business or making their way to or from their nearby homes. Puerto Ricos was fortunate as most of the apartments and townhouses were lived in more or less full time and were not used as occasional holiday homes, which would lie empty for long periods. The owners were a mixture of Spanish and British ex-pats with a smattering of Northern Europeans. The developers had been British, which explained the high percentage of British owners. Brodie had quickly become accustomed to hearing British and Spanish voices around the bar since he started frequenting it, these were interspersed with the occasional German or Dutch voices but very little else.

Today was no exception and as he sat toying idly with his, now empty, beer bottle he exchanged greetings and waves of recognition from a number of the local residents who he had become acquainted with as a regular visitor to El Puerto. Eventually, he rose from the table and walked slowly across the beach, and having slipped off his Havaianas, paddled along the water's edge to his house. He kicked up the warm Mediterranean water as he walked, reflecting again on his immediate future, his new venture as a bar owner, his remit to uncover a drugs gang and having the added pressure of a police officer as a member of his staff. Much as he was aware that Sergeant Malik was also a very beautiful young woman, who under different circumstances, he would be only too keen to get to know better, he could do without the added complication she introduced. That said, it was what it was, he knew, for Manuel's benefit.

Chapter 9

BRODIE SENT AND RECEIVED A FEW EMAILS, THEN SEARCHED THE internet for information he wanted on a number of subjects then showered quickly, changed and made his way back up to El Puerto, where he had arranged to meet with Manuel who would introduce him as the new owner to some of the regulars.

The bar was busy by the time Brodie arrived and although he quickly acknowledged Brodie's arrival, it took a few minutes for Manuel to free himself from taking customers food and drinks orders.

"Hey, Alan," he greeted Brodie, "I was beginning to think you were not going to come, I was thinking maybe you had cold feet, as you say."

"No, no, just had a few things to do first, but looking forward to tomorrow, so I wasn't going to miss tonight."

"Good, good, because I have put a bottle of Champagne aside for us in the chill, come with me."

Brodie followed Manuel over to the bar and the Spaniard gestured to one of the staff to open the Champagne as he pulled a tray of flutes towards him and began to pour the Champagne. Consuela left the bar and Carlos and Manolo appeared from the kitchen and joined Manuel and Brodie in a toast to the new owner before returning to their duties. Slowly but surely, the regular customers in the bar realised what was being celebrated and wished Brodie well in his new venture.

As the celebrations died down and the bar trade returned to normal, Brodie decided to eat and when a table became free he sat down in a quiet corner with a glass of his favourite, 'behind the bar' Rioja Reserva and a plate of Carlos's renowned paella, cooked, the chef claimed, to his grandmother's traditional recipe. As he enjoyed his last meal as a customer, Consuela cleared away his empty plate and he poured another glass of wine as he sat watching and listening to those around him while soaking up the warm, social atmosphere of the evening. Alan Brodie was a Scot and always would be, but he had chosen to make his home, and now his place of business, in the Almeria region of Spain. Sitting there on the terrace of El Puerto, he felt no regrets.

"Señor Brodie.?" A woman's voice invaded his thoughts

He turned to look in the direction of the interruption and was surprised to see the tall, slim, dark figure of Sergeant Anita Malik, wearing a pair of white shorts, a loose multi-coloured top and a heavy, white necklace similar in style to the one she had worn the previous night.

"Well, well, Señorita Malik. Here to engineer another assault charge?"

"No, the very opposite actually," she said hesitantly, "if you will allow me. May I sit?"

"Be my guest." Brody gestured with a flourish at the chair opposite.

"The Comisario said you would be here tomorrow."

"Yes, I know what the Comisario said, but I wanted to speak with you before then." She looked around to ensure that no one was within earshot. "I wanted to apologise for last night. That was not my doing, I was carrying out my orders as a police officer and as you know from your time in the military, there are times when you are told to do things which you do not like to do."

"So, who's orders were you following, Sergeant Malik?"

"That doesn't matter, although you know very well who arranged your predicament and please, I am here as a woman not a police officer and I came to apologise."

"As a woman or a police officer, Sergeant Malik."

"I'm sorry, I obviously misjudged you Señor Brodie and I am clearly wasting my time and yours." Malik said and stood up to leave.

"Wait! Hang on. Sit down."

Malik sat down heavily on the seat, folded her arms across her chest, crossed her legs and glowered at Brodie.

"You're right, I *am* being unfair, I'm sorry. You're perfectly correct, you were acting under orders and I *do* know whose orders and I get why he did it. Manuel is a friend of mine as well and I would have helped him anyway. What gets to me is that I could easily have killed one or both of these officers, in other circumstances I would have and Moreno knew that."

"You have killed people before?"

Brodie laughed, "You really don't know anything about me, do you?"

"Only that Comisario Moreno singled you out because you had been in the military and he wanted to test your friendship with Manuel Gutiérrez, he did not say why."

Brodie sighed and ran his fingers through his hair, then as Malik had done earlier, checked his surroundings before responding.

"I spent a great deal of my military life as a member of a Special Forces group and I really shouldn't be telling you this, but yes, I have killed many people before. I didn't take any pleasure in killing people, but it's what I was trained to do and I'm *very* good at it, which is why I am still alive. Moreno knows that, he made it his business to find out"

"I did not know."

"Do you know what? I actually think that your Comisario is a genuine, honest guy who is trying to protect a good friend. But what would he have done if I had inadvertently killed one of his officers? I somehow don't think we would be having this conversation now, do you?"

Malik hung her head, her hands covering her face. "Now I am even more sorry, I did not think. Comisario Moreno told me nothing of this."

"It's not your fault, you didn't know and to be fair to Moreno, I don't think he thought it through properly. I think he thought three police officers, four if we include you, would take me down before I had a chance to do them any real damage."

"I started it off, then left, I was not comfortable with what we were doing, so I did what I had been told to do then walked away. I did not see what you did to the others."

"Maybe just as well. Anyway, we can't change the past and we need to work together, so can I get you a drink?"

Malik held up a hand, "No, thank you, I think maybe I should buy you a drink. A Rioja?" she asked pointing to his empty wine bottle.

"OK, sure. Just tell them it's for me, they'll know what I want."

"We can share a bottle, maybe?" Malik lifted the empty bottle when Brodie nodded and carried it to the bar.

As she stood by the bar, Brodie noticed two men standing behind her. One was tall and well-muscled, probably in his mid to late thirties with long blond streaked hair tied back in a ponytail. He was dressed in a grey linen jacket over a white t-shirt, denim jeans and white trainers. The other was shorter, slightly older and dressed in a black t-shirt, black jeans and trainers. He had a slight paunch and was trying to hide a receding hairline by shaving his head. Both were well tanned.

Malik spoke to Consuela and she walked off to get a fresh bottle of Rioja. As Consuela disappeared, the two men took the opportunity to sidle unseen, so they thought, into the kitchen.

Brodie rose quickly and when Consuela returned, bottle in hand, he squeezed past her to the kitchen door.

"Al, what is it?"

"Not sure, Conchie, just checking," he replied, opening the kitchen door and stepping inside.

The two men he had seen coming in were standing with Manuel pressed up against a stainless steel kitchen worktop, the shorter one with his hand at Manuel's throat. On hearing the door open then swing shut, they all looked in Brodie's direction. The taller man moved to face Brodie.

"*Desaparecer* – disappear," he snarled at Brodie.

"Don't think so," Brodie took a step forward. "Although, maybe you guys should, while you still can."

"This has nothing to do with you, so get out."

"It's got everything to do with me. As of tomorrow, I own this bar, so if you've got anything to say, maybe you need to say it to me."

The older, shorter man let go of Manuel and said something to his taller companion in what Brodie thought was Russian. Ponytail lunged at him with a wild right hook which Brodie evaded by swaying back from his waist and blocking the punch with his left forearm. Before the man could react, Brodie pivoted forward from his waist and hit the man hard with a ferocious head-butt.

The man's nose exploded and his legs wobbled as he all but lost consciousness and could do nothing to stop Brodie's knee connect with his groin. As the man folded, Brodie swung a fierce right hook into the side of the man's head and he dropped unconscious to the kitchen floor. The second man, who because of the restricted floor area of the kitchen, had been unable to get to Brodie, now approached him, picking up a large kitchen knife from the worktop as he passed.

He roared at Brodie as he charged, the knife raised to strike downwards but Brodie stepped into the intended blow, grasping his arm, turned and drove his elbow into the man's soft midriff. The man loosened his grip on the knife as he fought for breath, Brodie twisted it from his grasp and holding his assailant's hand flat on a heavy wooden table, plunged the knife into the back of his hand. The blade passed through skin, bone, muscle, penetrating deep into the wood, pinning him to the table. The man screamed in agony and as he tried to pull his hand away he quickly realised that he would only cause himself more pain.

Brodie sensed movement to his right as the kitchen door swung open and Malik stood at the entrance, her expression one of horror. Consuela bumped into her as she tried to follow her into the kitchen.

Brodie held the handle of the knife as he swung round to look down at the trapped hand which was now bleeding profusely over the wooden surface.

"So, do you want to tell me what this is all about?"

....."Anybody?" he asked again, this time looking at Manuel

"They want to use the bar to buy and sell drugs, Alan"

"Do they now? We'll see about that."

Brodie pulled the knife out of the man's hand allowing him to fall to the floor, cradling his injured hand.

"Open the back door, Manuel. These two are leaving," Brodie snarled, grabbing the man's injured arm. He howled in pain, as Brodie pulled him to his feet and marched him to the rear door of the kitchen which opened out onto a narrow, dark alleyway. Brodie threw him out, watching as the injured thug fell against the far wall.

Brodie followed him into the alley.

"Tell your boss if he wants to do business in my bar, he talks to me. He doesn't send round a couple of second rate thugs to try to put the frighteners on me."

As Brodie walked back into the kitchen the second intruder was staggering to his feet. He looked first at Malik, who was still standing in front of the kitchen door, and then at Brodie. He chose Malik and tried to brush past her to get out of the kitchen, but she stood her ground and propelled him back towards Brodie

Grabbing hold of the man's ponytail he half pulled, and half dragged him towards the back door, tossing him into the alley beside his accomplice then watched as the two stumbled along the passage, away from the bar.

Chapter 10

HAVING MADE SURE THEY HAD GONE, BRODIE RETURNED TO THE kitchen and closed the door. He looked at the blood stained kitchen floor and table and then at Manuel.

"You OK, Manuel?"

"Manuel! What has happened, are you all right?" Consuela asked him worriedly as she crossed the kitchen and hugged her husband

"*Si,* yes, yes. I'm OK," Manuel sighed, obviously badly shaken by the scenario that had just unfolded.

He looked across to Brodie, an expression of concern on his face, "Thank you Alan, what you did..."

"Was nothing."

"But I think maybe you have made enemies tonight."

"Nah, they won't come back," he lied.

Brodie saw Manuel look across at Malik and frown.

"Manuel, this is Anita Malik, she will be working with me in the bar from tomorrow, ...if she still wants to after tonight"

Malik waved over to Manuel and Consuela who had also turned to look at her, "Hi, yes, I still want to work here." She smiled slightly

"Where are Carlos and Manolo?" Brodie asked.

"Kitchen is closed, so they both left about half an hour ago," Consuela replied.

Brodie looked at his watch, it was almost midnight.

"Is the bar busy?" he asked Malik.

She walked through to the bar area and came back with a shake of her head.

"Only two people finishing their drinks."

"OK, Malik, would you walk these guys round to their car and get them off home. Manuel, I'll clear up here and shut the bar."

Malik nodded and stretched out her hand to Consuela.

"Thank you Alan, thank you. I will see you in the morning." Manuel, clearly still distressed by the evening's events, patted Brodie on the shoulder as he ushered Consuela ahead of him out of the kitchen, followed by Malik.

Brodie followed them through to the bar as they left. The last two patrons of the night were just climbing down from their barstools and making for the door. Brodie followed them, brought down all but one of the outside shutters and locked the door. He picked up a few empty glasses and bottles, binned the bottles for recycle, put the glasses into the dishwasher. He then washed the kitchen floor and the bloodstained worktop. About to clean the bar area and the tables, he heard a soft knock at the door.

"Sorry we're closed," Brodie called.

"It's me," Malik's voice came in reply.

Brodie opened the door. Malik stepped in and he locked the door behind her.

"You got them off OK?"

"Yes, they are both a bit shaken but they're OK."

"I expected you to have just gone straight home."

"I thought you might want a hand to clear up."

"You sure?"

"Yes, I worked in bars in Madrid when I was at university and I have a hygiene certificate, believe it or not, so tell me what needs doing."

Malik cleaned the bar area while Brodie stacked the chairs on the tables, washed the floor, replaced the chairs then cleaned the tables.

On finishing the tables, he turned to the bar area to find Malik holding aloft what Brodie recognised as a bottle of his favoured Rioja Reserva.

"Consuela opened this but didn't get any further than that. Can I pour us both a glass?"

Brodie hesitated then shrugged, "Yeah, why not?"

Malik poured two glasses and they sat down.

"Thanks for doing that," Brodie said

"No problem, I think I owed you."

"Oh, you owe me way more than that Malik, way more," Brodie laughed as he sat at one of the newly cleaned tables. Malik sat quietly opposite him.

"So, Sergeant Malik, tell me your life story in the time it takes me to drink this glass of wine."

"That's easy. My father was from Sudan, he worked in the Sudanese Embassy in Madrid, met my mother, a Spanish lady, locally engaged by the Embassy. They got married, had me and my little sister. I grew up, went to school, then university and from there, joined the police and here I am. You're not finished your wine."

"That means I get to ask questions," Brodie countered. "How much younger is your little sister?"

"Five minutes, we are identical twins." Malik smiled.

"Wow, so there's another Malik who looks just like you?"

"She has shorter hair."

Brodie eyed her for a second, "Do you ever get fed-up being judged on your appearance?"

"No, I use it to my benefit. I am proud of how I look, I am a beautiful woman and I am black but if that is *all* people choose to see then that is their loss, because I am many other things too."

Brodie smiled and nodded. "I'll bet you are."

"What about your parents?"

"They still live in the outskirts of Madrid, both have retired now."

"How did Moreno find you, him being in Mojácar and you in Madrid?"

"For the last three years, I was working as part of a team looking at international drug smuggling and at the beginning of this year we had a big success and broke a huge smuggling network which was operating through Algeciras. Comisario Moreno had become aware of increased smuggling in this area and asked Madrid for access to some members of the team to help him here. One of my colleagues and I were seconded to Almeria, where Moreno reports to. My colleague is still in Almeria and I am in Mojácar."

"How much does Moreno know about these guys?"

"He knows that they are probably Russian and have recently set up an operation here. They are well organised and have a great deal of money behind them. We think that the ring leader is a Russian who has a large expensive yacht, which he keeps in Puerto Banús,, but sometimes sails to Garrucha or Puerto Ricas, sadly we have no proof. We have tried to get someone on the inside but so far we have got nowhere, then they approached Manuel, told him they were going to use his bar to buy and sell their drugs. Manuel pushed back at first, but they threatened his family. That's when he spoke with Comisario Moreno. I think tonight was meant as a reminder of what might happen if he did not co-operate."

"Didn't work out too well for them did it? Having said that, it might work in our favour."

"How come?"

"Well, when I chucked the first guy out into the alleyway, I told him to tell his boss that if he wants to do business in El Puerto, he needs to come and talk to me, not try to frighten me."

"You said what? Comisario Moreno will not be in favour of that. We cannot commit a crime to catch a criminal."

"You speak for yourself Malik and if you don't like heat, stay out of the kitchen, metaphorically speaking, of course."

"I take my orders from the Comisario, Señor Brodie, not from you."

"You're working with me, Malik, you take my lead or you're gone. This deployment has one leader, me, I call the shots in engaging with these smugglers."

"We'll see about that tomorrow." Malik finished her drink, stood up and strode out of the bar door slamming it behind her as she left.

Brodie took out his phone and hit a pre-programmed number.

"Moreno, we need a meeting tomorrow morning, you, me and Malik. We need to sort out some ground rules and lines of authority. We had a visit from two of the smugglers' heavies tonight. There was a confrontation in the kitchen, they were taken down and dispatched back to their boss with a message that we should talk if they want to do business in El Puerto. Malik's not happy and wants to take her orders from you, not me. I need this sorted out before we go any further. Nine o'clock at yours, good." He ended the call.

Ten minutes later, Brodie had locked the bar door, pulled the shutter down and was making his way back to his house along the now deserted beach. He loved the soft, relaxing sound of the waves breaking on the sand and very often sat in the darkness of his front terrace listening to the soothing sound while appreciating his surroundings.

He reached the house, showered and got ready for bed,

where he sat reading for a while before sleep got the better of him.

Chapter 11

Seven o'clock the next morning, Brodie was on his usual morning run along the beach, heading toward the village of Villaricos, formerly a Phoenician port. Forgotten by history for thousands of years, it resurfaced as a silver mining boom town in the 19th century before finally becoming the pleasant fishing village of today. Villaricos was now home to a number of bars and restaurants, regularly frequented by a substantial ex-pat British population. It was separated from Playa Marques, where Brodie lived, by a convenient three miles of quiet beach. When the mood took him, he could extend his six mile morning run by continuing along the paseo in Villaricos, coming out of the far end of the village and up onto the main road above the seafront. From there he could complete a circular route back to Playa Marques. That morning, Brodie had a lot to think about plus a meeting with Comisario Moreno and Malik to prepare for so he stuck with the six mile version of his run.

He returned to the beach house, showered quickly and dressed in a pair of black jeans and a white linen shirt, before sitting down to a hurried breakfast of orange juice, poached eggs, toast and coffee. He checked his email on his laptop, cleared his dishes and headed out to his meeting at the police station in Mojácar.

He bypassed Garrucha to avoid the usual heavy traffic through the town centre then dropped down on to the coast road at the far end of the town, following the free flowing traffic into Mojácar Playa where Moreno's office was situated. He watched his rear view mirror constantly, looking for anyone following him and doing a double detour round the block to give himself added confidence that he was not being followed. He finally parked in a small car park two streets away from his destination walking the rest of the way, still constantly watching for unwanted company.

He approached the front desk and told the officer behind the reception that he was expected by Comisario Moreno. One phone call and two minutes later, he and one of Moreno's officers were walking along a narrow corridor leading to Moreno's office. The Comisario ordered coffee as they entered his office and shut the door. Moreno signalled that Brodie should sit on a leather settee situated against the far wall of the office, facing a long low coffee table and two matching leather chairs.

"Good morning, Señor Brodie, I trust you are well."

"Yes, Comisario, I am. However, we need to get a few points of order sorted out before we get our little operation up and running."

"So I understand. Sergeant Malik and I had a long discussion this morning. She told me of your, 'slight altercation' last evening and the disagreement you had with her afterwards."

Moreno held up his hand to stop Brodie interrupting him.

"I did not ask her to visit El Puerto last night, she did that on her own initiative. She knows that you and she did not get off on a very good footing. She was keen to make amends and start again on a fresh page. She is keen to make this work, as we both are."

A knock came to the door and an officer brought a tray with coffee, biscuits and three mugs to the table.

"Ask Sergeant Malik to join us, please."

"Please help yourself to coffee and biscuits, Sergeant Malik will be with us directly."

"Thanks," Brodie replied, as again someone knocked on the door.

"Come."

The door opened and Malik entered, closing the door behind her. Moreno signalled her to the other leather chair. She nodded to Brodie and sat down.

"Coffee?" Brodie offered.

"Yes please."

"Señor Brodie, Sergeant Malik and I had a long discussion this morning, as I have said. It would appear that perhaps I did not explain properly what her role at El Puerto would entail. Her understanding was that as she is under my command here during her secondment, I expected she would take her instructions from me on a day to day basis, rather than from you. We both agreed that as you were going to be on the front line, she should take her instruction from you; unless of course, your direction was not what we had agreed in this office."

"Can I just stop you there, Comisario? On all successful missions I have been involved with, they were successful because everybody knew who was in charge, who to follow and, they reacted accordingly. Now, with all due respect, none of us knows how this little adventure is going to pan out and what decisions will need to be made on the spur of the moment; decisions that will determine whether we get the result we are looking for, or whether we fail and, worst case scenario, one of us is killed. On that basis, I need everyone to know that I am in charge and when I make a decision or give an instruction, that instruction is carried out without question or hesitation. No phone calls back to you for ratification or permission. I can tell you now, Comisario, that is the only basis that I will allow Sergeant Malik's involvement."

"Spoken like a true leader, Captain Brodie. Sergeant Malik and I have already discussed this and we have both agreed that is the only way forward. She argued your case very forcibly this morning. She has worked on assignments like this before, more so than I have and she has convinced me that the best approach is as you have just described."

Brodie looked at Malik, an expression of surprise on his face.

Malik smiled, "I have been in situations like this before, Señor Brodie. The senior officer in the field is best placed to make quick decisions which will affect the outcome of an operation, not someone operating remotely from the action. Comisario Moreno is a good police officer, an excellent strategist who can pick the right people to make difficult operational decisions quickly and get them right. I was not convinced he had picked the right person to carry out this operation against the drug smugglers, until last night.

Last night I saw why the Comisario was correct in choosing you. You think tactically, you react to situations as they occur and make positive decisions based on what you see. Until now, my orders were to report back to the Comisario and take instructions from him. This morning we discussed what happened last night and agreed that it is best if you have responsibility for tactical decisions and I will take my operational instructions from you."

"Without question, Sergeant Malik?"

"Without question!"

"And you're happy with that Comisario?"

"Before you arrived this morning, I showed Sergeant Malik some of the information I received from my sources regarding your past. She pointed out, very diplomatically I hasten to add, that you have past experience of situations like this and we should allow you to use that experience to our best advantage. So, yes, having discussed this with Sergeant Malik, I am prepared to pass the reigns of command to you in this instance."

"OK, so if I give Malik an instruction, she should take that as a direct order from you?"

"Yes."

Brodie looked at Malik for a second.

"I say that, Sergeant Malik, because I need to know that if I give you a direct instruction, you will carry it out, not go flouncing off in a strop the way you did last night. I need to know that, because your life or mine might rely on your response. I don't want to die because you want time to run a direct order from me past Comisario Moreno."

"We have agreed that you will lead this operation and I know from experience how a chain of command works, so yes, I am happy with taking a lead from you. Last night, my chain of command was through Comisario Moreno, but we have discussed this and that is no longer the case. I will now take my instructions from you."

"Without question?"

Malik looked directly at Brodie, "Without question," she replied.

"OK, you're hired." Brodie stood, signalling that the meeting was over. Malik and Moreno stood also and Brodie shook hands with Moreno.

"Thank you for your trust Comisario Moreno."

He turned to Malik and smiled, "Don't be late for work on your first day and don't dress like a police officer," he shook hands with Malik and left the office.

Chapter 12

BRODIE DROVE BACK TO HIS HOUSE, PARKED HIS CAR, AND WALKED the short distance to El Puerto, once again taking care to watch the people around him, convinced that before very long he would have another encounter with the Russian drug smugglers.

He entered the bar and was met by Manuel and Conchita Gutiérrez.

"Hey, Big Al" Conchita welcomed him, "We thought you were having a change of mind after last night."

"No, no! I had some business to take care of this morning. What happened last night Conchie? Brodie joked.

"Manuel told me what happened last night...those two men in the kitchen."

Brodie ushered the couple to a quiet table where they sat down.

"Look guys, I know about the drugs smugglers and I know why you tried to put me off buying El Puerto. I have spoken with Comisario Moreno and we have discussed what to do about these guys. Last night was just the start of what they can expect if they try to get heavy again. We will work with Moreno to get rid of them, so don't worry about that. OK?"

Manuel and Conchita looked at each other, then at Brodie.

Manuel spoke first, "I did not want to sell you the bar without you knowing about these people, so I spoke with Xavier and he said he would speak with you. I have known Xavier since many years; he is a good man and a good friend."

"It's fine guys, seriously. You did the right thing. I know what I am getting into. Hopefully we'll get these guys sorted out quickly and I can get on with running El Puerto.

Speaking of which, here comes Comisario Moreno, hopefully with my licence."

Manuel and Conchita looked round as Moreno walked onto the bar's terrace area.

"Please, don't get up my friends, he said, as he sat at the table.

"Señor Brodie, it is good to meet you." Moreno reached over the table and shook Brodie's hand.

"I have brought you the licence for El Puerto, transferred into your name. It is a good excuse to visit my friends and sample their lunchtime menu, which I will continue to do, Señor Brodie, if you will have me."

"Of course, Comisario, you will always be welcome at El Puerto."

"Please, call me Xavier."

"OK, Xavier, and as you know from the licence, my name is Alan, although my smaller friends call me Big Al." Brodie smiled as he gently squeezed Conchita's shoulder.

"I think maybe this young lady is looking for you, Alan," Moreno nodded to someone standing behind Brodie.

He turned and saw Anita Malik, who had just arrived. She was dressed for work in black shorts and a white t-shirt, a pair of black and white trainers. Brodie couldn't help thinking that regardless of what she wore, Anita Malik was a beautiful woman.

"Anita, hi. I wasn't expecting you for another half hour or so," he finally managed.

"I thought I would try to impress my new boss on my first day," she smiled down at him.

Brodie stood and turned towards her.

"Anita, you met Manuel last night," Manuel smiled and waved.

"This is Conchita, Manuel's wife. Conchie, this is Anita. She will be working with me behind the bar. Last but not least this is Comisario Moreno. He is going to be one of our regular customers, he tells me."

"In that case we had better take good care of him." Malik smiled.

"Anita, let me show you where to find things behind the bar, Alan has worked here many times to help us, so he knows where to find everything," Conchita said, rising from the table and gesturing for Malik to follow.

As the two women went off, Manuel leaned into the table.

"Alan, I hope you know what you are doing here, I am already having regrets at what I have done. These men can be dangerous. Please be careful, both of you."

"Manuel, you've sold me a bar that I wanted to buy, I approached you, if you remember, and Xavier has told me about the small problem we need to overcome. I know what I'm getting into and I'm quite capable of facing off a few bad guys. It's what I did for a living for years."

"Manuel, Alan is also a very dangerous man. I know this because I made it my business to find out before I allowed him to put himself in this position and Sergeant Malik is a very capable officer. They will work well together."

Manuel's head almost fell off as he spun round to stare at Malik.

"*Sergeant* Malik? She is a police officer?"

"She is, and a very good one. She has a black belt in karate and uses a firearm with amazing accuracy. It is difficult to be a female officer in a mainly male police force, but to be female and black, well, you need to be among the very best to succeed."

"Oh, you need to behave with this woman Alan. Otherwise you will be in big trouble!" Manuel laughed.

"Don't you worry, Manuel. Work and play; two different things."

"I have seen a few men try their luck with Malik and come off worst. As I say, Anita can look after herself," Moreno smiled.

"I've worked with female officers in the military and they get my utmost respect. You're right Xavier, they *do* need to be so much better than their male counterparts to get recognition. Speaking of work, I suppose I had better go and do some and you need to do a final handover for me, Manuel," Brodie said, rising from the table.

"Were you serious about lunch, Xavier?"

"Yes, of course!"

"OK, we better get you fed then." Brodie reached over to the bar and handed Moreno a menu.

"No need, Alan, I see you have *cocido montañés,* mountain stew, on the Menu del Dia. Carlos's *cocido montañés* is better than they serve on the Camino de Santiago pilgrimage."

"You've done the Camino?"

"*Si,* yes, about five years ago. I did the Camino Frances from Pamplona, about six hundred and sixty kilometres. I made very good friends with my feet."

"I would love to do the Camino one day; I know a couple of people who have done the walk."

"It is wonderful, beautiful scenery and you meet the most engaging people."

Just then, Manuel appeared with a large steaming bowl of *cocido montañés.*

Manuel laughed when he saw the expression on Brodie's face

"I do not need to ask this man what he will eat when Cocido Montañés is on the menu."

"Apparently not, that can be my first El Puerto lesson of the day. I'll leave you in peace to have your lunch Xavier. Enjoy!"

Manuel took Brodie into the kitchen and they spent some time speaking with Carlos and Manolo. Brodie assured both that their positions were safe and he looked forward to working with both. Carlos floated a few ideas as to how he thought the menu could be updated and improved.

Maria, Mateo and Diego were making sure the lunchtime customers were well looked after. Brodie was already well acquainted with the trio, as a former regular customer. He liked all the waiting staff and had no problem in reassuring them all of their job security.

Chapter 13

THE DAY PASSED INTO EVENING, DARKNESS FELL AND CUSTOMERS came and went. Brodie and Malik worked behind the bar and front of house as required. Brodie was impressed by Malik's work ethic and her easy manner with the customers. While the rest of the staff cleared and cleaned their work areas, Malik and Brodie cleared the bar area, took the bottles out to the large bins at the rear of the building and restocked the bar for the next day.

"So, what did you think of your first day?" Brodie enquired.

"Good. I worked in bars in Madrid when I was at university. I had forgotten how much I enjoyed it. It's hard work but it can be good fun if you have the right clientele and the bar is busy like today; time passes quickly."

"Does that mean you'll be back tomorrow, then?"

"Oh yes, I'll be back, tomorrow and the next day and the day after that. You don't get rid of me that easily."

"I don't know if I want rid of you after today. We worked well together considering it was the first day for both of us, so, thanks."

Miguel, a stocky, energetic young man, who Brodie had

discovered was Carlos's cousin, pulled down the roller shutters and everyone left for the night, leaving Malik emptying the dishwasher of glasses and Brodie cashing up the till.

"Hey, listen, you get away if you're finished with the glasses. I'll be done here in a couple of minutes," Brodie said.

"OK, thanks," Malik answered, closing the dishwasher.

She picked her small shoulder bag from behind the bar and slung the strap over her head to rest across her body.

"When do you think we will get another visit from the drug dealers?" she asked.

"Soon, they won't let last night pass without another visit."

"That does not worry you?"

"Sure, it worries me but I think we can handle them. I told these guys last night that I was willing to do business with their boss, but I won't be bullied or threatened into it. I told them if they wanted to do business, they should come and talk to me. Hopefully they got that message loud and clear and they'll come back to talk, not to hurt anyone."

"OK, I will see you in the morning, Señor Brodie,"

"Alan, everyone else calls me by my first name. It sounds strange if you don't, so no more, 'Señor Brodie'."

"Sure, till tomorrow, Alan," Malik smiled and left, pulling the door closed behind her.

Brodie finished counting the cash, bagged it and put it in the small safe under the bar.

He had decided that he would move some of his belongings over to the apartment the next day and gradually move in over the next few days. As he always did when he bought a new property, he would have the locks changed and a small safe built into one of the wardrobes.

On a last minute whim, after he locked up the bar, he decided to go round and have another look at the apartment which was to be his new home. He walked round the corner and was standing in the doorway having just unlocked and opened the carved wooden door, when he became aware of someone moving in behind him. He turned to find three men standing, one of them, the tall ponytailed man from the previous night, his nose covered by a large plaster. The other two he had not seen before. One of them, was a man of medium height, who looked slim, fit, around fifty years old and dressed expensively in a beige Armani linen suit. The third, was tall, slim, wore his hair long and sported a dark beard. He was dressed in a pair of denim jeans and a black leather jacket over a pale blue shirt. He was pointing a suppressed Glock G17 pistol at Brodie's navel.

"I think we need to talk," the well-dressed man addressed Brodie.

"You think?"

"You told my friend here and his colleague that we needed to talk. I am here at your bidding, Señor Brodie, it would be bad manners not to invite us in."

"Of course it would," Brodie held out his hand to the man, "Alan Brodie, but you know that already and you are?"

"You do not need to know who I am for the moment. We will talk, then I tell you who I am."

Brodie stepped aside to allow the men entry to the apartment and as he did so, he spun round taking the man with the Glock completely by surprise. He grasped his wrist in one hand and the gun in the other, pointing it at the gunman's foot. He had already taken note that the safety was off and the man's finger was resting on the trigger. Brodie jerked his hand and heard the satisfying, suppressed pop of the shot. His assailant roared in pain as the nine millimetre bullet shattered his foot and he loosened his grip on the pistol and Brodie grabbed it from him.

He swung round to the man in the Armani suit and held the gun to his forehead.

"OK, now we can talk. Tell your friend to take his buddy

here to get his foot attended to and not to come back until you tell him to come and get you. Tell him in English so that I hear what you are saying to him. Any Russian and I will shoot your kneecap off, do you understand?"

The man nodded and did as he was told, his companion with the broken nose hesitated and looked from his boss to Brodie and back.

"Don't even think about it. One wrong move from you and I will take his kneecap off."

His boss repeated his instruction, again in English, this time with a little more urgency, fearing that he was about to do something reckless, which would result in Brodie carrying out his threat. "Take him away, now, and wait till I tell you to come back."

The second instruction got through to him and he lifted his injured colleague to his feet, still writhing in pain, and helped him hobble away from the apartment.

"OK, inside," Brodie told the Russian.

He walked up the wide marble faced stairs into the apartment, looking to see where to go as he got to the top step and into a large square hallway.

"Stop there, take your jacket off and hold it up in the air. Now turn around. Pull up your trouser legs."

Brodie was satisfied the Russian was not armed.

"Go left," he instructed and he followed him into the lounge.

"Phone, give me your phone. Now sit," Brodie ordered, pointing at a mid-blue armchair. He went into the kitchen and poured two glasses of water from the cold water dispenser in the fridge/freezer, carried then back to the lounge, and handed one to his visitor.

"I'd offer you a drink but the cupboard is bare, as they say. No one lives here at the moment, although I will be moving in shortly."

"Now, who are you and what do you want?"

"I am Alexei Markov and I was told you wanted to do business with me," the man said calmly.

"Do you normally point guns at your business associates?"

"I work in a very dangerous business, Señor Brodie."

"I don't like people pointing guns at me Mr Markov, let's be clear about that."

Brodie dropped the magazine from the Glock, slid it into his pocket, and tossed the weapon to the Russian, who fumbled to catch it.

"I think we can dispense with that," he said, sitting on the matching mid blue settee,

"Manuel told me last night that your heavies were there to remind him that you wanted to do business with him in the bar," Brodie continued, "but he didn't elaborate..., although I don't imagine for a minute you want to be his supplier of choice for frozen peas.

Let me guess at illegal substances, drugs maybe?"

"Maybe. Would that trouble you?"

"I'm in business to do business, Alexei and I've never been too squeamish about how I make my money. Proceeds from El Puerto aren't going to keep me in the manner to which I have become accustomed. I bought that as a base to do other business, if not with you, then with someone else. It's up to you."

"That will not be my decision, or yours Señor Brodie, I am only here to assess if you are friend or foe. My employer will decide if we are to do business or not."

"No Alexei, your employer might make me an offer, but I'll decide if I want to take it, or not. There are plenty more fish in the sea. Plenty more Russian gangs out there looking to do business with local partners. I worked with a Russian oligarch in London and in Puerto Banús. He has a lot of contacts in Russia and in Europe who I could partner with."

"I will tell my employer, now, I need to go," Markov said

reaching to take his phone from the low table at his side, where Brodie had placed it.

"Sure, tell your buddies to come and get you, Alexei." Brodie stood as Markov called his lackeys.

"And, Alexei, tell your employer if he sends his heavies again, I'll kill one of them. I could have killed your sidekicks earlier. They're still alive because I chose not to kill them."

Markov left and Brodie watched from the shadows of the side balcony as he walked over to a large dark coloured Audi saloon. He sat in the back and the car drove off at speed.

Brodie returned to the lounge, picked up his glass of water and drained it. He retrieved the glass he had given Markov and dropped it into a plastic carrier bag he had found in a kitchen drawer.

Taking out his phone he called Moreno, who answered on the fourth ring.

"Xavier, I've just had a visit from a guy calling himself Alexei Markov and two of his minders. I sent the minders on their way, one of them with a bullet hole in his foot and brought Markov up to the apartment above the bar"

He related the conversation to Moreno, "Oh, and by the way, I've got a present for you. I gave Markov a glass of water, as I had nothing stronger and he very kindly left us his fingerprints on it. His oppo also left some blood on the cobbles outside the apartment, I'll get some of that and you can test for DNA."

"Excellent, I'll pick it up from you when I come for lunch to the bar. Thanks for letting me know and mind how you go, Alan."

Chapter 14

BRODIE HAD DECIDED WHEN HE WOKE IN THE MIDDLE OF THE night that he would move into the apartment that day, so when he woke again later that morning, he pulled on a t-shirt and shorts, slipped on his trainers and hit the beach for his morning run. He ran more quickly than his normal relaxed jog, knowing that he was going to have a busy day, but still wanting to cover the miles.

The morning was sunny and warm, with only a hint of a breeze and the odd thin wisp of cloud spoiling an otherwise perfect blue sky. It might only be springtime, but feeling the heat of the sun even at that early hour, Brodie could sense that Costa Almeria was in for another very warm day.

He ran to the start of the paseo at the harbour in Villaricos and turned to head home. Ahead of him he could see a few of the local fishermen setting up their rods close to the water's edge. In his peripheral vision he noticed a tall figure get out of a car and begin running in an almost parallel direction to him. As he neared Puerto Ricos, the figure came closer to him on his right hand side. He smiled as the runner came within a few metres of him although slightly behind him.

He picked up his speed slightly and the other runner responded. After a short distance, he lengthened his stride again; the other runner matched his increased pace.

He turned his head as he ran. "Good morning, Anita," he laughed, "I didn't know you ran."

"There's a lot you don't know about me."

"True. To what do I owe the pleasure of your company this morning?"

"The Comisario said you have some samples for him and he wanted to get them and have them processed as quickly as possible."

"Ah, and here was me thinking it was the attraction of an early morning run along an almost deserted beach and the thought of my company on the run. I'm disappointed, Malik."

"I prefer to keep our relationship professional, Señor Brodie...., Alan. I am here because Comisario Moreno instructed me and for no other reason."

"Wow, you certainly know how to deflate a man's ego, Malik. I will consider myself chastised and put back in my box."

"I did not ask to be involved in this deception at El Puerto and I am still not happy with how you are handling it. I think it is dangerous."

"Well, feel free to go back to Madrid any time you want. If you're not committed, I don't want you here."

"I am a police officer, I do not choose my deployments, my superior officers do, and Comisario Moreno has said I need to be in El Puerto."

As they spoke they arrived at Brodie's house and he let them in.

He went through to the lounge and picked up a small package from the TV cabinet and handed it to Malik.

"There's a glass in there so don't break it."

"I'm not stupid, I know what is in it."

"I didn't say you were stupid, although I do doubt your

commitment, so maybe we need to talk to Moreno about your continued involvement."

"My involvement has nothing to do with you. That is between the Comisario and me."

"No, no, it's got everything to do with me, Malik. Your lack of commitment could cost you your life, or even more importantly to me, it could cost me my life, so by lunchtime today you, or Moreno, need to tell me whether you are in or out, with full commitment. If you don't appear at the bar by lunchtime, I'll take that as your answer."

Brodie held the front door open, Malik stood in the centre of the room for a second before storming out, the loud bang of the slamming door following her as she left the house. She walked to the car which had dropped her off earlier and was now waiting just out of sight of the beach house.

Two hours and a shower later, Brodie was on his way to the apartment above the bar. He had loaded as much as he could of his personal effects into the confines of the Mustang and had driven into the underground car park. It took him three trips from car to apartment to empty his car and four trips from beach house to apartment to take what he wanted to his new home. By the time he had finished, he was badly in need of a beer.

"Marie, *buenos dias, que tal?*"

"Good morning to you too. I am very well thank you," She smiled at Brodie.

"I need a beer, it's hot and I've been up and down from the car park to the apartment a dozen times this morning." Brodie poured a cold beer from one of the fonts and sipped at it to quench his thirst. Maria looked puzzled.

"Sorry, I should have said, I'm moving in upstairs today."

"Really? I didn't know."

"Neither did I.... till about three o'clock this morning. Kind of makes sense though."

"Yeah, I suppose."

"Right, I better get on, get a bit more done before lunchtime. If you need me, give me a call and I'll pop down."

Brodie looked at his watch as he walked round to his new home; almost eleven thirty and no sign of Malik. He wasn't sure if he was relieved or disappointed, but either way, it was what it was. He climbed the stairs into the apartment and started to unpack more of his belongings.

A few minutes later the door buzzer sounded. Brodie picked up the wall mounted handset.

"*Diga?*"

"Brodie, we need to talk," a familiar female voice said.

"Come up," Brodie pressed the button and replaced the handset. A few seconds later, there was a knock at the inner door. When Brodie opened it, Anita Malik stood on the top landing.

"Alan, we need to talk."

"You already said that."

"Can I come in?"

"Sure." He stood back from the door as she walked past him into the hallway. Brodie gestured toward the lounge and Malik walked through and stood facing him as he followed her into the room.

"This better be good."

"I should not have said what I did this morning."

"Oh, but you should have, Malik; in these circumstances; you should always say what you think. That way people whose lives might depend on you know how much they can rely on you, or not, as the case may be, and right now, I wouldn't trust you with my budgerigar."

"Señor Brodie, I have been a police officer for almost twelve years, four of those working undercover and during the last two, breaking up an international drugs cartel. In all that time, I have never broken the rules, I have never lacked commitment and I have never let anyone down. I have always obeyed instructions from my superiors, to the letter and I have earned.... yes earned, the respect and trust of my fellow officers. How dare you say that I am not committed or cannot be trusted! Is it because I am a woman? Maybe you only want to work with big, strong, macho men like you? Maybe you don't like black people. Is that it?"

Brodie strode over to the door and swung it open.

"Get out! Get out now and don't ever darken my door again."

Malik crossed the hall towards the door and swung her right foot at it kicking it shut with a loud bang, which resonated throughout the apartment.

"I will not get out! I will not let you ruin my reputation or my career. I have had to work very hard to get to where I am. I am a black woman in a white man's world and I will not lose what I have worked for because of you."

"Now that's impressive, Malik. At least I know that you're committed to you. But let me tell you, I've worked in battle zones with some amazing female soldiers, some of them officers, a few of them black, but all of them, all of them, committed, so don't you dare try to play the race card or accuse me of sexism. Man or woman, I don't care if you are black or sky blue pink with purple spots, but I do need to know that if I'm in trouble, you've got my back and I don't see that in you."

Malik stood for a moment looking at the floor in front of her, slowly she lifted her head and looked at Brodie. She had tears in her eyes.

"Señor Brodie, I have spent the past two years breaking up a very dangerous international drugs network. It was not easy, but we did it. We did it, not I did it. We worked as a team, some of us gave orders, others obeyed them. Two of my colleagues thought they knew better and decided to go against orders. They both died, not quickly and in great pain. I found their bodies. It was horrible...I never want to see that again. I never want to walk into El Puerto to find you lying dead on the floor in a pool of blood, with pieces of your body cut off. Now you know why I do not agree with the cavalier way you are handling this. My commitment is not in question, but I do believe you are taking unnecessary risks."

"Oh Anita, I have seen fellow soldiers and Special Forces operatives killed and I've helped put some of them in body bags, sometimes in one piece, sometimes not. A few have even been killed carrying out my orders, and I remember every one of them, I have the greatest of respect and admiration for my fellow combatants. I would never ask anyone under my command to do something that I would not be prepared to undertake myself. That's why anyone who has ever been in a combat situation with me will tell you that I always lead from the front. Some will charge me with being reckless, but I have a nose for danger and, yes, sometimes I *do* appear to take unnecessary risks, but believe me, I will have assessed the situation and done everything to mitigate it before I put anyone's life in danger unnecessarily, including my own. There's nothing wrong with taking risks, provided you manage them properly"

"And you think you do that?"

"I went into the military straight from university, went from there into Special Forces, I've got two awards for gallantry in combat situations and I'll reach the ripe old age of forty in a couple of years, so I must be doing something right." He smiled, lightening the mood.

"Look, Anita, we both took up careers that meant we would be exposed to a higher risk of being injured, or worst case, killed. On top of that, we volunteered to put ourselves in even more dangerous situations. I didn't need to apply to join a Special Forces group; you didn't need to take on undercover work, but we did, and the best way to survive that is by managing each situation as it arises and watching out for each other.

Now, I need to finish up here and I'm sure you have places to be and things to do. If you are committed to this job, I'll see you down in the bar. If you're not, it's been nice knowing you."

"Just like that?"

"Just like that. I'm safer in this on my own than with a partner I have no confidence in."

"OK", Malik shrugged, opened the door and closing it behind her, walked down the stairs and out into the warm Almanzora sunshine.

Chapter 15

Twenty minutes later when Brodie walked into El Puerto, there was no sign of Malik but the staff were busy putting final preparations in place for another busy lunchtime, so Brodie started to change one of the kegs of beer at the back of the building. He heard a noise behind him and turned to see the door of the ladies toilet open revealing Anita Malik.

"Girl can't serve behind a bar with smudged eye makeup," she smiled.

"Hi!" Brodie couldn't help but sound surprised.

"You thought I had gone?"

"It had crossed my mind."

"Oh no, you don't get rid of me that easily."

"Who said I want to be rid of you?"

Brodie turned away, finished connecting the beer keg and started toward the bar.

"Do you really have a budgerigar?"

He stopped and looked at Malik over his shoulder.

"No."

"That's good."

"Why's that good?"

"My father always told me never to trust a man who had a budgerigar."

"Really?"

Malik laughed and slipped past Brodie to serve two customers at the bar.

El Puerto had a good, steady, year round lunchtime and evening trade. The area was recognised as the hottest part of Spain and as such, attracted a steady stream of tourists almost twelve months of the year. With its beachfront site and close proximity to the small harbour and marina it attracted visitors easily. That coupled with the high percentage of UK and northern European residents in both Villaricos and Puerto Ricos meant good all year business to the bar.

This lunchtime was no exception and for the next two and a half hours the staff worked hard to keep on top of the demands of hungry and thirsty customers, both regular and visiting. So much so, that Comisario Moreno was halfway through his lunch before Brodie noticed him sitting alone at a table in the corner of the internal restaurant area.

"Xavier, I didn't see you sitting there," Brodie welcomed him, "*Como estas* - How are you today?"

"I am very well, my friend, and you?"

"I'm good."

"Can you sit for a moment?"

"Sure"

Moreno dropped his voice, "The finger prints you gave us, they are not from a man called Alexei Markov. They belong to Yuri Kuznetsov, he is Russian, a very dangerous man, Alan. You must treat him with great caution. Europol are very interested in him. He has been linked with drugs cartels and people trafficking in Amsterdam and Hamburg. He is basically a hired killer. I say, linked, because nothing has ever been proved against him. We are still searching the DNA of the blood you have on the paper handkerchief, but no match yet."

"You and Sergeant Malik have had a long chat today, no?"

"That's one way to put it."

"She told me this morning that she was not happy with the way you were handling these people. She said you were putting yourself into dangerous situations and would get yourself killed. She lost two of her team in Algeciras... both were tortured and murdered. I think I underestimated how badly that affected her. She said you and she argued this morning when she picked up the samples from you and you said, maybe she should go."

"True, and I told her to get out of my apartment later on but she stood up to me, which I didn't expect. Accused me of being sexist and racist, didn't want to work with her because she was black and a woman. We had quite a set to."

"Apartment?"

"Yeah, I've moved into the apartment upstairs as of today."

"Ah, OK and you and Malik?"

"Oh, we kissed and made up."

"You kissed?"

Brodie laughed. "No, Xavier, just a figure of speech. I don't think Malik and I will ever kiss, but we've made up, I think."

"She is a good officer, Alan. She will put her all into this, she wants revenge for her two dead colleagues."

Moreno rose from the table, "I must go, crimes to fight, villains to catch," he laughed.

The two shook hands, Moreno paid his bill and waved at Malik as he left.

The lunchtime trade was starting to tail off, Brodie suggested that the staff take their lunch breaks in turn, while the bar was quiet. Eventually he and Malik sat at one of the small tables at the back of the restaurant to take their lunches. Malik sat with a prawn salad and a bottle of still water, while Brodie favoured a portion of Carlos's renowned Chilli con Carne and a bottle of chilled beer.

"You seem at ease with Comisario Moreno."

"I think he is a good man, trying hard to do what's best, despite having set me up for this. I can understand why he did it though."

"So you have forgiven him then?"

"Almost," Brodie smiled.

"But maybe you have not forgiven me yet. Is that why you do not want to work with me? I should not have called you a racist or sexist, I am sorry."

"Anita, I have no problem working with you as long as I know you are committed and that I can trust you for your support when I need it. Yes, I was more than a bit angry about that night in Barril Rojo, but I understand that you were doing your job and carrying out orders, so I don't have an issue with you for that."

"Did Moreno have any feedback on the samples you gave him?"

"Yes and no. He has identified the finger prints as belonging to a Russian called Yuri Kuznetsov, a hired gun as Xavier describes him, well known to Europol but never any evidence. No information on the blood yet."

Brodie rose from the table, "Look I'm going to go sort out some more stuff in the apartment. Why don't you get off for a couple of hours and I'll see you back here about six."

"OK, I'll see you then."

Chapter 16

As Brodie walked round the corner to the apartment, he became aware of someone behind him; he stopped suddenly. His follower stumbled into his back, surprised by Brodie's action. He turned to find an attractive, tanned, blond, woman that he guessed she was in her mid to late thirties. She was wearing a white cotton dress and a red, straw, Stetson with a red and white ribbon around the brim, and carrying an oversized red and white striped beach bag over her shoulder with a compact Glock 9 pistol in her left hand, partly hidden by the bag.

"Please keep walking, Señor Brodie," her English heavily accented.

Brodie looked down at her, standing his ground.

"I said...."

"I know what you said."

"Then do what I say, unless you want that I use this." She poked the Glock at his midriff.

"So, you poke me in the ribs with a gun and ask me to walk with you. That means someone sent you to persuade me to go somewhere, probably to meet that someone who sent you. Now if you were to shoot me as you just suggested, a) that person is going to get really hacked off, and b) everyone here is going to know you've just shot me. Either way that doesn't sound clever to me. Guy who sent you won't get to talk to me and you'll get yourself arrested by that policeman over there," Brodie nodded over the woman's right shoulder and she looked round to check.

As she did so, Brodie grabbed the Glock and pointed it in the air.

"Oh sorry, it's not a policeman," Brodie smiled, holding on to the gun. The woman struggled to release his grip on the weapon, all the time conscious of people walking past.

"Tell you what. Someone obviously wants to see me very badly, so why don't we just put the gun away and we can go see what the man wants? Other option is, we fight over your gun, you get shot or I have you arrested and handed over to the police. What do you think? Either way your boss is going to be pretty pissed off."

Brodie twisted the Glock in the woman's hand, she let go of it with a gasp of pain.

He slipped the gun into his pocket.

"Right, now that we're friends, why don't we go and see the guy who sent you. Where's your transport?"

The woman rubbed her wrist, then pointed to a light blue SEAT Ateca, parked, engine running, on the roundabout at the end of the paseo

"OK, let's go," Brodie walked briskly towards the SEAT and quickly ejected the magazine from the Glock then dropped the weapon into the woman's bag.

"Best you keep that, I'll let you have the magazine when we get to where we're going. Don't want you getting into trouble, do we." He smiled down at his totally confused abductor.

Brodie slid into the back seat and the woman followed him. They both clicked on their seatbelts.

"Right, Fangio, let's go," Brodie tapped the driver on the shoulder and sat back.

The driver looked at his other passenger who said something in what Brodie recognised as Russian. The driver moved off from the kerb and drove back down the street.

"What's wrong with laughing boy?" Brodie asked.

"He doesn't speak English."

"Not at all?"

"Not a word."

"Oh good, 'cause that means you can tell me where we're going and he won't know."

The woman ignored Brodie and continued to look forward through the car's windscreen.

"No? OK. You're going to be mysterious. I like mysterious in a woman. So if you won't tell me where we're going, at least tell me your name."

Still the woman ignored him, staring this time out of the side window of the SEAT.

"Oh, this is getting boring, I think I'll just leave. Next time he stops, I'm off."

The blonde woman still stared out of the window as the car left the village and sped out into the country, heading north, along the coast road.

"Two things, Señor Brodie. One, the car will not stop till we get to our destination and two, even if it did, the doors are locked and cannot be opened from the inside."

The driver looked at the woman in his rear view mirror and said something to her in Russian.

She put her hand in her bag and pulled out a brown, rough fabric hood, "Put that on," she demanded.

"No I will not. Listen, I'm here because I want to be. Your little kidnapping manoeuvre didn't exactly go to plan and I could have either shot you with your own gun or had you arrested, but I didn't, I chose to come with you instead, so you can stick your hood back in your bag, lady,"

The driver suddenly braked hard, pulled onto the side of the road and in one quick movement, got out of the car, pulled a Glock pistol from a shoulder holster and opened the rear door of the car, pointing the Glock at Brodie's head.

"Get out of the car! Move," he barked.

Brodie looked at the woman sitting beside him, "You lied to me. You said he didn't speak English."

"I was told he didn't. You better do as he says."

"Get out of the car!" the man shouted.

The driver was tall and of a broad build. He had long dark hair pulled into a ponytail and a few days growth of beard darkened his chin. He looked as if he would use his Glock if pushed too far.

"OK, OK, keep your hair on," Brodie retorted as he climbed out of the SEAT.

The man moved behind Brodie and as he stood, brought the Glock down hard on the back of his head. He felt a sharp pain, before the world started to spin, and everything went black.

Chapter 17

Brodie woke, confused. He felt as if the whole world had hit him. He reached up and held the back of his head; it felt wet and sticky with blood. He moaned as he opened his eyes.

He was lying on a beige marble tiled floor and became aware of other people standing around him. He counted four pairs of trouser legs and one pair of bare legs resting on top of red, high heeled sandals. He sat up slowly on the floor and looked around.

There were four men in the room as well as the blond woman who had tried to kidnap him earlier. They stood in a semi-circle, all staring down at him.

He found himself in a large living room of a modern villa, with full width bifold doors that opened out onto a swimming pool area surrounded by extensive gardens. The furniture looked expensive and comfortable; two off-white settees sat facing each other across a low glass-topped table with matching occasional furniture that filled the room.

"Señor Brodie, please, take a seat, Vasily, fetch Señor Brodie a drink," a detached, Russian sounding voice said.

Brodie climbed onto one of the settees and looked up at the speaker.

He was a small man, who Brodie guessed would be early to mid-fifties, he had long, white hair and a matching goatee beard. He wore a pink linen shirt and navy trousers.

The man Brodie knew to be Yuri Kuznetsov, stood just behind him as he spoke. They were flanked by the driver of the car and the man who had been referred to as Vasily, who had just placed a glass of clear liquid on the table in front of him.

Brodie picked up the glass and as he raised it to his mouth, realised from the smell that he had been given a substantial measure of vodka, not water as he had expected. He took a large mouthful and put the glass down.

"Please excuse my colleague's over enthusiastic approach to chauffeuring. Unfortunately, some of my employees lack the social skills and refinement of people such as you and I."

"Yeah, I was always told that men were like ponies. Nine times out of ten, when you lift up their tail, you'll find an arse underneath." Brodie glowered at the man responsible for his headache.

Pink shirt laughed, "Very poetic, Señor Brodie, I must remember that one. But I should apologise for the clumsy way you have been brought here. My wishes have unfortunately been misinterpreted. I will ensure that does not happen again."

"I understand you now own El Puerto in Puerto Ricos and I am given to believe that on two occasions you have expressed an interest in some, shall we say, extracurricular activity. Profitable extracurricular activity, of course.

I believe that you told Alexei here, that you were in business to do business and were willing to potentially work with us on that. You told Ivana, that you were coming here of your own free will. You are either a very stupid man or a very brave one to walk into what could be a lion's den for you."

"I'm not stupid. If Alexei had wanted to kill me or harm me he would have done so that night, but he didn't. He was obviously there because I had told the two guys you sent round to intimidate Manuel Gutiérrez that I was open to do business. Then today, why would you want to bring me out here? To kill me, I don't think so, you could do that in Puerto Ricos. You wanted me out here to see if I was someone you would want to do business with; I came because I didn't buy El Puerto to fill tourists' bellies with cold beer. So what more do you want to know?"

"Nothing, I just wanted to look you in the eye, to see if I could trust you. I already know all about you."

"I doubt that, but if you're happy thinking that, then knock yourself out." Brodie chuckled.

The man turned to a bookcase and pulled out a thick file.

"This is my dossier on you; Captain Alan Brodie DSO and bar, ex-SAS and Special Forces who fought in Iraq and Afghanistan. Very impressive. Oh, and the icing on the cake," he pulled a single sheet of paper from the back of the file, "a personal recommendation from my friend Alexander Salenko, who you worked for in London."

"You *have* done your homework."

"I always do my homework, Señor Brodie. I would not have done all this, if I was just going to have you killed." He waved his dossier in the air,

"So, why did you?"

"As I said, I wanted to see if I could trust you and I think I can. Alexander speaks very highly of you, by the way. He said you saved his life in Nice."

"That's what he pays me for."

"Walk with me, come and see my gardens."

"My mother always told me never to walk in gardens with people I don't know."

The man laughed, "Alexander told me you were a man who liked to make jokes sometimes. I am sorry, I have forgotten my manners. My name is Ivan Romanov. Do you mind if I call you Alan?"

"I've been called worse, so no, I don't mind," Brodie smiled.

Romanov walked through the open bifold doors and into the garden, gesturing for Brodie to follow him. Despite the throbbing pain in his head, he slowly followed.

"I believe you have fought against terrorists and jihadists, Alan, so you will be aware of their cell strategy. They keep knowledge to within small groups and information on a strictly need-to-know basis. These people in the house, they do not need to know what we are discussing and sometimes you will not need to know what I have discussed with them. It is safer that way, for everyone."

"Makes sense."

"Good, I am glad we understand each other. I have a consignment of merchandise coming into Puerto Ricos tomorrow morning. It will arrive on a small fishing boat and I would like you to pick it up from the boat, take it to El Puerto and keep it till my courier comes to pick it up from you. Can you do this for me? You will be paid 10,000 euros cash by the courier for your trouble."

"OK, sounds simple enough, you'll need to give more detail of course."

"Of course."

Romanov spent the next twenty minutes giving Brodie instructions on the pick-up procedure, how to find the payment in the goods, store the packages safely and how to recognise the courier.

Romanov and Brodie walked slowly back to the house under the watchful eye of Alexei Markov, who stood with two of Romanov's men at the patio doors, out of earshot of the conversation in the garden, but still watching Brodie and their employer as they spoke.

"So, Alan, my people will take you back to Puerto Ricos, I

hope you will not suffer too much from your head trauma and again, I apologise for that. I look forward to doing business with you."

Romanov opened a drawer in his sideboard and took out a cheap, burner phone.

"My number and only my number, is in there. Take it and use it to call me if necessary. I will also use it to call you."

He held out his hand to Brodie and gave a good firm handshake as he showed him out of the front door to a waiting car.

Chapter 18

BRODIE WAS SHOWN INTO THE BACK SEAT OF THE SAME SEAT which had brought him to the house and found himself seated beside the man referred to as Vasily. The man with the broken nose and ponytail sat in the front passenger seat. The driver was the man who had earlier hit him with the Glock.

They drove past a set of wrought iron gates and turning right towards the coast and Puerto Ricos. Romanov's villa was built on a steep hillside, giving it spectacular views over the countryside and on down to the coast. There were wooded areas and open ground dotted with other Mediterranean style villas.

The Russians sat in silence as they drove down the hill until they entered a mature wooded area, which blocked the sea views. They came to a narrow track leading off the main road and into the trees. The driver turned into it.

"Think you'll find Puerto Ricos is the other way, guys." Brodie suggested

Silence.

Once out of sight of the main road, the driver pulled into the side of the track and stopped. All three Russians got out of the car. The driver held the rear passenger door open for Brodie.

"Get out," he ordered, once again pointing his handgun at Brodie.

Brodie stood carefully, not allowing the driver to move out of his sight.

"So, you will work with Mr Romanov, eh? But first we have a lesson we would like to teach you. You do not hurt our friends without paying a price, Brodie. We will see how brave you are now," he nodded to his two compatriots and waved the Glock at Brodie.

"When I was in the Forces," Brodie explained, "I was always told to get my revenge in first and not wait to be attacked."

As ponytail held back slightly, the other Russian stepped forward. Brodie lunged at him, his right foot connecting with the Russian's knee joint, causing a loud crack as the joint snapped. The man screamed in pain as he lost his balance and fell to the ground. Brodie stepped over him and swung round to face the man whose nose he had broken in the bar kitchen hitting him with a vicious punch to the solar plexus. As the man bent forward struggling for breath, Brodie hit him hard on the back of his neck, just below the base of the skull. As the Russian fell, unconscious, face down into the long grass. Brodie silenced his fellow attacker with a well-aimed kick to the side of his head.

The driver was still processing what had just happened when Brodie rounded on him.

"I take it Mr Romanov doesn't know about this little diversion you and your pals have decided on. You know he wants me to work with him, so you wouldn't dare shoot me. Never point a gun at someone unless you're prepared to use it."

The Russian backed away, still pointing the Glock at Brodie. As he stepped back, he caught his heel on a large stone at the side of the road and his inbuilt reaction was to look down to his foot. Brodie moved fast, grabbed the gun and twisted it, catching the man's finger inside the trigger guard, snapping the bone. The Glock fell from the Russian's grasp allowing Brodie to retrieve it, and point the weapon at his attacker.

A look of disbelief crossed the Russian's face as he nursed his broken finger and saw Brodie standing with the gun pointed at his head.

"I think you've rather shot yourself in the foot, comrade. Oh no, wait a minute," Brodie lowered the Glock, squeezed the trigger and sent a bullet crashing through the man's right foot, "It's me who's shot you in the foot."

The man fell to his knee, looking in horror at his shattered, bleeding foot.

"OK, I'll tell you what's going to happen now. I'm going to borrow your car to get me back to Puerto Ricos and you're going to call your boss to have someone come and get you lot before you bleed to death. I'll leave the car where you picked me up, with the keys still in it. What Romanov decides to do with you guys is totally up to him. Don't wait too long to call him."

Brodie wiped the Glock clean of his finger prints, ejected the magazine, tossed it into the bushes and dropped the gun at the side of the road. He walked to the SEAT, slotted it into reverse and drove back to the road, leaving the three Russians to their fate.

He returned quickly to Puerto Ricos, parked the car as he had promised and walked back to the apartment above El Puerto. Once there he showered and changed, then took a couple of paracetamols to ease the pain of the Russian's recent assault on the back of his head.

He called Moreno to give him an update on the events of the day and outlined the planned drugs pick-up for the next day.

"How do you want to play it tomorrow, Alan?" Moreno asked.

"Discreet surveillance only, Xavier."

"No, we must arrest them, take the drugs."

"That would achieve nothing. We watch and follow the trail. It should lead us back to Romanov and if played right, we could end up with the top man."

"You think that is not Romanov?"

"It's not Romanov. He has a boss, the top man, I'm sure of that. Romanov may be important in the scheme of things but he's not the 'high heid yin', as we say in Scotland, and until we get *him*, we haven't won the day."

"OK, we'll play it your way, but be careful, Alan. You are playing a very dangerous game."

"I'll be fine. Nothing about this is new to me. These guys may be dangerous but not in comparison to the Taliban."

Brodie ended the call and went down to El Puerto. He greeted a few of his regulars as he passed the outside tables and walked into the bar. The staff were busy serving up food and drinks while Anita Malik was tending the bar and chatting with the customers as she served drinks. She paused as she saw Brodie arrive and watched as he began to serve two young women who were at the bar. As he poured their beers, Malik approached him.

"Where have you been? You didn't tell me you were not going to be here today?"

"I didn't know I wasn't going to be here. I'll explain later, too many people around."

Brodie bent down to fill an ice bucket.

"Your head, Alan, what happened?"

"Tell you later."

That evening was busy, time flew past and in what seemed like no time, the kitchen was closed, staff were clearing up and Brodie was sitting in a quiet corner, devouring a fillet steak, that he had cooked to perfection once Carlos had left for the night. Malik stood behind him and touched the large lump on the back of his head.

"Ouch! Careful, you'll hurt my brain, Malik."

"Sorry. What happened, Alan?" Genuine concern in her voice.

"My head bumped into a Glock. I'll tell you when everyone has gone."

The burner phone that Romanov had given him earlier rang in his pocket. He retrieved it and looked at the screen. All it said was, 'unknown number'. Brodie answered it.

"Diga mi!"

"Ah, very Spanish, Alan, I'm impressed," Romanov remarked

"Ivan," Brodie replied.

"I am calling to make an apology to you. I understand the men I asked to take you back to Puerto Ricos had ideas of their own."

"Yes, they did. I managed to dissuade them, though. I hope I didn't damage them too much."

"No matter. They are dead now. I do not tolerate disobedience, so I have made an example of them. That way none of the others will make the same mistake."

"Bit drastic was it not?"

"I think not Alan. I am very loyal to those I work with and I expect the same in return. You are not harmed, I take it."

"No, I'm fine. They didn't get a chance to hurt me."

"You are still OK to pick up the merchandise tomorrow?"

"Of course, are you still OK to pay me?"

"Of course."

"Then I look forward to doing business with you, Ivan."

"And I with you, Alan." Romanov ended the call.

Brodie sat looking at the phone. "They are dead now."

Romanov had been so matter of fact about needlessly killing three people.

"You've got a new phone?"

"Sorry?" Brodie was brought back to the present.

"New phone?"

"Eh, yes. Long story, we need to talk."

"Miguel, can you lock up, tonight?"

"*Si,* sure thing, I have keys."

"Good man, thanks. Anita and I are going for a late night swim. Malik, walk this way!"

Chapter 19

"Late night swim, I don't think so!" Malik replied softly, following Brodie out of the bar.

She caught his arm, "I'm not going for a swim, I don't have a costume!"

"Why do you need a costume? Its dark." Brodie smiled at her obvious panic.

"Brodie, I'm not going swimming with you without a costume."

"Spoilsport. Actually we're not going swimming, I need to update you on what went down today and the bar has cameras and microphones which I installed a while ago for Manuel. It's better we talk in the apartment."

Malik punched Brodie hard on the back of his shoulder. "You pig!"

Brodie opened the door of the apartment and they climbed up the stairs to the large lounge area.

"Can I get you a drink? I haven't got that much in, only what I brought with me from the house. I've got some beers and a couple of bottles of Rioja," Brodie explained as he started to open a bottle of Rioja for himself.

"Rioja's fine," Malik replied as she followed him into the kitchen, leaning against the doorway, arms folded and wearing a frown.

"So how did you get the head injury?" she asked, looking at the back of his head. "Have you cleaned it yet?"

"Yeah, I had a shower earlier and put some antiseptic on it. The cut's not bad, the lump makes it look worse than it is."

Malik walked over and stood behind him. She fingered the wound and nodded.

"It's not bleeding now and it does look clean."

"There you go, nurse Malik," Brodie handed her a glass of wine and gestured towards the lounge. "Grab a seat and I'll bring you up to date."

Once seated, Brodie went over the events of that day. He told her of the plan to retrieve a delivery of drugs from the fishing boat in the morning and the payment he was to receive. As she started to object, he told her of his conversation with Moreno and his eventual agreement to allow Brodie to run with it for the time being to see where the trail led. He explained to her about the burner phone and the call from Romanov. She did not seem in the least phased when he told her that the three men who had attacked him had been killed.

"These men are ruthless, Alan, they will kill anyone who threatens their supply chain. As long as you are a link in that chain, he will protect you, but when he no longer needs you, he will kill you too."

"I'm well aware of that," Brodie replied, stretching over to pour a second glass of Rioja for each of them.

"I shouldn't really, I have to drive home," Malik said.

"Grab a taxi."

"OK, I suppose I could. Thanks then.

This is a beautiful apartment, I didn't know you had bought it as well as El Puerto."

"Made sense. It's handy for sure and when the bar's open,

I'll be downstairs working so the noise won't bother me. Having said that, it's obviously well insulated because when I was moving in I was up here and the bar was open and I wasn't conscious of noise."

"Are you going to work every night?"

"No. I will do at the moment, but once this drugs thing is sorted out, I won't be. I don't want to be needed downstairs, I want to work when I want and not be relied on. I'll still be away a good bit, security work pays too much to just ditch at the moment. Last job I did was for an old friend, took less than a week and I walked away with a six-figure sum of money."

"Wow, maybe I should try private security, if that's what it pays."

Brodie laughed, "Doesn't always pay that much and you find yourself working in some real hellholes from time to time."

"How did you come here?"

"I'd done some security work occasionally for a Russian oligarch who lives in London, looking after him and his family if they are travelling, sometimes its business, other times its leisure. He owns a huge villa just outside Malaga and I was looking after his wife and kids on holiday there a couple of years ago. When I saw them off at the airport, I grabbed a rental car and decided to do the tourist bit for a couple of weeks. I've always liked Spain and never really had the chance to see much of the country. I drove up the coast intending to drive up to Bilbao and fly back from there. Two days into my road-trip I found Villaricos and fell in love with the place. I stayed for a few nights and met a Belgian couple in a bar one night. They were moaning about the property crash and the fact that they were going to be forced to sell their house here and couldn't get a buyer. They said they would need to take a massive hit moneywise but had no choice as they needed cash for another business investment.

The guy's wife had a brochure in her bag. When I saw the

house and where it was, I bought another bottle of Rioja and talked a rock bottom price out of them, on the basis that I would pay them in cash as soon as the legalities could be completed. I was in a notary's office the next morning and flew back to the UK at the end of my two weeks with the keys of the beach house in my pocket. I never did make it to Bilbao."

Anita Malik laughed, "You really are a man of action then."

"I believe life's for living. It presents you with once-in-a-lifetime opportunities. If you don't grab them there and then, they're gone. I've stood beside too many men, Anita, who were there one minute and gone the next. If I see an opportunity and it's within my reach, I'll grab it."

"You have not made any mistakes?"

"Sure I have. Thankfully none that I haven't been able to rectify. I bought the beach house. If it turns out to be a wrong move, I can always sell it on. Property prices have started to recover, so it wouldn't have cost me any money. Might even make a small profit."

"What about women? Have you made mistakes there?"

"None that I regret. I love my lifestyle. I like that I can make my own decisions and not have to worry about anyone else. Don't get me wrong, Anita, I love women too... just never met one that I am willing to give up my lifestyle for."

"Maybe one day you will."

"She'd need to be a very special lady. Who knows? My friend Rob has just married a lady who's a bit special and I looked at them with a bit of envy and thought, maybe one day. But now, here I am, chasing sun kissed tourists in bikinis from behind my own bar overlooking a Spanish beach."

Malik put down her glass and rose to her feet. "I should be going, Alan, I need to grab a taxi. Where is best to find one?"

Brodie stood, "I'll show you, come on."

They left the apartment and walked across the plaza past the obligatory fountain to the road which took traffic to and from Villaricos to Garrucha and Mojácar. The traffic was heavy during the day and through the evening, but was currently fairly quiet. Nevertheless there were still two taxis standing on the rank just beyond the plaza.

Brodie opened the rear door for Malik.

"Thank you, Alan," Malik hesitated, "I enjoyed tonight, maybe we can do it again, sometime."

She stood on her tiptoes and kissed Brodie lightly on his lips.

Brodie, slightly taken aback, smiled, leaned towards her and they kissed once again.

"What happened to professional?" Brodie teased.

"You could pay me. A six figure sum of money would be nice, Señor Brodie. Good night, Alan." Malik smiled at him as she curled her long legs into the taxi and Brodie closed the door.

He walked back to his apartment, the taste of Malik on his lips.

Chapter 20

BRODIE SLEPT FITFULLY THAT NIGHT, HIS MIND SWITCHING between the memories of an unexpectedly pleasant evening spent with Anita Malik, ending with an even more unexpected kiss, plus the prospect of the drugs pick-up the next morning.

He rose early, showered and dressed, then made breakfast. He sat at the breakfast bar, checking his email as he ate and drank a mug of strong black coffee.

At nine o'clock, he stepped out of the apartment into the warm morning sun, dressed in a pair of denim shorts and a pale blue, linen shirt, striding purposefully towards the harbour. The shops displayed their merchandise on the paseo; the upmarket boutiques had their windows displaying expensive ladies' clothes and accessories.

As he turned towards the little harbour, bustling with small local fishing boats whose owners were now throwing their catches onto the harbour side. Brodie homed in on the boat described to him by Romanov. He passed one of his regular customers, carrying his freshly caught fish, and smiled quickly to acknowledge him. His move was also designed to surprise anyone following him. He saw a small, rotund man dressed in black jeans and t-shirt suddenly turn away and look into the harbour, before turning his attention back to Brodie.

Brodie looked away, not wanting to alarm the man any more than he already had, continued along the harbour to his target boat.

"*Buenos dias,* Pedro. I hope you had a good catch this morning." Brodie recited the opening gambit he had been told to use by way of introduction.

"*Buenos dias,* Señor, I have your order ready," Pedro pushed a large, thick, blue, plastic bag onto the quayside.

"A pleasure doing business," Brodie recited, as he stooped down to pick up the bag and turned to see the man in black standing behind a pile of plastic fish boxes, doing his best to look disinterested.

Brodie carried the large fish filled plastic bag, trying hard not to let it come into contact with his clothing. As he walked, he took out his phone and put it to his ear as if taking a call. He held it up to look at the screen and seeing the reflection of man following him, quickly reversed the camera, took a quick photograph of him, then pocketed his phone.

El Puerto was not particularly busy as Brodie stepped into the kitchen. Manolo was prepping for the day and Carlos would probably be down at the harbour looking at the day's catch. Surprisingly, Brodie had not seen him as he passed the little fish market.

"Manolo, go take a break. I'm sure you would welcome a coffee."

Manolo looked surprised. "*Si,* no problem," he said eventually, and wandered through to the bar.

Brodie took the first fish out of the bag and using one of the sharp kitchen knives, carefully cut it open to retrieve the drugs as Romanov had instructed. The fish was empty. Brodie lifted out the four other fish, one by one and repeated the process.

They were all empty, except one, which contained a clear plastic bag filled with 10,000 euros.

Brodie picked out the cash and took it through to the small safe under the bar and making sure he was unobserved, stashed the money in the safe. He then placed all five fish back in the bag he had collected them in, sealed them in a plastic bin bag, and deposited them in a large rubbish bin at the back of the kitchen.

He took out his phone to call Moreno. The call was answered almost immediately.

"Did you send someone to follow me this morning, Xavier?"

"No, why?"

"Because I had a tail when I went down to collect the drugs. If you didn't send him then Romanov must have. The fish were all empty by the way. No drugs. I'm just about to call Romanov but needed to know about my short fat friend before I do."

"You're sure he was following you? It wasn't just a coincidence?"

"No, he was tailing me for sure. I took a photograph of him on my phone. I'll forward it to you. See if you know him."

"OK, do that."

Brodie ended the call.

He picked up the burner phone Romanov had given him and pressed a button. Romanov answered after four rings.

"Did you make the pickup?"

"You know I did. Your little fat friend will have confirmed that. By the way, tell him that black jeans and t-shirt are not a good look when you're wandering around a harbour and trying not to stand out."

"I'm sorry you spotted Igor and he will be too."

"You know there was no merchandise in the bag."

Romanov laughed. "You do not think I would risk valuable merchandise when I try a new partner? He or she might decide to keep it or to go to the authorities with it. Not that I think you would be so stupid, my friend, but you must understand my caution. It's what keeps me in business. You have been paid for your trouble and now that we know we can trust each other, the real pickup can take place, same time and place as today, if you are in agreement."

"OK, same payment?"

"Of course."

"No tail?"

"I think we are past that."

"Good, I'll call you again tomorrow when I am in receipt." Brodie ended the call.

"Where is Manolo?" the question came from the back door.

"Carlos! I needed to make a couple of calls and asked Manolo to go get a coffee."

"OK, that explains. You are finished now?"

"Yes, you can have your kitchen back." Brodie smiled and patted Carlos' shoulder as he passed.

He stepped through to the bar and was met by Anita Malik, who was filling ice buckets in readiness for the lunchtime trade.

She looked at Brodie, somewhat embarrassed, "Alan, I am sorry for last night, for what I did."

"What did you do?"

"You know what. I kissed you. It must have been the wine. Maybe I should not drink wine in future, if that's how it affects me."

Brodie smiled as he walked past her, she carried on with the ice, until Brodie reappeared at her shoulder.

"If that's what the odd glass of wine does to you, maybe you should have this," he suggested with a smile, handing her a glass of Rioja. "I rather enjoyed last night, I had hoped you did too."

Malik looked flustered, somewhat surprised by Brodie's

reaction and more than a little baffled by the offer of a glass of Rioja. Then the penny dropped and she smiled coyly.

"You did?"

"You sound surprised, Malik. What's not to like?"

"I don't know. I wasn't sure. I didn't think.... I just did it." Malik stammered.

Brodie took her hand and led her through to the back of the bar area. He turned to face her, cupped her face in his hands and smiled as he bent forward to kiss her. She responded after a few seconds, kissing him back as he pulled her to him.

"Good to see you two are getting along at last," a voice came from behind them.

Both turned in surprise to find Moreno leaning against the door frame, arms folded.

"Comisario!" Malik jumped backward.

"Xavier, good to see you. We are trying to give anyone watching us the impression that we are close. It would seem very strange otherwise. It has to be said that Malik took a bit of persuading, but she eventually agreed that to all and sundry she should be my girlfriend. Otherwise, why would we spend time talking in dark corners as we tend to do in here?"

"You certainly had me fooled, Alan, I didn't realise Sergeant Malik was such a good actress."

"Lives are at stake, Xavier. In this game you're either good or you're dead and you told me Malik was here because she was good."

"Mm, yes, I suppose you are right."

"Can we talk about this morning?"

"No, not here. It would look strange if we were seen having an in-depth conversation through here. After the lunchtime biz, Malik and I will go up to the apartment and call you. Say 2.30?"

"OK, that would probably be best as you say. You will send me the photograph you took?"

"Photograph?" Malik sounded puzzled.

"I still haven't had time to tell Malik about this morning. It's difficult in here. That's why we need to look like we're close, if we're going to have cosy little chats."

"Yes, yes, I can understand."

"OK, I take it you came here for some lunch?"

"Yes, that is indeed why I am here," Moreno laughed.

"Good!" Brodie replied, placing his hand on Moreno's shoulder and leading him through to the front seating area.

"Your usual, Comisario?"

Moreno nodded his agreement.

"Manolo, *tostada con tomate para Comisario Moreno, por favour.*"

"*Si,* coming up." Manolo shouted back from the kitchen. "*Y un cafe con leche, mas caliente.*"

Having finished his tomato toastie and extra hot, white coffee, Moreno waved goodbye and left.

Malik approached Brodie, her hands at her mouth, her dark brown eyes wide.

"How could the Comisario find us kissing?" she uttered in total disbelief. "Of all the times for him to walk in. You have never kissed me in the bar before!"

"I think we got away with it, though. He seemed to buy that we need people to think we are close."

"That was good. I would never have thought of that."

"Just as well I was here then!"

"Wait a minute, if you had not been here, you would not have been kissing me!"

"Um, I suppose there is that. Just as well I was here then." Brodie winked and smiled as he kissed her again.

Chapter 21

THE LOUNGE IN BRODIE'S NEWLY ACQUIRED APARTMENT HAD TWO, three seater settees facing each other across a long, low glass topped table. Brodie and Malik faced each other, both looking at Brodie's phone on the table which was set to speakerphone. Brodie debriefed both Moreno and Malik on the events of that morning. He had taken time to send Moreno the photograph of the man who had been following him during his trip to the fishing boat.

"We have no match for him so far with facial recognition, but we are still looking. If he is known to any police force in Europe, we will know soon enough," Moreno had informed them.

"It will be interesting to see if he follows me tomorrow. Romanov says he won't. He knows I clocked him this morning."

"Do you think he will?"

"Yeah, I think so, Anita. I might be wrong, although I hope not."

"Why so?" Moreno asked.

"Because if he does, I'll send Romanov a photograph, tell

him that he is surrounded by amateurs and that he needs to be very careful for both his organisation and his own personal safety. My hope is he will see me as a solution to that problem."

"You need to be careful, Alan, these are dangerous people."

"We want to get to the top of the tree; we won't do that by being too careful. We'll need to take a few risks, but we'll manage them as best we can, don't worry."

"Don't worry, he says. You have one of my best officers working with you, Alan. You are responsible for her safety as well as your own. I don't want anything to happen to either of you. I will ultimately be held responsible for both if things go wrong"

"Comisario, I am quite capable of looking after myself and I will look out for Alan as well," Malik protested.

"I'm glad you said that Malik, because up until now you have been pretty much in the background. We have only been seen together in the bar, but we need to be seen more now as a couple, as we were in the bar today. You need to become more involved so that we're both getting closer to the top man, not just me. Are you both OK with that?"

"There is no point in me being here just to serve beers. The whole idea was for us to work as a team, use our joint experience to crack this," Malik replied before Moreno could interject.

"She's right, Xavier. You insisted on her being here because she was a good officer who was part of the team that broke up a big drugs cartel in Algeciras, not because she was a good barmaid."

Moreno hesitated, considering what Brodie and Malik had said.

"You're right, of course," he said eventually. "OK, but please be careful, both of you."

"We will," Brodie assured him and ended the call.

He looked across at Malik. "You OK with that?"

"If you are."

"If I am?"

"You said you did not trust me to do what you needed me to do."

"Yes, I did, I'm sorry, I was wrong. Even now, you showed that you are willing to put yourself in the firing line. You could have backed off with Moreno, but you didn't. You did the exact opposite. I appreciate that."

"So we are a team now?" Malik asked standing as Brodie picked up his phone from the table.

"Looking that way," he smiled.

"Speaking of teams, I need to rearrange the team downstairs. I never intended to work full time in the bar but we both have to try to get ourselves attached to the Russians. We need more flexibility, to come and go without leaving the bar understaffed, so I need a manager and a bar person. I'm going to ask Miguel if he will step up as manager. He's capable and honest. He's Manuel's nephew and has worked here for a while so he knows the business."

"And the bar."

"I'll replace one sexy lady with another sexy lady, to bring the customers in."

Malik laughed and stood close to Brodie draping her arms around his neck.

"You think I am a sexy lady, Señor Brodie?"

Brodie pulled her close. Malik was tall, probably only six inches or so shorter than his six foot four, so he only had to bend his head down slightly to kiss her, which was unusual for him, "I think you're an incredibly sexy lady, Sergeant Malik, but right now, we have work to do."

"You are a slave driver. What about my employee's rights?" Malik pouted.

"That's the first time I've heard it called that," Brodie chuckled. "We can discuss those later."

The two laughed, descending the stairs to street level and from the square round to El Puerto. The bar and restaurant were quiet and the day staff had gone, replaced by the evening shift.

Malik went behind the bar and started to help with the preparation for the busier evening trade. Cutting lemon and lime slices, stocking up on mixers, ensuring spirit optics were well charged, filling ice trays, all took time. Advance preparation of these went a long way to making for an easier shift behind any bar.

Brodie called Miguel over and sat with him at one of the quieter tables.

"Miguel, when I bought this place from your uncle, it was never my intention to work here full time. I planned to help out rather than run it on a day-to-day basis. Sometimes I might need to be away for a few weeks at a time, although I hope that will happen less and less. What I'm trying to say, is that I need a full-time manager to run the place and make decisions when I'm not around.

You know the business, probably better than I do. You do your job well, the rest of the staff get on with you and you're someone I can trust. It would mean longer hours but obviously more money too. Would you take on the job?"

"Wow.... I did not expect this," Miguel stammered, somewhat taken aback, "But, of course I would love to take the job, Señor Alan. My uncle Manuel would be so proud of me, thank you."

"Good, we can sort out the hours and your salary tomorrow. I thought a salary, plus commission based on profit. Listen, I could do with some extra cover behind the bar as well. I want Anita to be freed up to work less hours, so if you hear of anyone looking..."

"Ah, my cousin, Christina. She works for Uncle Manuel in Mojácar and she lives in Palomares. She has told him that it is too far to travel late at night and she is looking for a job closer to home. She had thought Villaricos but this would be even closer. Can I ask her to come down and speak with you?"

"Sure, sounds ideal. I'd rather have someone you know than a total stranger."

Chapter 22

BY THE TIME MIGUEL AND BRODIE HAD SPOKEN, THE EVENING customers had begun drifting into El Puerto. Food orders were being placed with Carlos and Manolo in the kitchen and drinks were being prepared behind the bar. A few of the regulars stopped to speak to Brodie as they passed. They laughed, joked, and told stories as the friendly, convivial atmosphere of El Puerto, gradually built up in the warm, balmy Andalusian air, enveloping Brodie, and reminding him of what had motivated him to buy the bar in the first place.

The mood created by people enjoying good food and animated conversation, lubricated by their choice of drinks was enhanced by the constant clicking of the cicadas in the nearby trees and the rhythmic sound of the waves breaking on the beach. It was this atmosphere that Brodie had enjoyed from the first night he'd stepped into the bar as a customer, an ambience a million miles from the hot sands of Iraq or the cold nights in the mountains of Afghanistan, together with the bullets and roadside bombs of these war zones. War zones that had claimed the lives of too many of his friends and brothers in arms.

He looked over at the bar and at Anita Malik; she seemed to sense his eyes on her and returned his gaze. She smiled, then turned to face a customer she was serving. Malik would be used to being looked at by men and women. Admiring looks from men and perhaps looks of envy from some women, or stares of jealousy from others, who caught the admiring glances she warranted from the men by their sides.

Brodie returned her smile. "God, you're beautiful," he murmured quietly, to no one in particular.

"I hope you're not talking to yourself, Mr Brodie," a voice from the beach behind him said, "Please don't turn round and if anyone comes over, please walk away."

Brodie continued to look at the bar, but instantly recognised the voice, "Alexei, good to meet you again. To what do I owe this pleasure? I assume you are not building sand castles down there."

"Bridges, more than sand castles, Captain Brodie, and I assume the object of your appreciation was the delectable Sergeant Malik, who it has to be said, is an object of rare beauty."

"Black, female police sergeants are allowed to be beautiful, and I am allowed to have a girlfriend."

"I am sure that this is all true Mr Brodie, but I did not come here to discuss your sexual preferences. Your little ruse to collect my fingerprints on a glass was very admirable, but it leaves me in a very difficult position. I cannot have Romanov find out that I am not Alexei Markov, as that would put a complicated Europol operation in jeopardy and my life in great danger, as I am sure you understand."

Brodie casually swung his legs over the paseo wall to look down at the Russian.

"So Yuri, you can't decide whether to kill me, Malik and Moreno, who all know your real identity, or to bring us on board with your operation ....and you want my advice on what to do."

"I would not have put it that way but in essence, that is my dilemma."

"Well, I've just bought this place." Brodie gestured toward El Puerto. "So I obviously don't have a death wish, so you might want to convince me to keep my mouth shut, as I have done up until now."

"You know who I am, so you therefore know what I am and what I do."

"Mm, you kill people"

"Maybe. Europol arrested me for killing four people in Amsterdam about eighteen months ago. They had some very strong evidence against me that would have put me in prison for the rest of my life. However, they also knew that I had contacts in the drugs cartels that could be very useful to them. Normally, the people who order assassinations are very high in their organisation and I know many of them. Your sergeant, who you obviously admire, was part of a team which took down a major drugs organisation in Algeciras at the end of last year. I gave her bosses the intelligence to act on. That is how I know of her. When you managed to get my fingerprints and sent your enquiry to Europol, they alerted me, and I looked at you and Malik. I saw that you were getting in on Romanov's organisation and that you had Malik at your side. I put two and two together, then factored in that Moreno and Malik knew who I was. I saw the danger."

"It's not Romanov's organisation, he's just the front man."

"I know, but I do not know who the top man is and it is important that he is found and dealt with."

"Is that why you're here?"

"To find and kill him, yes."

"What do you want from me?"

"I think you also want to find the top man or you would

have interrupted the drug courier who you met with this morning. I think you are not interested in stopping the drugs by arresting a few Russian bullies, you want Romanov's boss, the top man and that is what Europol want. They want to take down the whole organisation, not just the couriers. That's what we did in Algeciras."

"Yeah, Malik told me."

"She is good, but she has not killed before. You have, I have seen it in your eyes. You are dangerous, Mr Brodie. Romanov is soft. He gets other people to do his killing and believes that gets him respect. He surrounds himself with killers and he likes you. He knows Alexander Salenko from the big yacht club in Puerto Banús, sometimes they party together. If you are good enough for Salenko, you would be good enough for Romanov. He will test you out on small things then introduce you to bigger things. Just try not to kill for him."

"OK, I hear you."

"I should go, before someone sees me talking to you. Tell Moreno and Malik we have spoken. I do not want them arresting me. Tell them to talk to the Europol office in Madrid, they know what I am doing here."

"OK, I'll do that."

"I will keep in touch, Alan Brodie. Oh, by the way, I have told Romanov that I do not like you. It is what he would expect of me if he thinks I see you as a threat."

Markov turned, walked into the darkness and was out of sight almost immediately, leaving Brodie to his thoughts. Only Europol would know what Markov had just told him, but he would talk to Moreno, tell him of this conversation and ask him to check out Markov's story.

Chapter 23

BRODIE DECIDED TO WAIT UNTIL HE COULD SPEAK WITH MORENO and Malik together. He texted Moreno and asked when it was good to call him, letting him know it was urgent. After a couple of further messages. It was agreed that they would speak once El Puerto's evening trade had eased off allowing the rest of the staff to cope without them for a while.

By ten o'clock, the kitchen was closed and many of the customers were starting to leave.

"Miguel, can you and the guys cope for an hour or two without Anita and me?"

"Sure, no problem. Everyone's served now. Maybe a few more drinks but that's OK."

"Malik, your boss needs words!" Brodie raised his eyebrows, "can we go upstairs?"

"Of course," Malik smiled in reply.

They climbed the stairs to the apartment and Brodie motioned Malik to go through to the lounge. Brodie didn't speak.

"What's all this about?" Malik asked. She was beginning to know Brodie's moods and mannerisms

"We're going to call Moreno," He hit the speed dial button on his phone and put it on speaker phone, before placing it on the table as before.

"Moreno," came the response after two rings. "This sounds serious Alan."

"It is. I need to tell both of you about a development earlier tonight."

Brodie related his earlier conversation with Markov to Malik and Moreno who both listened quietly as Brodie spoke.

"OK, first reactions?"

There was no immediate response.

"Xavier?" Brodie prompted.

"I do not understand. Yes, I sent the fingerprints to Europol and they came back with the identification, which said that they belonged to Yuri Kuznetsov, who was a Russian hitman wanted by Europol. I have heard nothing since then, but I have contacts in their office in Madrid. I will call them."

"Either Markov has an informant in Europol who is feeding him info or he's a Europol plant, but one way or another he knows things only Europol could tell him, and if he spills his guts to Romanov and his cronies, we're dead."

"Yes. I will contact Madrid now. Give me an hour and I will call you back."

The phone went dead.

Malik looked stunned, "Wow, do you think he is telling the truth?"

"Markov? I've no reason to doubt him. He was telling me things only Europol would know. He knew you were police, how? He knew about your involvement in Algeciras, how? He knew of my involvement here, how? He might have got lucky and figured out one of these, but not all of them. That had to come from Europol."

"Kuznetsov is a killer Alan. We need to be wary of him."

"No, no! Not Kuznetsov. He is Markov, always Markov. If he

becomes Kuznetsov in your head, you'll call him Kuznetsov one day and that could be fatal for him *and* maybe you too."

"Sorry, yes, you are right."

A few moments later, Brodie's phone rang.

He stabbed the answer button. "Xavier, what have you found?"

"Markov is a Europol plant, pretty much as he described to you. I have spoken with Madrid and Amsterdam. He is deep into the drug cartels and yes, he was involved in the Algeciras operation for Europol. Some of the intelligence you acted on, Anita, came from Markov. He heard your name mentioned after that operation and when he started to get involved with Romanov, he saw your name crop up again and put two and two together. Then he noticed you at El Puerto and knowing that Brodie was about to be used as a courier by Romanov, again he started to do sums. He reported all this back to Madrid, who spoke to Amsterdam. Amsterdam picked up my enquiry about his fingerprints. They did some digging, joined up some dots, told Madrid. They told him to approach you before you blew his cover."

"Who did you speak to in Madrid?" Malik asked.

"I spoke with Comisario Hernandez, who you know. Hernandez was the man who suggested Sergeant Malik to us for this operation, Alan. However, the man who came back to me was Comisario Principal Alonso. He was aware that you had been seconded to me in Mojácar to work with me against Romanov. He also thinks that Romanov is not the top man in the organisation."

"He's not, Xavier, he hasn't got the brains to set up and run an organisation like this. He does what someone else tells him to. He's too busy looking in his vanity mirror to see what's going on around him. That's why he can't control his own people. They don't respect him. He thinks ruthless gets him respect, it doesn't. Somebody is running an organisation made up of cells, same as terrorists do, small groups acting autonomously, under orders from above."

"That's what Comisario Principal Alonso says he gets from Markov."

"OK, listen, I need to go and close up the bar. If you find out any more let us know."

"*Si,* I will, good night and be careful, both of you."

"Will do. Good night."

Brodie ended the call and stood up, "I better go and help Miguel. I don't think he knows the combinations."

"I'll help you."

"No, it's fine, it won't take me long. Before I do though, I'm going to get you a taxi to take you home. I don't want you wandering about on your own at night till we get this Markov thing sorted out."

"I'm a big girl, Alan, I can look after myself." Malik protested.

"I know you are and I know that I'm maybe being a little bit over protective, but humour me here. I just need to know that you're safe, OK?"

"Hey, that almost sounded like someone who cares."

"Of course I do. I care about everyone who works with me."

"And that's all I am to you.... someone who works for you."

Malik walked out of the room, down the stairs and out into the plaza, closely followed by Brodie.

"Hang on, that's not what I meant. Anita, please."

He watched in disbelief as Malik's long legs propelled her purposefully towards the taxi rank and into a waiting cab.

Just then his phone pinged and he stopped to read the message.

"Hey, Señor Alan, I have closed up and am just leaving now. I have all the combinations."

Chapter 24

AT SIX THIRTY THE NEXT MORNING, BRODIE ROSE, PULLED ON A pair of black running shorts, a black top and a pair of trainers. He picked up a pair of Ray-Bans, made his way down to the beach, and began to run along the water's edge towards Villaricos. Alone on the beach, at that time of the morning, he was still annoyed with Malik for storming out of his apartment the night before. He ran at a punishing pace, his feet stamping into the wet sand as he took his mood out on the beach.

The morning had not yet reached the high temperature it would within a few hours but it was warm enough to cause Brodie to sweat profusely as he reached the far end of his usual morning run, just short of Villaricos. He turned and started back for Puerto Ricos, the sun now in his eyes as he ran.

Nearing Puerto Ricos, he became aware of another runner coming towards him, but with the sun behind the figure, all he had was a profile of someone running. He altered his direction to take him closer to the water's edge, the figure coming towards him followed suit. Alarm bells started to ring in Brodie's head.

As he got closer to the figure, he heard a familiar voice.

"Alan, Alan, stop, please!" Malik called to him.

Brodie kept running and as he passed Malik, she shouted to him again.

"Alan, Alan, please!"

Brodie kept running and became aware of Malik running just behind him.

"Alan, we need to talk, please. Alan don't ignore me."

Malik caught up with Brodie and caught his arm.

"Don't you dare ignore me you arrogant...."

Brodie suddenly stopped, causing Malik to bump into him, he quickly picked her up and started towards the water.

"Put me down!"

Brodie kept walking and soon the water was lapping around his knees, as Malik kicked and wriggled.

"Brodie, put me down. Do you hear me? Put me down!"

The water was now at the top of his thighs.

"Put you down, OK." Brodie tossed Malik unceremoniously into the water.

"That'll cool your temper, madam." he shouted above the sound of the waves and turned away as Malik surfaced and staggered to her feet, spluttering water.

"You arrogant, self-centred bastard, Brodie."

"Oh right. Water not cool enough," Brodie turned and picked Malik up again and walked further into deeper water, with her still kicking and shouting to be put down.

Eventually, Brodie tossed her into the water again. As he did so, Malik wrapped her arms round his neck and the weight and momentum of her body pulled him under the water with her. They both struggled to find their footing and as they surfaced, Malik kept her arms tightly round Brodie's neck to stop him from throwing her into the water again. Brodie tried to break her hold but she had no intension of letting go.

"That was sneaky, Malik," Brodie spluttered.

Malik panted for breath. "No choice," was all she could manage.

They suddenly seemed to realise how close they were to each other and both backed away slightly, although Malik refused to let go of Brodie's neck.

They stared at each other, both catching their breath; slowly Malik pulled Brodie to her and kissed him. Taken by surprise, Brodie stepped back and looked at her. She smiled at him, Brodie kissed her, tentatively at first, till he felt her kiss him again and suddenly they were lost in each other.

After a while, they became aware of other people on the beach, walking past, watching them. They pulled back, both looking slightly embarrassed.

"You want to come back to mine and dry off?"

Malik laughed. "Yes, please."

Brodie looked around in the water, eventually finding his sunglasses and they walked, dripping wet, up to his apartment.

"There's a robe hanging up in the second bedroom. Go take your wet things off and put that on. Our clothes can go in the dryer. They won't take long to dry.

"OK, thanks. I'll only be a minute."

She was as good as her word and soon emerged from the second bedroom, wearing one of the robes. There had been two, a man's and a woman's. Malik was wearing the latter, and carrying her wet clothes.

"Great, I'll stick them in the dryer."

"If you want a shower, help yourself. There are towels in the bathroom. I'm going to grab a shower too."

Brodie walked through to his bedroom and into the ensuite shower room. He was rubbing shampoo into his shoulder length, wavy, fair hair when he heard a discrete cough from behind him. He turned quickly to find Malik standing in the middle of the shower room wearing the pale green robe. As

Brodie watched, she untied it, letting it drop slowly to the ground.

"You said if I wanted a shower, I could help myself," she smiled.

"I meant.... that you could use the...the other shower." Brodie stammered.

Malik stood naked then did a slow, 360 degree pirouette with her arms extended. She was a stunningly beautiful woman.

"You do not like naked black women, or is it just me you don't like? Last night you said I was just like anyone else who worked for you. Now you want me to use the other shower," she stated.

"That's not what I said, either last night or just now." Brodie held out his hand. "So, get your sexy backside in here now."

Malik smiled and walked into the spacious shower, Brodie clasped her slender waist as she wrapped her arms around his neck, for the second time that morning.

"You think my backside is sexy?" she asked looking up at him.

"I think every inch of you is sexy, Sergeant Malik."

"Prove it then!"

Chapter 25

MAKING LOVE WITH ANITA MALIK CAME AS A VERY PLEASANT surprise to Brodie. He hadn't realised that they had become so close. He was aware he had started to really care for her, but had been totally blindsided by the fact that her feelings for him ran so deep.

He had discovered that morning that Sergeant Malik and Anita Malik were two totally different people. Sergeant Malik was professional, impersonal, even distant. She had obviously had to work hard against both sexism and racism among her peers and was immensely proud of what she had achieved professionally. The fact that her beauty had, if anything, strengthened resistance to her professional progress because so many male officers could not see past her sensuality.

Anita Malik, on the other hand, when she encountered the racism that many women like her had to tolerate, treated it totally differently. She used her looks as a weapon, no sitting in a corner hoping that people wouldn't notice her; she dressed to be noticed, wearing brightly coloured, sexy clothing, with her almost black, curly hair worn big and long.

As Brodie had also discovered that morning, Malik could

show a vulnerable, insecure side which was very much at odds with her public persona. She had offered her nakedness to him, not sure of the reaction she would get, wanting to be wanted but not sure if she would be.

Later in the morning Brodie retrieved their clothes from the drier. Malik dressed reluctantly, and went back to her flat to get changed for work. Brodie had called Miguel to make sure he was OK with opening up the bar.

He sat on the balcony, drinking a cup of coffee, going over in his mind, the mornings turn of events, as he toyed with his phone. Then he decided.

"Malik, quick question."

"OK."

"How would you feel about moving into my apartment? You're in a rented room so no great loss there, from what you said. I'm not happy with you walking to get buses home, late at night on your own at the moment, until we get this situation resolved. It's too dangerous. Now, I'm entirely flexible, Anita. You can have a choice of bedrooms, or if you prefer, I'll move back to the beach house and you can have the apartment. Whatever suits you." Brodie realised that he had said all that without stopping for breath, so he breathed in deeply.

Malik was silent for a moment. "Do you not want me to sleep with you, Alan?" she asked hesitantly. "I thought you were happy this morning."

"Of course I want to sleep with you, but I don't want you to feel pressured into sleeping with someone you don't want to be with and the last thing I want is for you to think I'm using the walking at night thing as an excuse to get you into my bed. I'd like you to move into my apartment because I enjoy your company and I want you to be safe. The sleeping arrangements are entirely up to you."

Malik laughed, sensing Brodie's discomfort. "You're not very good at this, are you?"

"No I'm not, but only because I've never asked a woman to move in with me. I've had loads of relationships with women, but I've never asked any of them to live with me."

"I need to think about it, Alan. Mm, OK, I've thought about it and have already started to pack."

"So you'll move in?"

"Yes."

"Tonight?"

"This afternoon."

"OK, let me know when you are ready and I'll come and pick you up."

Brodie headed down stairs with a spring in his step and walked into El Puerto in the middle of the lunchtime rush. The restaurant was busy, with most tables occupied. A few regulars were perched on bar stools with cold beers and assorted tapas, which was their normal lunchtime diet.

Xavier Moreno was sitting at one of the tables with coffee and his traditional tostada de tomate as there was no *cocido montañés* on the menu that day.

Brodie walked round some of the tables, chatting to a few of the customers. He felt that personal contact between owner and patrons was important. He got to read the mood of the customers, get feedback on all aspects of his business and helped to create a relaxed social, atmosphere around the eating and drinking experience for both him and his clientele.

As he approached Moreno's table he and the Comisario shook hands as they always did. Brodie sat down.

"How are you, Alan? Business seems to be booming. You are very busy today, but no Malik."

"Long story there, Xavier," Brodie began.

"Please don't tell me you and she have fallen out again."

"No, no, on the contrary. Since Markov visited, I have been really worried about Malik walking for buses to get home at night after her shift, so I've told her I want her to move into the spare room of the apartment upstairs until we are both happy that it is safe for her to walk around on her own at night. She understood my concerns and has agreed, so she's at home packing some clothes and so on and I will pick her up later."

"Your *spare* room, Alan?" Moreno raised an eyebrow.

"Yes, why. Do you see a problem there?"

"No, your spare room may be a very wise decision, but I would want you to keep it to the spare room, if you know what I mean. I do not think that a romantic involvement is wise in a small team working on a case like this. "

"I wouldn't do anything to jeopardise our operation, or any of my colleagues. I've offered to move back to the beach house if she would be happier with that arrangement, but she said no, she was happy to share."

"That's very good of you Alan. Now I really must get back to work." Moreno said, catching a waiter's attention and making the universal sign for "may I have my bill please".

Brodie left him and signalled to Miguel.

"Hi Miguel, you OK with everything?"

Si, no problem. You were OK with me shutting up last night?"

"Yeah, yeah, I wasn't sure if you had the codes so I was going to come down but your text saved me a journey."

"When my uncle was in Mojácar, I looked after this place for him so I needed the codes. I have asked my cousin, Christina, to come down to meet you after lunchtime. She has been here for five minutes. Do you want to speak to her now, or should I ask her to wait?

"No, we should talk to her now."

"She is over there at table six."

Brodie looked over and saw a, slim, attractive young woman of average height, aged he guessed, in her late twenties, early thirties. Her dark hair was cut short and she wore a short cotton sun dress. She smiled nervously when Brodie looked over.

"Hi Christina, I'm Alan Brodie," he said as he sat at the table and gestured for Miguel to join them.

"Pleased to meet you, Señor Brodie," the young woman replied.

"I told Miguel I needed someone to look after the bar for me and he said that you worked behind the bar with Manuel, but were looking for somewhere closer to home than Mojácar."

"That is correct. I live in Palomares and could walk from there. I have told my uncle he said he understands and when I said I was coming to talk to you he said that was good and that if you wanted a reference you should call him."

"When is your next day off?"

"Tomorrow, I have two days off before I go back to work."

"OK, why don't you come down tomorrow and we will give you a trial shift. You'll get paid of course."

"Yes, I can do that. Thank you."

"Good that's settled. Miguel will tell you when to come down."

"Miguel, I'm going in to Garrucha this afternoon, but I'll be around tonight, you've got my number if you need me. Christina, I'll see you tomorrow."

Brodie left and went upstairs to get his car keys and make sure the apartment was clean and tidy for his new flat mate.

He walked down to the secure underground car park, becoming aware as he opened the door with his swipe card that someone was walking behind him. He looked round.

"Alexei, to what do I owe this pleasure?"

"We need to talk."

"OK, walk this way," Brodie replied holding the door open, while searching the outside area for any watchful eyes.

"Did you speak with Moreno to verify what I said about my involvement with Europol?"

Brodie held up his hand to stop Markov and clicked a button on a little plastic fob on his keyring.

"What is that?" Markov demanded.

"Just a precaution, Alexei. It jams phone signals or wires you may want to transmit from. Sorry, but I'm not big on trust... helps to keep me alive. What can I do for you, this fine day?"

"Have you spoken with Europol?" Markov demanded again.

"Moreno has, yes."

"And they have confirmed what I have said?"

"Yes."

"He spoke with Comisario Principal Alonso?"

"Yeah, if you know that why ask?"

"I need to be sure Europol are keeping their part of our deal."

"And what deal is that?"

"The deal that gives me immunity from prosecution if I help them against the drug cartels that I have contacts with or access to. If they want to break that deal all they need to do is hang me out to dry to one of the cartels and I will be dead within hours, so I need to check they are doing what they tell me they are doing."

"I understand. What happens if you come good with your side of the deal?"

"They let me walk; new identity, cash payment, protection."

"You think?"

"I hope."

"What's to stop you going back to your old ways if they cut you lose?"

"Let's just say that the package they offered me is a good one, I would have no need to earn money ever again."

"So what do we need to talk about?"

"Romanov is planning and organising something down in Puerto Banús,. I don't know what and I'm not sure exactly when, only that it is important that he gets it right. I think it involves someone at the top of the organisation, because Romanov very rarely goes out of the villa for anything. He hasn't told me much and I don't want to press him on it, although he says he wants me to be there "*for security*". I think it could give us a shot at the top man and I want you to be there too, so I think we need to work out a way to get you closer to Romanov, and soon."

"I'll be talking to him tomorrow morning, I have a package to pick up at the harbour."

Brodie thought for a minute, "Could you persuade him that he needs to put a tail on me to check that I do what is expected of me?"

"I suppose so, why?"

Brodie explained.

Just then, Brodie's phone rang and he retrieved it, noticing a look of surprise on Markov's face.

"Sorry. Doesn't affect mine," he held up his key fob.

"Brodie," he answered.

"Alan, it's me," Malik said, "Can you pick me up?"

"Sure, I'm on my way, text me your address."

"OK, see you soon."

"Can you do that, Alexei? You don't mind me calling you Alexei?"

"Sure." Markov smiled then nodded, "It's my name, is it not?"

Chapter 26

Markov left and Brodie went over their conversation in his head as he sat in his car, waiting for the hood to power down.

Malik had texted her address which Brodie entered into his satnav. He drove out of the carpark into the late afternoon Andalusian sunlight. He flicked his sun glasses down from his head and made for Garrucha.

It didn't take him long to find Malik's accommodation, above some shops, in a whitewashed building behind the harbour. His satnav was able to give him directions to the building but not to a parking space, so Brodie decided to call Malik and tell her he was going to go round the block and would meet her at the kerbside. As he approached Malik's accommodation for a second time, he was amazed to find her standing by the side of the road complete with two huge black suitcases and a large backpack. Obviously dressing to be noticed entailed having a large selection of clothes.

"Sure you've got enough clothes, Malik?"

Malik stood hands on hips. "Girl needs her clothes, Alan."

"OK, let's get you on board," Brodie said, raising the

Mustang's boot lid and lifting one of the two large cases into the confined space and the other onto the back seats. Malik dropped her backpack onto the seat beside the case, they both climbed into the car and Brodie drove off.

Malik looked around the cockpit of the Mustang as the throaty exhaust note of the big V8 engine reverberated off the high walls of the buildings bordering the narrow street.

"Not exactly your ideal surveillance vehicle, is it?"

"Never intended it to be. I was so fed up with driving a white, 4x4, Japanese, SUV, military vehicle and more lately, black, armoured German SUVs, there was no way I was ever going to buy anything like that. I wanted something colourful, a boys toy that *would* stand out in a crowd.

I was out in Houston, Texas, with a major oil company client and was sitting on the outside terrace of a coffee outlet. I was just traffic watching when I heard, rather than saw a car pull into the drive through. It was one of these. The model had just been released in the States. I sat and stared at the thing as the guy got his coffee and listened to the sound of the big V8 when he pulled away! I fell in love with it there and then, so when I moved over here, I bought one. Couldn't quite bring myself to replicate the bright orange paintwork of the one I saw in Houston, it didn't look out of place in the Galleria but it would have been a bit over the top in Mojácar."

"So you opted for blood red."

"Lucid Red."

"Ooo, sorry! Looks like blood to me," Malik teased, as Brodie joined the traffic on the main Mojácar to Villaricos road. He accelerated hard, away from the junction in the direction of Puerto Ricos.

"Philistine," Brodie shouted over the growl of the exhaust and the wind noise as the big car picked up speed.

It took only about ten minutes to complete the journey to Puerto Ricos.

"Wow, that was an experience," Malik enthused as Brodie presented his plastic entry card to the electronic barrier at the entrance and dropped down the ramp into the underground carpark.

"I can see why you bought this baby. I love it! We should go for a drive one day. We could find a nice quiet beach."

"Sounds good. We could drive up the coast, find somewhere quiet, go for a swim, and just relax for the day."

"That would be great, Alan."

A small elevator took them up to street level, Brodie wheeling both of Malik's large black cases to his apartment entrance while Malik wore her backpack over her shoulder. Brodie carried the two large cases up the stairs and deposited them in the second bedroom, which drew a frown from Malik.

"Don't you frown at me, Malik. Two reasons. Firstly, Moreno knows you are moving in here and he was a bit 'big brother' about it. I assured him that you were moving in to the spare bedroom, so in case he comes into the apartment at any stage, he will see your stuff in here. Secondly, I don't think there is enough free space next door to house everything in these cases... and I know I said two reasons, but thirdly, you still have a choice of where you are comfortable sleeping if you have second thoughts."

"You want me to have second thoughts?"

"You know I don't, but I want it to be your choice, Anita."

"It is my choice, Alan." Malik smiled, moved close and kissed him.

"Good, please don't feel pressured." He kissed her in response, then looked down at her.

"Sadly though, all that is going to have to wait, I need to update you on a conversation I had this afternoon and then we're going to go to work," he said pointing to the floor and bar below.

Brodie brewed some coffee and the pair sat on the two

settees while he called Moreno and took time to brief him and Malik on his encounter with Markov in the carpark and the outcome of their conversation. They discussed the possibilities of the unexplained event in Puerto Banús,, what it might be, and why Romanov was getting so animated about it. Brodie had decided that if this event involved someone further up the tree in the organisation, he should try to be present as Markov had intimated.

Moreno was more apprehensive and warned Brodie about the dangers of getting too deeply entrenched, but, surprisingly, Malik supported Brodie's thoughts and ideas, saying that the only way to get to the people at the top was to eat at their table. Eventually Moreno relented and reluctantly agreed with the plan which Brodie had outlined and Malik supported. They ended the call and had a final discussion around the issues,

Brodie wanted to reply to a few emails and make one or two phone calls. This allowed Malik time to unpack some of her clothes, personal effects, and toiletries, which she arranged in the second bedroom as they had agreed. She knew they were expected to help out in El Puerto that evening so decided to leave the rest till the next morning.

Miguel was taking orders from the tables and passing them to the bar and the kitchen. The others were delivering drink and food orders to the appropriate customers Malik slotted in behind the bar while Brodie fitted into his front of house role, clearing and setting tables. This also gave him the opportunity to spend time talking to customers as they arrived and departed or when they chatted to him during their stay.

Most of the staff had been with Manuel pretty much from day one when El Puerto had opened, one or two having previously worked in his bar in Mojácar; they worked well as a team, helping each other when needed, communicating easily and naturally with the customers. Brodie appreciated that good staff were as important to repeat business and building a regular clientele as good food was. He was aware that Manuel had paid his staff above the going rate and that he did so to ensure that they all felt valued and their input to the business was appreciated; it was paying off.

It was a busy evening and time passed quickly as it always did when there was a steady flow of customers. In what seemed like no time at all, the restaurant and bar customers had gone, the kitchen had been cleaned, tables cleared and polished and the bar was being restocked in readiness for the next day. With everyone pitching in, the cleaning was soon completed and the shutters were pulled down on another busy day.

Chapter 27

AFTER THE OTHERS LEFT, BRODIE AND MALIK WALKED ROUND TO the plaza and up into the apartment. Malik disappeared into the second bedroom to sort out a few remaining things while Brodie poured two glasses of Rioja, leaving one on the breakfast bar for Malik.

Being a warm night, Brodie opened the balcony doors and strolled out to lean against the balustrade and look out towards the harbour and marina, listening again to the clacking of the cicadas in the trees and bushes and the lazy splashing of small waves as they broke against the sandy beach. He was soaking up the atmosphere as he sipped his wine, when he became aware of Malik standing beside him. He looked across at her.

"You found your wine then."

"Yes, thank you," she smiled up at him.

"You are a lucky man to be able to work and live in a location like this. How many beach front bars are available, especially ones with beautiful apartments like this, and views like that?" She looked across to the beach.

"Oh, this is just living the dream for me, Anita. Everyone

warned me about all the expats who come out here looking to run bars in the sun and who fail miserably because they haven't a clue what they're doing. They said I would be the same if I wasn't careful. But I was careful. Look at Mojácar. How many bars and restaurants are there along the front? Garrucha, the same. Even Villaricos, which used to be a small fishing village. How many bars are there in Villaricos? Puerto Ricos, only one, and developed in the ways it was, that's not likely to change. That's why I waited for the right premises in the right location and even better, as it turned out, it was a business I knew. Although I didn't know that Manuel owned this apartment, buying it was an afterthought."

They were both quiet for a few minutes, taking in the view from the balcony while listening to the gentle lapping of the sea below

"I'm sorry we didn't get off to a very good start when we first met. The Comisario's deception was unfair. I can understand why he did it, but it was unfair to you and I can understand why you were angry with him, and me."

"Moreno did say that you were only acting on his orders. I just wasn't in the mood to listen to him. Having said that, you *were* a bit prickly at that stage which didn't exactly endear you to me."

Malik laughed, "I thought you were arrogant when I first met you. I thought you were just another, sexist racist, who was judging me by my gender and the colour of my skin."

"Do you get that a lot at work?"

"Oh, yes. If we are working as a team, I'm the one who gets told to make coffees and tidy up. Nowadays I just pass the buck to someone who isn't wearing three stripes and eventually everyone gets the message."

"I was just generally pissed off with you and Moreno at that stage. It was obvious you didn't want to work with me and wanted to take your instructions from Moreno. I can't work that way in a hostile situation, I need to know that my team works together, acts on instruction and covers everyone's back under attack. You weren't showing me you were prepared to do that, but that's in the past. We seem to understand each other better now." Brodie smiled at Malik.

"I understand that we need to support each other and work as a team of two people. I see that you are not arrogant but you have confidence in your abilities, which is different. I see that you are not sexist or racist. You don't have a problem that I am black and a woman."

"I have to tell you, if you were white and a man, you wouldn't have been sharing my shower the other morning."

They both laughed as Malik rested her head on Brodie's chest.

Brodie put his arm round Malik's shoulder and pulled her closer.

"Anita, you're a very beautiful, highly intelligent young woman who, I think, has a tendency to be a little insecure because of her race. Believe me, you have nothing to feel insecure about. Don't let anyone put you down because of your skin colour. Sadly, I know from experience that very often, particularly in a male dominated environment, women need to work twice as hard to achieve their goals, but you've already proven yourself capable of doing that."

"Can you repeat that, maybe six more times?" Malik smiled as she leaned up to kiss him.

"I'm going to grab a shower before I go to bed. Care to join me, Sergeant Malik?"

"We may be under attack, Captain Brodie, so I will need to look after your back."

Brodie closed the doors. Walking through to his bedroom, he undressed, turned on the shower, stepped under the spray of water immediately followed by Malik. They kissed as they explored each other's bodies. Later they dried each other, slowly made love, and much later fell asleep in each other's arms in Brodie's bed.

Chapter 28

BRODIE WOKE EARLY THE NEXT MORNING, CONSCIOUS OF ANOTHER body lying beside him, breathing softly. The sheet partially covered her upper body, rising and falling slowly with each breath. Malik looked so peaceful; her face gave the impression of a slight smile. Slowly and quietly he slipped out of bed, pulled on his running shorts and a t-shirt, picked up his trainers and sunglasses and headed for the beach. He ran with a spring in his step. He was happy, unexpectedly so, never in his wildest dreams had he thought when he first encountered Malik in the bar in Villaricos that a few weeks later she would be living with him and sharing his bed.

Brodie went over in his head the plan to collect a genuine consignment for Romanov that morning. He hoped that Markov had managed to persuade Romanov to tail him again giving him the opportunity to return the inept watcher to Romanov as he and Markov had discussed.

He completed his run in, what for him, was a good time and climbed the internal stairs to the apartment. As he opened the door, he was greeted by the aroma of freshly brewed coffee and toast and by the sight of Malik. She was setting out two places on the breakfast bar, wearing a pair of very small panties and one of his t-shirts, which looked about three sizes too big for her, her hair tied back in a loose ponytail.

"Good morning," she greeted him, "I have made us coffee and toast and poured some orange juice. You don't mind do you? How was your run? Do you do that every morning?"

"Don't mind, good, and almost." He smiled back at her

"I don't understand."

"You asked me three questions, I just answered them. I don't mind you making us breakfast, my run was good and I do it most mornings."

"Oh, right, sorry, I must be a little slow this morning," she laughed.

"You're wearing my t-shirt," Brodie pointed out.

"Yes, sorry. I didn't think you would mind. It was lying on the floor. Do you want me to take it off?"

"I'd love you to take it off, but maybe wait till after breakfast?"

"Sure, let's eat," Malik smiled.

They discussed their plans for that morning as they ate. Malik suggested that she sort out the rest of her things and Brodie was to pick up another package from the fisherman at the harbour, checking to see if he had a tail again.

"You need to be careful, Alan. Maybe I should come with you."

"No, its fine. All the guy will be doing, if he turns up, is watching to make sure I behave. If he is there, I've told Markov that I'm going to take him back to Romanov and suggest that he gets decent security. Markov's going to set the scene for me. He's the one encouraging Romanov to involve me in his security at this mystical Puerto Banús, do."

Malik was still unhappy but she could see that Brodie was committed to his plan.

"I'll give you directions on how to get to Romanov's villa

and If I'm not back by mid-afternoon, you and Moreno come looking for me, but don't go off half-cocked and turn up at Romanov's if there is no need. That would screw up the whole thing.

I'm going to take a small GPS transmitter with me so give me your mobile so that I can download an app that will let you track it. OK?"

"Sure," Malik agreed and passed him her phone.

Brodie downloaded the app and explained it to Malik

He cleared the dishes into the dishwasher and turned to find Malik pulling his T-shirt over her head, "You wanted me to take it off after breakfast, you said." She tossed it over for him to catch. "You need a shower and as I haven't had mine either, I thought maybe we could...."

Brodie stepped forward, and slid his arms round her waist, pulling her toward him, "You're a wicked woman Anita Malik, trying to lead me astray."

"I'm not having to try too hard." She kissed him, turned, took his hand and led him through to the shower.

Chapter 29

AT NINE O'CLOCK, BRODIE PARKED BEHIND THE SMALL FISH market, watching for the same fishing boat he was expecting as it slid up to the quayside. As its catch was being lifted onto the harbour, he got out of the car and walked back to the paseo, taking care not to be seen at that point. Having reached the end of the pier, he about turned into full view of everyone there. He started to walk slowly back up the pier toward the small fishing boat. He stopped twice, turning to talk to regular customers; on the second meeting, he spotted his tail, the same man as before, duck quickly out of sight, two seconds too late. It didn't take Brodie long to reach his target boat.

"*Buenos dias,* Pedro. I hope you had a good catch this morning." Brodie recited the opening gambit he had been told to use by Romanov.

"*Buenos dias, Señor,* I have your order ready." The tall, thin fisherman looked at him, showing little or no signs of recognition and again, as he had done the previous morning, handed Brodie a large canvas bag containing the consignment of fish.

"Gracias, mi amigo," Brodie answered, turning away from the boat, heading back towards the paseo and El Puerto, stopping again to pass the time of day with one or two people to ensure that his shadow was still behind him. As he reached the end of the small building that was used as a fish market, he suddenly turned off the main quayside and walked along the narrow alleyway formed by the building and the stacks of fish boxes. He stopped behind a stack of boxes, close to the parked Mustang and pulled a Glock 19 hand gun from the waistband of his shorts. He didn't have long to wait till his tail followed him down the same route. As the man passed, Brodie stepped out behind him and poked the Glock into his lower back.

"Walk over to that red car," Brodie hissed, pointing to the Mustang while prodding the man in the back with the Glock.

The man walked over to the car as instructed, then stopped.

"Open the door."

He opened the door.

"OK, sit in the car with your feet on the ground."

The man complied.

Brodie fished a large black cable tie out of his pocket.

"Wrap that round your ankles."

Again, compliance.

Another cable tie, "Put that round your wrists and hold out your hands." Brodie, pressed the Glock into his forehead to reinforce the dangerous position he was in.

The man obeyed and presented his wrists to Brodie.

Brodie stretched out to pull the cable tie tight, but the man suddenly lunged forward in an attempt to head-butt him. Sadly for the Russian, Brodie had done this procedure many times before and was aware of the dangers it presented. He hit him with a vicious right hand to his solar plexus. The man sank back down onto the Mustang's seat, gasping for breath as Brodie pulled the black cable tie tight round his wrists.

While the Russian was fighting to catch his breath, Brodie opened the boot of the car pulling out a roll of duct tape. He proceeded to wrap the tape round the man's wrists and his ankles, then pushed his legs into the passenger foot well and shut the car door. He retrieved the bag with the fish, placing it in the boot of the car. He searched the bag, found the package of cash which was his payment, stashed it beside the spare wheel, closing the boot lid. Getting into the car beside his captive, he dropped the Glock into the driver's door pocket.

"OK, let's get you home, sunshine," Brodie gave his prisoner a sardonic smile.

"No, no, he will kill me," the Russian pleaded.

"Not my problem. Now, sit there and shut up."

Brodie drove quickly through the built up area, keeping well within the speed limit, not wanting to attract the attention of any local police, having a bound prisoner sitting in the car. Once on the open road, he used the power of the big Mustang to ease past anything that was in danger of slowing him down. He was soon climbing the narrow, largely unused road leading to Romanov's villa.

As they approached the gates of the house, his prisoner began to get more agitated,

"Please don't do this, he will kill me." The man pleaded.

"Told you, not my problem."

They pulled up at the gates and were greeted by two armed guards, both brandishing AK-47 assault rifles.

"Tell Mr Romanov that Alan Brodie is here and has a present for him,"

"Mr Romanov is out, so get lost," one of the guards snarled.

Brodie pulled the Glock out of the door pocket and held it at his prisoner's left temple, as both turned their AK-47s on him.

"Don't even think about it, guys. Your boss man isn't going to like you killing me. Now, tell him I'm here before I spread his tiny brain over your nice white wall."

One of the men put down his rifle and spoke into his radio. Brodie couldn't hear what he said but he seemed to get a quick answer. He spoke to his fellow gate keeper and they opened the gates to allow Brodie in to the grounds. As he passed the two guards, he deliberately hit the throttle sending a shower of gravel up from the spinning rear wheels and showering them with small sharp pieces of gravel.

Brodie pulled up at the front door and got out of the car. He opened the boot of the car, retrieved the bag of drug filled fish, walked round to the passenger door, and opened it as Romanov and two of his heavies came down the steps of the house.

"Do you know what, Ivan? I was disappointed that you felt you couldn't trust me after our little conversation yesterday, but today I'm insulted that you thought you could send the same halfwit to keep an eye on me and I wouldn't recognise him. Do I come that far down in your estimation?"

Alexei Markov appeared at the top of the stairs and walked down to join them.

"I told Novak not to send the same man as yesterday, Ivan. This man is too good not to notice. You know that he has been a security advisor to Alexander Salenko in London. We should have this man on board, not that fool Novak."

Markov sneered in disgust and walked away.

Romanov signalled to his men to retrieve Brodie's prisoner and invited Brodie to join him in the house. He followed the Russian up the steps into the large lounge area.

"I've brought your dinner, Ivan," Brodie said and dropped the bag of fish onto the marble floor. "Your goods are still intact."

"We just wanted to see if everything went to plan, Alan, no insult was intended, I can assure you. My so-called head of security was responsible for arranging it, I had no idea he would send the same idiot who you spotted yesterday. I too might be annoyed if I were in your position. Please accept my apologies."

"Apology accepted."

"Good." He waved to Markov, indicating that he should join them. "You have met Alexei."

"Yes, some time ago."

Markov nodded to Brodie. "Good to meet you again, Brodie."

"Alexei has been very impressed by you and the way you operate, so I let him have sight of some of the file I have on you. He said that explained many things he had seen with you and when we spoke afterwards he suggested that we might offer you some extra work, and maybe some fun as well."

"Fun? I remember fun. I think I enjoyed it if I remember rightly." Brodie smiled. "What kind of work? What kind of fun?"

Markov stepped forward. "Ivan needs some extra protection for a couple of days. We are planning a party in Puerto Banús, next weekend, with some of our biggest clients and a few of our business partners. If you could be persuaded to act as close protection for Ivan for the trip, we would invite you and a partner of your choice to attend the party, you would enjoy the party, I am sure."

"Mm, sounds interesting. I've provided close protection for a number of fairly high profile clients, your friend Alexander Salenko included, as you know."

"Alexander speaks very highly of you, which is why we are making this offer to you. How do you say *'better the devil you know'*."

"We would need to discuss money of course. I don't come cheap."

"No discussion is needed, Alan, I know your rates from Alexander. We would pay you seven thousand euros per day for the three days and we will provide full accommodation for you and a partner should you wish to bring one."

"Cash, upfront and you've got a deal."

Romanov snapped his fingers at Markov, pointing to one corner of the room.

Markov walked over, folded back a tapestry on the wall uncovering a safe. He opened it and took out a bundle of large denomination euro notes, which he handed to Romanov.

"I always pay cash," he said as he handed the bundle of fresh, new notes to Brodie. "Although very rarely upfront. But for you, I will make an exception, this once. Alexei will be in touch." Romanov turned to walk out of the room, he stopped at the doorway, "Do not let me down, Alan."

Chapter 30

BRODIE WAVED THE WAD OF CASH AT MARKOV AND STRODE BACK down the stairs to his car. He climbed in, fired up the big V8 engine and drove out towards the entrance. As he approached the gates, he noticed a cheap, mobile phone lying on the front passenger seat. He picked it up, looked at it for a moment, then the penny dropped, Markov.

The two guards opened the gates allowing Brodie out and onto the public road, turning right toward Puerto Ricos. He accelerated quickly, enjoying the sound of the exhaust note as much as the power of the car forced him back into the leather seat. Mission accomplished. He had the invite to the Puerto Banús, event, which appeared to be a lavish party possibly on board one of the luxurious yachts which were commonplace in that area. That would surely put most of the hierarchy of the drugs gang in one place that evening. Also, he had been paid 21,000 euros to be there, little wonder he was in a good mood as he sped down the twisting, winding road to Puerto Ricos.

His own phone began to play, Springsteen's "We Look After Our Own", as he slowed down for a roundabout at Vera Playa, he hit the button to answer.

"Brodie?" Xavier Moreno's voice held a hint of concern.

"Yes, Xavier, how are you?"

"I'm very well, Alan. Where are you?"

"Roundabout at Vera Playa, on my way back home. Why, what's wrong?" Brodie was starting to sound apprehensive.

"Nothing's wrong. I was just worried about your safety. Anita told me where you were going."

"Oh, that's very sweet of you, Xavier. I didn't know you cared," Brodie laughed.

"Brodie, you are an asset involved in a very important case. Of course I'm concerned and for some unknown reason, Malik also seems to care what happens to you."

"Of course she cares, I'm her landlord. Anything happens to me, she's homeless."

"I think it is a bit more than that, which worries me."

"No worries there, Xavier. I care about Anita and I would do nothing to hurt her, trust me."

"I hope not, Alan, and yes, I do trust you. You are a very decent man. Changing the subject. How did this morning go?"

"It went well, I collected Romanov's drugs, then delivered them, plus the guy he had tailing me, up to his villa."

"Please, Alan, I cannot hear that. I did not hear that. Your signal broke up."

"Sorry Xavier, I forgot you needed to be a wise monkey."

"A wise monkey?"

"Sure, Hear no evil, speak no evil..."

"OK, OK, the three wise monkeys. Carry on." Moreno chuckled.

"Romanov wasn't too happy initially, but Markov turned things round, slating a guy called Novak as being useless for allowing this situation to evolve, and telling Romanov he would be better with me looking after his security. I think Romanov had already decided to involve me, not sure why, but I have my suspicions. Anyway, the upshot of all that is that Romanov wants me to provide him with close protection at a big party in Puerto Banús, next weekend and he has extended the invitation to a partner, so we can get Malik along as well, and he's paying me 21,000 euros for my services, which I got up front in case he doesn't make it back."

"Only you would have the audacity to ask for payment upfront from a man you are plotting against." Moreno laughed.

Brodie's phone beeped to indicate an incoming call.

"Need to go, I've got another call coming in. Talk later." Brodie answered the incoming call.

"*Dígame.*"

"Alan, are you all right. Where are you?"

"I'm fine, I'm just coming in to Puerto Ricos. You all right, you sound agitated?"

"Agitated, how can I not be agitated? You are going into a lion's den and I should not be agitated?"

Brodie laughed. "You worry too much. Look, I'm just going to drive into the carpark under the apartment so I'm going to lose signal. I'll be with you shortly."

Malik started to say something but as Brodie had predicted, when the nose of the Mustang dipped into the entrance to the carpark, his phone signal broke up and her voice disappeared. Movistar had apparently promised a new mast in the Puerto Ricos area but had problems with finding a site and getting the necessary permissions, so work had only just recently started on the tower.

He parked the car, retrieved the package containing the 10,000 euros he was being paid to deliver the drugs to Romanov from the boot of the car, picked up the bundle of notes Romanov had given him, stuffed the Glock into his waistband, and made his way up to the apartment.

The apartment was empty when he got there so he deposited the cash into the freezer, grabbed a quick shower and got changed, ready to go down to the bar. Miguel's cousin,

Christina, would have started her trial shift that lunchtime and he was keen to see how that had gone. On the way out, he collected the cash from the freezer and made his way down to El Puerto.

The late lunch customers were finishing off their meals as he walked into the bar. He waved to Malik as he passed her and made his way directly to the safe to deposit the cash and closed it again. He stood up as Malik walked over to him.

"How did this morning go?"

"Can't say too much here, but all went according to plan."

Miguel crossed the floor to speak to Brodie.

"Señor Alan, Christina has been working behind the bar with Anita over lunchtime. She says she has enjoyed it and is still keen to work here."

"She's good, Alan," Malik offered. "She knows how to take orders, pour drinks, and talk to customers, sometimes all at the same time," she added with a smile.

"Good. As someone said to me earlier today, 'better the devil you know', I'll talk to her. Oh, by the way, Miguel, Anita and I will not be here next weekend, we are going to a big party in Puerto Banús,."

"We are?" Malik asked with a tone of surprise in her voice.

"We are. Did I not tell you?" Brodie grinned and turned away.

"Christina, I'm told you enjoyed today."

"Señor Alan, yes. El Puerto has a lovely atmosphere, everyone is very friendly... the rest of the staff and the customers."

"Boss is a bit of an ogre though, or so I'm told. Eats bar staff if they don't do as they're told," he joked. "So, did you enjoy it enough to want to do it again?"

"Yes, I would love to work here."

"Good, consider yourself one of the team. Talk to Miguel,

figure out when you can start and have a chat about your hours."

"Thank you, Señor Alan. My uncle knows I am here and said I can leave on Tuesday, so I can start on Wednesday."

"Good, so you'll be able to cover next weekend. Excellent."

"Miguel, can you just pay Christina cash for today and we can start her wages as of Wednesday."

Brodie turned to Malik. "OK, we've got some shopping to do, young lady."

Chapter 31

"Where are we going, shopping, I mean?"

"Mojácar. This time next week we will be in Puerto Banús, and you will need to be dressed in clothes that good, honest, police officers just can't afford, otherwise you are going to stick out like a sore thumb."

"Excuse me," Malik stopped in mid-stride. "What's wrong with the clothes I wear? You don't like the way I dress, is that what you're saying?"

"God, you're beautiful when you're angry," Brodie smiled at Malik and pinched her cheek playfully. "Please believe me there is nothing wrong with the way you dress. I love your clothes. You'd look good in a bin bag with a hole cut out for your head but in Puerto Banús, yacht society, every last article of clothing a woman wears to a party needs to have a designer label and a hefty price tag. I know. I've been to some of these parties, working I might add, but I know what they're like."

"I can't afford clothes like that!"

"No, but I can, if we use some of the cash I've been paid to act as Romanov's bodyguard for the weekend."

"What do you mean, act as his bodyguard?"

"Exactly that. He wants me to provide close protection for him over the weekend at this party in Puerto Banús, and I can bring a partner to the party. I was going to ask Moreno, but people would talk, so then I thought you might do instead, but if you don't want to go, I can still ask Moreno."

Malik slapped Brodie's shoulder playfully. "You want to buy me dresses?"

"A dress."

"And shoes?"

"And shoes."

"Maybe a handbag."

"Don't push it, Malik."

"A girl's handbag needs to match her shoes."

"OK, a handbag."

"Why are we waiting," Malik hooked her arm round Brodie's, smiling up at him. "And you can tell me what happened this morning while you take me to buy my dresses."

"A dress!"

"We'll see."

Working as a member of a Special Forces group and later in the private sector, Brodie had got into the habit of constantly checking around himself for people or actions that were out of context or rang alarm bells with him. This was a habit that he found difficult to break, which was why he noticed the blue SEAT Leon behind them. It had pulled out from the kerb as he passed it and was now following them at a safe distance. It slowed down when Brodie slowed down and increased speed when Brodie accelerated, always careful not to get too close.

As Brodie was following the Leon in his mirrors, Malik looked over at him.

"Are you looking at the blue Leon?"

"Yes, you'd seen it too?"

"I wasn't sure but yes, I have watched it in the wing mirror."

Brodie became distracted as he heard a mobile ringing,

then realised it was the burner that Markov had given him. He retrieved it from the door pocket and answered it.

"Brodie, we need to meet. Where are you?" Markov sounded concerned.

"We're on our way into Mojácar."

"Do you know where Valle del Este golf complex is?"

"Yeah, is off the AP-7, near Los Gallardos."

"Can you meet me there in half an hour?"

"Probably, but I've got a blue SEAT Leon tailing me at the moment. Let me get rid of it and we'll be right with you."

"We? You are saying we."

"Yeah, Anita Malik's with me."

"OK, bring her with you."

"No choice, Alexei."

"Who is in the Leon? Can you see?"

"Two men, I think."

"You need to lose them, then go to Valle del Este. Pass the hotel then turn right. Drive on down and I will wait there for you." Markov ended the call.

Brodie looked across at Malik, "That was Markov. He wants to meet at Valle del Este the golf resort, but we need to lose the Leon first."

Malik was watching the blue SEAT in the wing mirror on her door as Brodie spoke.

"I know where that is, I've seen it from the motorway. How do we get rid of the Leon?"

"Oh, that's easy," he smiled across at her.

On arriving at a large, busy roundabout, Brodie eased into the traffic and drove round, exiting for the town of Vera. The Leon followed them at a distance. The Vera road was constantly busy, with traffic heading to or from the AP-7 *Autopista del Mediterráneo*. Europe's longest motorway, it ran from close to the French border to Algeciras in the south of the country. The constant flow was supplemented by local leisure and business traffic. As Brodie drove towards Vera, the Leon sat three cars behind the red Mustang, until it reached the outskirts of the town and the retail park which stretched along both sides of the road. Immediately, Brodie pulled off the road and stopped quickly, forcing the Leon to pass them. The driver of the Leon drove for about two hundred yards and pulled off the road as Brodie had done, just before another busy roundabout, close to the Plaza de toros de Vera.

Brodie sat for a few minutes, the engine of the big Mustang idling. Then, as he started to slowly move forward and back on to the road, he turned to Malik.

"Get your phone out and take a photograph of these guys when we pass them. Make sure they see you taking it."

Malik held up her phone as Brodie pulled level with the SEAT and as Brodie had asked, made a show of taking a photograph of the two occupants of the blue car. Brodie approached the roundabout and took the first exit. The blue SEAT again pulled onto the road and followed the Mustang, only now making no effort to conceal their presence as Brodie approached another roundabout and turned left, following signs for the AP-7 Autopista.

Once clear of Vera town, Brodie picked up his speed, slowing down twice when he was held up by other traffic, which on both occasions he overtook. The blue SEAT was still right behind him as he reached the junction that allowed access to the Valle del Este Golf complex and the AP-7, both north and south. Brodie passed the entrance to the golf resort, drove under the motorway then swung sharp left, accelerating hard onto the AP-7 South, the Leon still in pursuit.

The Autopista was busy and a good deal of the traffic consisted of heavy goods vehicles, making their way, closely packed, at a steady pace along the inside lane of the motorway. The outer two lanes had fairly constant, faster moving, lighter traffic, some of it matching Brodie's outer lane speed of just in excess of hundred and fifty kilometres an hour, a speed which the attending SEAT matched, sitting right on Brodie's tail.

A few kilometres later both vehicles were fast approaching the junction at Los Gallardos, with the heavy, slower trucks forming a convoy in the inner lane, but the traffic in the centre lane was very light. Brodie pulled the Mustang into that lane and the SEAT followed.

Suddenly Brodie gunned the big Mustang, leaving the SEAT in his wake, and at the last minute, pulled the wheel to the right, cutting in front of a large red truck and swerving into a tight space between two trucks.

Malik, caught totally unawares screamed when the rear end of a blue container loomed large in her vision for a few seconds, the loud blare of a truck's air horns filling her ears as the motorway crash barrier flashed past, inches from the left hand side of the car as it shot down the off-ramp from the motorway. Brodie stood hard on the Mustang's brakes as the big car careered towards the small roundabout at the end of the exit road at over one hundred and twenty kilometres per hour, stopping just short of front end contact with the high kerb.

The driver of the SEAT, caught totally off guard, tried to follow but there was no gap in the traffic, and unable to stop because of the pressure of traffic close behind him, the driver was forced to overshoot the junction.

"Shit, Brodie, you almost killed us there!" Malik shouted from behind her hands, which were covering her face.

"Didn't take you for a panic merchant, Anita," Brodie smiled across at her, then negotiated a tight turn to allow him to cross over the AP-7 and swing back onto the motorway heading in the opposite direction.

"Panic merchant? The back of that container was centimetres from my head, so was the crash barrier. I shudder to think how close the truck behind you was."

"He hit his horns, not his brakes, so he wasn't that close."

"You obviously don't know Spanish drivers. They blast their horn at you first to tell you they are about to hit you, it's got nothing to do with not being close."

"What happened to the Leon?" Malik looked around.

"Oh, he's about thirty clicks away from us by now."

"What?"

"Well the next junction at Los Gallardos is closed because of roadworks. I found that out the other day. So, he's going to need to drive to the next one and that's about fifteen kilometres from here, so fifteen there, fifteen back, leaves us free and clear to head to Valle del Este.

Do you play golf Malik?"

"No."

"Shame. I'd have liked to play around with you."

Malik punched Brodie's upper arm. "Don't be so flippant, Brodie. You almost killed us both back there."

"What? Do you think I'd risk putting as much as a scratch on this baby just to get rid of two goons in a SEAT?" Brodie patted the Mustang's steering wheel.

Chapter 32

BRODIE TURNED INTO THE ENTRANCE OF VALLE DEL ESTE GOLF Resort and followed the road towards the hotel. The lush green fairways and greens were in sharp contrast to the arid, brown hills that surrounded the area. Little white golf carts whizzed up and down the trails and fairways, carrying eager golfers from all over Europe. He turned right, past the hotel, as instructed by Markov. A minute later, a black BMW X3 parked in a layby, flashed its headlights and Brodie pulled up alongside. He buzzed down the driver's window as he looked up into the SUV from the low interior of the Mustang.

Markov glowered down at Malik, then Brodie. "I am not happy that you have company, Brodie."

"Alexei, she is putting her life on the line, same as we are, so she has every right to see the whole picture. Please go with me on this. You trusted me and I trust Anita. If you can't, then we should go our separate ways."

"It is too late for that, Brodie. Things are moving ahead with the plans for Puerto Banús,. Romanov will ask to see you tomorrow. This is why he asked his people to follow you today.

He wanted to know what you were up to. Where is the SEAT, I hope you lost them properly?"

"Oh, don't worry about them. We turned off the motorway without indicating and they ended up heading for Almeria. You just can't get the staff nowadays, Alexei. Now, much as I would love to stay and chat, what was so important that we needed to talk today?"

"I told you. Romanov wants to see you tomorrow. He will call you to arrange a meeting. He wants you to provide him with close protection, as you have done for Alexander Salenko in the past. Oh, and by the way, Salenko will be at this party on Saturday. I think he is more than a friend to Romanov, just a feeling I have. I think Salenko has banned all partners from the get-together. Romanov says he has changed his mind but I think he has been told that only the group will be at the meeting. Romanov is organising the meeting so he will have his security there, including you and I. He will give you all the detail tomorrow when he meets you. He knows you are taking Malik and he has people checking on her so if you are going to be with him, it is best that you do not take her with you. You should keep her well-hidden if she is on her own, out of harm's way. Just in case he finds something and knows she is police."

"My police record shows that I was dismissed for misconduct, four years ago. This was done in case someone like Romanov found out I was in the police. I will not show as a serving officer to anyone who looks, but as one who took bribes from drug dealers. The system will also show an alert with details of who has been looking."

"Clever," Markov smiled slightly. "I should go, Romanov does not like me to be off his radar for too long at the moment. Too many things going on. Just one more thing," Markov tossed a mobile phone to Brodie, "Get rid of the old one and use that one to contact me, my number is already in it."

"OK, I'll keep in touch if I need to and you do likewise. Thanks for the heads-up."

Brodie drove forward and watched as Markov eased out of the layby and headed for the main road.

"You know this Salenko?" Malik enquired.

"Yeah, I've worked for him in the past, providing close protection. I've been in Russia, Saudi and Turkey with him and out here in Puerto Banús, keeping an eye on him and his family when they are out at his villa on holiday. He's got a second wife and a son who is two years older than she is."

"Looks like I'm not going to Puerto Banús,. No party, no new dress, no..."

"Who said you're not going to Puerto Banús,?"

"But Markov just said, no partners."

"Romanov might have said that but I want you there watching my back and acting as my eyes and ears around the place. Romanov doesn't need to know you're there. We'll keep you well under the radar."

"OK, Puerto Banús, but no party dress."

"Oh, I think we can still get you out on the town once all this little adventure is over, so let's go get you a posh frock."

"Posh frock? What is a posh frock, I don't understand?"

"A party dress to a girl like you, Anita." Brodie laughed as he turned the car and drove out of Valle del Este, heading for Mojácar.

As he drove, he mulled over how best to handle the weekend in Puerto Banús, and how to approach it with Romanov. He knew he was potentially stepping into a lion's den and needed as much information on the bigger picture as he could get as the weekend unfolded. This meant that he needed Malik there, although out of sight if Romanov was insistent on no partners. It also meant that he might need some other police cover.

"Just thinking about Puerto Banús,, Anita. Romanov's 'no

partners' edict changes our plans a bit. I still need you there, but keeping out of sight somewhere you can still keep an eye on what these guys are up to. Do you think Moreno would give us some extra bodies as watchers?"

"He has access to some of the team from the Algeciras operation. We could ask for some of them. They are experienced in situations like this."

"That would be good. Can you ask him?"

"*Si,* I will speak to him."

"Good. Here we are," Brodie said as he pulled into a parking space at the side of the road, beside Mojácar's *Parque Comercial,* "Let's go get you a posh frock, lady."

Brodie took Malik's hand as they crossed the road and walked into the shopping centre. They passed a café and some other shops as he led her to the very upmarket dress shop he had suggested.

The lady who owned the shop fussed over Brodie and Malik. She listened to their requirements and disappeared behind a bamboo curtain, returning a few minutes later with a selection of dresses. The lady showed them to Malik and the two women discussed the options as Brodie sat checking his emails.

"Sir, may I get you a coffee while your partner is trying on some dresses?"

"Mm, please. That would be good, thank you."

Two cups of coffee later, Malik had modelled a number of dresses for Brodie and with his approval, she settled on an elegant blue dress a pair of matching shoes and handbag. Brodie paid the bill. Malik also picked out two tops and a pair of pale blue silk trousers from a sale rail, she paid the bill before the two headed back to the car.

Brodie held the passenger door open for Malik and closed it as she sat in the cream leather seat. He was just about to move round to the driver's door when his phone rang.

"Diga mi." Brodie answered.

"Señor Brodie?"

"Si"

"It's Ivan. Can you speak?"

"Yes, Ivan, I'm good to talk."

"OK, I need you to pick up another fish for me tomorrow, same supplier, same time. Can you do that for me?"

"Sure, no problem."

"Good, and can you bring it out to me? We need to talk about next weekend."

"Yeah, I can do that. Just head straight out to yours?"

"That would be good. We will talk then."

The line went dead as Romanov ended the call.

Chapter 33

BRODIE ENJOYED HIS MORNING RUNS. OUT OF BED BY SIX THIRTY, pull on his running gear, gather up his phone and earbuds then head out onto the deserted beach. He loved the solitude and the relatively lower temperature of the early morning air. The rolling of the waves as they broke on the white sand was the only sound as he headed along the beach, up on to the paseo, past El Puerto and the small harbour, then back down on to the sand heading towards Villaricos. His pace was steady, his breathing not in the least bit laboured, his thoughts centred on the coming weekend in Puerto Banús.

He wanted to bring this scenario to a head, put Romanov and his fellow drug dealers where they belonged, behind bars or into the soil. The longer these low lifes were allowed to continue to make large sums of money from their illegal trade, the more innocent people would get hurt or killed. Brodie didn't want that on his conscience.

He had a few ideas on how to achieve a satisfactory outcome but was unable to connect them into a coherent plan until he had spoken with Romanov.

Without realising it, he had reached his marker just before

Villaricos, turned and started to head back along the damp sand close to the water's edge. As he ran, he looked up towards the area where some of the local fishermen who favoured this stretch of beach with their rods, would occasionally park. Today there were no fishermen, but instead a parked, a blue SEAT Leon.

Brodie continued to run without breaking his stride, he did not look back at the Leon. He retraced his steps, along the paseo and turned into the apartment entrance, just as the Leon pulled up in the square. He stepped into the covered doorway to the apartment, pulled out his phone and pushed the camera button. He quickly held the phone close to the wall allowing the lens a view of the plaza and clicked the camera button. He looked at the phone and checked his photograph. He smiled as he saw that he had managed to capture the Leon sitting by the kerb. He made his way up to the apartment.

He walked through to the kitchen and as he didn't hear any movement from Malik, made a coffee. As he lifted the cup to his lips, a voice sounded from the doorway.

"Good morning," Malik murmured, her voice still thick with sleep.

Brodie looked up to see her standing by the door, wearing a pair of silk pants and one of his t-shirts, her long curly hair still bed tumbled, her eyes sleepy.

"Hey sleepy, I've set up a coffee for you, just press the button."

As Malik passed him on the way to the coffee machine, she looked over at his phone lying on the worktop.

"What've you got there?"

"I've been car spotting. You got the registration of that blue SEAT that was following us yesterday, didn't you?"

"Sure."

"What's the number?" he asked as he zoomed in on the photograph he had just taken.

He waited till Malik fetched her phone and laid it on the worktop beside Brodie's, showing the photograph of the car. He looked at both phones, then smiled.

"Same car, it's sitting out in the plaza just now." Brodie swung his phone round for Malik to see.

"Really!"

"Yeah, I spotted it earlier, when I was running and it pulled up in the plaza as came round to the apartment door. Can you send these to Moreno? Ask him to run a check on them, see if we can find out who the car is registered to."

Brodie finished his coffee, then headed towards the bedroom.

"OK, I'll do that while you get your shower," Malik said picking up her phone.

Brodie undressed and wandered into the shower room, turned on the shower and while the water reached temperature, he cleaned his teeth. He became aware of someone standing behind him and turned to find Malik standing watching him, smiling.

"Come, I need to show you something I think will interest you"

Brodie turned off the shower and followed her out to the bedroom.

Malik, tuned to face him, pulled Brodie's t-shirt over her head and dropped it to the floor, sliding her underwear down to join it.

"Now that is interesting," Brodie held out his hand to her and pulled her to him.

Chapter 34

JUST AFTER EIGHT O'CLOCK, BRODIE LEFT THE APARTMENT, making sure that the SEAT was blindsided by a white van squeezing through a gap in the parked cars. He walked quickly along to the alley behind El Puerto, and made his way round two blocks of townhouses, approaching the square from the reverse angle. The two occupants of the SEAT were intent on watching Malik, wandering up and down the balcony, her phone at her ear, talking animatedly. Brodie opened the rear door of the car, slipped in behind the front passenger and poked his suppressed Glock17 into the side of the man's bald head.

"Just nod if you speak English."

Both men nodded.

"OK, drive out of here. Just go! I'll tell you where, once we get moving."

Having seen the Glock, the driver started the car and pulled out of the square without a word.

"Let's go back to where you were watching me when I was out running this morning. If you make one wrong move, driver, your friend's brains are going to make an awful mess of the inside of your car. Do you understand?

"*Si,* I understand," The driver nodded, as he turned right on to the main road, heading back towards Villaricos. He drove towards the beach area where they had been parked earlier, stopping at the same spot.

"Now take the keys out of the ignition and hand them to me, over your left shoulder with your right hand."

The man did as he was told.

Brodie poked the passenger in the shoulder. "You, get out of the car."

As the man stepped out, Brodie did likewise.

"Now, walk round to the other side of the car."

Brodie followed, until they were both facing the driver. Brodie stood back from the men, neither of whom were wearing a jacket.

"Get out," heordered the driver.

"Both of you, empty your pockets and throw your money, wallets, everything, back to me."

They did as they were told.

The driver's door and window were both open. Brodie told the driver to stand with his back to the open door.

"Put your hands behind your back with one arm through the open window

He pulled two cable ties out of his pocket and handed one to the passenger.

"OK, tie his wrists together with that. Tight!"

The passenger did as he was instructed, the driver winced as his arms were forced into an awkward position behind his back.

Brodie swung the Glock and smashed the rear passenger door window. The passenger winced.

"Open the door," Brodie ordered, holding out a cable tie to him.

"Put your left arm through the window and tie your arms together with this."

The man again did as he was told. Brodie stepped forward and pulled the cable tie tight.

"OK, now that we're all comfortable, let's have a nice cosy little chat. But first, we need to find out who you are."

Brodie walked round the car and picked up the wallets the two men had taken out of their pockets, opened them and stared at the identity cards shown inside.

He looked at the two men and then again at the photos on the IDs.

"Europol! You're Europol?"

"Yes Señor Brodie," the driver replied.

"Oh ho! This is priceless. So, tell me, why are you tailing me?"

"It is complicated, Señor Brodie."

"OK, let's uncomplicate it." Brodie pulled his phone from his pocket.

"Wait, who are you calling?"

"Comisario Moreno, that's who!"

"No wait, call Anita Malik, she knows us. We worked together in Algeciras, we were part of the same team. Please trust me on this, Señor Brodie. Do not telephone the police, please."

Brodie looked at the driver who repeated, "Please."

"OK, Malik it is."

Malik answered after four rings.

"Hey, what's up, Alan? I wasn't expecting to hear from you. Is something wrong?"

"Does the name, José Ramirez mean anything to you?" Brodie asked, reading the name on the man's ID card.

"Yes," Malik replied hesitantly, "Why do you ask that?"

"Because he and his sidekick are the two guys in the blue SEAT. I've got them both here and when I made to call

Moreno, he begged me not to and to call you first. Says you know him."

"Sure, we worked together in Algeciras, but why is he following us?"

"Hang on, let's ask him," Brodie switched his phone on to speaker and gestured to Ramirez to speak.

"Careful what you say, José," the balding passenger offered, before Ramirez could speak.

Ramirez nodded to his companion, "Anita, José Ramirez here. We think there is a cartel plant in the local police department. I'm not at liberty to give you any more than that at the moment, but the local police should not know we are here and looking at the investigation. We know you are dedicated to finding and arresting the leaders of this gang but we know that Señor Brodie was brought in by the local police department and we need to know if he can be trusted."

"Are you saying Moreno is bent?" Brodie demanded.

"No! I am not. We do not know." Ramirez replied quickly, "but we have been following you to try to see what you are doing and who you are meeting. Anita, help us out here with Señor Brodie."

"I trust Alan Brodie with my life, José. He is a good and honest man who is helping the police because the cartel was putting his friend in danger. He was asked to do so by Comisario Moreno, I was there when the arrangement was made. Alan has managed to infiltrate the cartel. Romanov likes him and trusts him. Who is your senior officer, José?"

"Alfredo Suárez. You know him."

"Yes, I know him."

"I'm sorry to break up this little reunion, but I have something I need to do at nine o'clock," Brodie interrupted. "Anita, can you meet with these guys later and bring them up to speed?"

"Sure, let me have a number to call."

"I'll text it to you and we can talk later." Brodie ended the call.

"So, you guys going to keep off my back now, or do I just leave you out here to fry?"

"OK. If Anita Malik speaks for you that is good enough for us, I think," Ramirez replied, looking to his colleague, who nodded." My partner, Diego Gonzales," he added pointing over to the other man.

Brodie produced a small knife from his pocket and cut the cable ties attaching the two men to their car.

"Sorry about that guys, but you must admit, you were acting a bit suspiciously. I needed to know who you were and why you were keeping tabs on me." Brodie glanced at his watch.

"I need to be at the harbour at nine o'clock. Can you guys drop me off behind the shops?"

"Sure, I guess," said a rather hurt sounding Gonzales.

The three men sat back in the SEAT and Ramirez started the engine and headed to the main road.

On the way, Brodie exchanged mobile numbers with Gonzalez and gave him Malik's number to set up a meeting with her.

Chapter 35

FOR THE THIRD TIME, BRODIE WALKED DOWN TO THE HARBOUR, to make his nine o'clock rendezvous with the fisherman. He walked purposefully towards the little fishing boat.

"*Buenos dias,* Pedro. I hope you had a good catch this morning," Brodie recited for the third time.

"*Buenos dias,* Señor, I have your order ready," the tall, thin fisherman repeated once again, handing Brodie another substantial canvas bag, containing a number of large fish, stuffed with drugs. Brodie walked back to his car with the bag, checking for a tail as he had done previously.

He sat in the car for a few moments, surveying his surroundings to see if anyone was watching him. Satisfied that he was clear, he took a small package out of the bag, checked that it contained his 10.000 euro fee, pushed the packet under the passenger seat, started the car and drove off.

Brodie enjoyed the winding road which led to Romanov's villa, there was very little traffic on what was basically a series of fast bends around which he powered the big Mustang. He finally stopped at the gates, was eventually admitted by the security guard, and parked close to the front door of the house.

Romanov sat at a table shaded by a large red parasol, on the wide rear terrace of the villa overlooking an expansive paved area which housed the swimming pool and was dotted with a random array of sun loungers.

"Alan, my friend, it is good to see you. Ah, you have brought me my dinner again. Let me take this to the kitchen," Romanov said, rising from the table and taking the bag from Brodie.

"Sergei!" he shouted and a man appeared from the far side of the lounge.

"Take this to the kitchen, put the fish in the fridge for now, and bring us some coffee."

He turned.

"Sit, sit, Alan, we must talk."

As the two men sat, the woman who had tried to kidnap Brodie and bring him to the villa appeared from the side of the house, wearing her Stetson hat and a red beach dress. She walked across the paved area to one of the sun loungers, dropped her bag and hat on the adjacent table, pulled the dress over her head, revealing a skimpy white bikini, and sat on the lounger. She fished a magazine out of her bag, lay down on her stomach, undid her top and proceeded to read her magazine.

"You have met Illy, I asked her to bring you here once. Beautiful, isn't she?" Romanov remarked, as he poured two cups of coffee and slid one across to Brodie.

"But maybe not as beautiful as your police officer girlfriend, Alan."

"Anita?"

"You think I would not find out she is a police officer, my friend?"

"Ex police officer, ex police officer." Brodie laughed, then his demeanour changed and his expression hardened. "Did you think I wouldn't know about her past? No one gets close to me, Ivan, unless I know exactly who they are and that, my friend, includes you. I know you almost as well as you know yourself.

Why? Because you're a potential threat to my life, so I need to know who you are, and I have sources who can tell me these things. I am nearly forty years old, and the reason I am still alive is because I recognise risks and potential threats. Then I either eliminate them or make sure they're no longer actual risks to me.

When I met Anita, letting her get close to me was a risk, so I needed to know who she was. I used my contacts to get access to her background and eventually her police records. She was a good officer, so when she was a bit naughty, she was given the choice of 'resign or be fired and charged'. She resigned as you would imagine. Now she is no fan of the authorities but she likes her designer clothes and the finer things in life, all of which cost money. So, I actually found a kindred spirit, someone who was fed up risking their life for little reward and was looking to make some real money.

You just paid me 10,000 euros for one hour's work. In the military, I would put my life on the line for two months to earn that. In the police Anita would work for almost twice as long to pay her rent and still no designer dress. Ivan, I trust Anita with my life, she will not let me down."

"What did she do to be sacked from the police?"

"You don't need to know that."

"Yes, I do!"

"No, you don't. I've told you all you need to know. If you don't trust my judgement, you should not be asking me to look after your security in Puerto Banús. Maybe you should let Alexei Markov handle that and I should just leave now," Brodie countered and stood up, retrieving his car keys from his pocket."

"I don't trust Alexei Markov the way I do you. He is a 'yes' man," Romanov sighed, staring into space. "Please, sit down, Alan."

"Sounds to me like you don't trust me either."

"I do, because nobody ever tells me I am wrong or says no to me. You are brave enough to do that. You are your own man. I respect that."

Brodie sat down again and stared hard at Romanov.

"This whole thing is all about trust. If I am going to look after your security in Puerto Banús,, you need to take my judgement and my advice and if I tell you to do something, you do it, without question, because that might just save your life. If you've done your homework on me, you will know that I have never lost a client. Our mutual friend Alexander Salenko, found it difficult at first to do what I told him. He doesn't like to be told what to do, but he found out one night in Kiev that it is not a good idea to ignore my instructions on security. He has never gone against my advice since. Ask him, he will tell you."

"I have asked him. He says you are good, but you don't take shit from him. He has respect for you."

"Why don't you trust Markov?"

"I do trust Alexei, but not as much as you. He never tells me I am wrong, he just says 'yes, Ivan', all the time. Even I cannot be right all the time, but don't tell anyone." Romanov smiled.

"OK, tell me about Puerto Banús. I need to go down and make a plan before the weekend. I need to know where we are staying, what we are doing, who will be there, why they are there. I need to be able to tell when someone is not behaving as they should, and also when they are not where they should be."

"There has been a change of plan. We were going to have a big party with our wives and partners but that has been cancelled. Some people were uncomfortable. They said we would be too conspicuous if the police knew any of the people there, so we will now arrive on Saturday afternoon and have our meeting on Saturday evening. We will stay in Puerto Banús, overnight then leave on Sunday morning."

"Will Alexander be at the meeting?"

"Why should he be?"

"Because he is part of this," Brodie raised his hand as Romanov started to protest.

"Don't treat me like a fool. Remember, I know Alexander, I've worked for him. I know what he gets up to."

"Alexander will be there."

"Thank you."

"Do not tell him I told you."

Romanov spent the next half hour or so relating the plans for the weekend meeting and answering questions from Brodie. When he was satisfied he had everything he needed, Brodie stood and smiled down at Romanov.

"Thanks for all that, Ivan, I can plan things out now to make sure you are kept safe."

"Will you have Anita Malik with you?"

"Yes, she will be a help to me and Alexei on Saturday and Sunday, if that's OK with you."

Romanov hesitated.

"Remember what we said about trust."

"OK, bring Malik. Alexei will be with us at the weekend."

"Great, I will talk to him on Friday and we will contact him once I have done my recce in Puerto Banús,."

The two men shook hands and Brodie walked back round to his car. He left the villa grounds via the well-guarded gates and drove quickly down the winding road back to the coast heading for Puerto Ricos.

Chapter 36

BRODIE AND MALIK SAT AT THE BREAKFAST BAR IN THE APARTMENT with Spanish tortilla, cheeses and bread that Brodie had brought up from the bar together with a bottle of chilled Sauvignon Blanc. As they ate they talked about the meetings they had had that morning; Malik with the two Europol officers and Brodie with Romanov.

"These guys are convinced that there is a mole in the local police department who is feeding information to the cartel, but they do not know who it is." Malik sipped her wine.

"I hope not, because if there is, we have a problem, and Markov is a dead man, now that we know who he really is and his links to Europol. This doesn't add up, Anita.

Romanov told me that you were a police officer. Almost the first thing he said to me when we sat down to talk."

"He what? What did you say to him?"

"I told him you were ex-police and that you had been a bit naughty and because of your previous good record, were told to resign or be sacked. He asked me what you had done but I told him he didn't need to know that, nevertheless, you can bet he'll be doing his best to find out. Might be best if you feed that back up to your bosses in Madrid so that they can amend your record temporarily with a cover story. Something about grabbing some of the drugs from a raid and selling them on might work for now."

"Did he buy that?"

"Yeah, I told him you were in on what we were doing and liked the designer dresses and other luxuries it paid for. I told him I needed to do a recce in Puerto Banús, before the weekend and that you would be with me and Markov when we were there. He was a bit reticent at first, but I told him he either trusted my judgement or I would step away and let Markov do the job in Puerto Banús,. He eventually agreed, so you're coming with me. Now tell me about these two guys from Europol."

"Not much to tell. They wouldn't tell me anything about what they were doing, "operational protocol" they said, but they were desperate to know what we were doing and where our investigation was going. I told them you were the main man and only told me what I needed to know, which wasn't very much."

"That worries me. When you are talking to Madrid, ask the guy who was your boss about them. What was his name?"

"Alfredo Suárez."

"Yeah, ask him about them and ask him about Moreno. I need to put some money in the safe. I'll be back up in a couple of minutes."

Brodie scooped up their empty plates and made his way down to the bar with the packet containing the 10,000 euros.

As he entered El Puerto, he noticed Xavier Moreno sitting at one of the tables with a coffee and a tostada con tomate, a man of habit. Brodie smiled to himself and then to Moreno as the Comisario noticed him.

"Xavier, how are you. We haven't seen you for some time?"

"Alan, I am very well. I still come here quite often for lunch.

Maybe you are doing other things when I am here."

"Give me a couple of minutes, and we can catch up. Would you like another coffee while we chat?"

"Yes, please. That would be good, thank you."

Brodie took the plates through to the kitchen, chatting with the staff as he walked, then quietly as no one was watching, put his package in the safe. He poured two coffees and returned to Moreno's table.

Brodie checked their surroundings before asking, "Does the name Alfredo Suárez mean anything to you?"

"Yes, he is the man heading up our operation against the cartel. Why do you ask?"

"His name came up in conversation. Is he trustworthy?"

"Yes, he is. I have known him and worked with him for many years. You are starting to worry me now, Alan."

"What about Jose Ramirez, or Diego Gonzales? Do those names ring any bells with you?"

"No, should they?"

"Maybe as part of the investigation team?"

"No they are not part of the team that I know. Why are you asking about them and Alfredo?"

Before he could reply, Brodie heard what he thought to be a crash of furniture, maybe a bar stool from the flat above and reacted immediately.

"Malik," he said quietly rising quickly from the table and running back to the apartment door. The door was open. Brodie kicked off his light shoes and pulled the compact Glock17 from his waistband, making his way silently up the stairs, two at a time. He could hear noises from the living area and as he stepped into the doorway, firearm raised, he saw the two men, known to him as Jose Ramirez and Diego Gonzales. Ramirez was standing in the middle of the room, holding a handgun by his side as he watched his colleague Gonzales in the process of tightening a length of cord round Malik's neck.

As she tried to get her fingers inside the loop to counter him, she did not see Brodie. Ramirez did see him and immediately began to raise a pistol in his direction. Without hesitation, Brodie fired off two quick shots at the man. Ramirez staggered back with a look of surprise on his face as two holes appeared in his upper left chest; he was dead before he hit the floor.

Taken by surprise, Gonzalez unintentionally loosened his grip on the cord round Malik's neck, then gasped for breath as Malik sunk her right elbow into his midriff, freeing herself from his grasp. Despite gasping for breath herself, Malik turned to face her attacker and unleashed a vicious and debilitating kick to the man's groin, following up with an equally vicious kick to the side of his head as he slumped to his knees, falling unconscious to the floor.

Malik coughed, holding her throat as she surveyed the two men, lying prone on the floor of the apartment.

Brodie sensed movement behind him and whirled round, raising the Glock, only to be faced by Moreno, a look of shock on his face. Brodie lowered his gun and turned back to Malik, who was still staring at the man who had tried to strangle her.

"You ever played football, Malik?"

"What? Football, no!"

"Tell you what, you kick a ball like that, Real Madrid would snap you up. You're good."

"What? I don't believe you, Brodie. You've just shot a man. This one was trying to kill me. Now you are making jokes."

"Just saying." Brodie shrugged, "Xavier, meet Jose Ramirez and Diego Gonzales... and if they are who they claimed to be, I've just blown away a Europol officer who was watching his buddy strangling a police officer."

"I think you are safe enough, Alan. Anita are you all right?" Moreno asked as he walked across the room and inspected Jose Ramirez.

"I'm OK," Malik replied with a cough, "I just need a drink."

"I'll get you one," Brodie offered. "Water OK?"

As Malik drank her glass of water, Moreno cuffed Gonzales, who was still unconscious, then on Brodie's suggestion, called Alfredo Suárez to notify him about Ramirez and Gonzales. He spent a good few minutes on the phone, mostly listening and nodding, before thanking Suárez and ending the call.

"Suárez knows both of these men and has been looking for them for a few days. He says they have been suspected of feeding information on the investigation to the cartel. They were found downloading Anita's service record and when they traced the IP address they sent it to, learned it is located in Puerto Banús,. The thing is, it didn't send, Suárez stopped it. Ramirez and Gonzales knew the team was onto them and once the team found out about the copying of Anita's record, they were in trouble, so they disappeared. He said that you spoke to him earlier, Anita. He has amended your record temporarily and sent it to Puerto Banús."

"Where does that leave us and more urgently, where does it leave Alexei Markov?"

"He says they didn't know of Markov, or of your involvement; that must have been what they were trying to find out."

"They asked me if Alan was working with the police or the cartel. I said I didn't know. That was when they grabbed me and he started to strangle me with that piece of cord."

"That makes sense. On an operation like this, Europol works in a series of cells so that if there is a leak, no one knows too much. Only the senior investigating officer and those he chooses to tell will know the full picture." Moreno added.

Gonzales was regaining consciousness and obviously in severe pain.

"Suárez has asked if we will hold this one," Moreno said, nodding in Gonzales's direction. "He will send officers down to pick him up and take him back to Madrid. We had better get him back to the station, and his friend to the mortuary."

Chapter 37

THE NEXT MORNING, BRODIE ROSE AT HIS USUAL EARLY HOUR, slipped quietly out of bed so as not to wake Malik, who had had a restless night's sleep and began his usual morning run to Villaricos at a pace which would leave most men struggling in his wake. Doing an about turn, he then headed back to Puerto Ricos, listening to a double album of Joe Cocker's greatest hits.

By the time he got back to the apartment, Malik was up and showered, but not dressed. She was standing in the kitchen with a bath towel wrapped around her, cradling a mug of coffee. There were wet tear tracks on her cheeks.

"Hey, you OK?"

"No, no I'm not. That man would have killed me yesterday. If you hadn't come in when you did, I would be dead. But you just shot and killed Ramirez, without a second thought. Then you make jokes. How can you do that?"

"When I was in the military, I fought in wars, I was paid to kill people and these people were paid to try to kill me and my colleagues. Special Forces is a different life, as a soldier I would use a rifle, a grenade or an armoured vehicle to kill my enemies. In undercover ops I would sometimes use a gun, but often it was a knife or my hands that killed my enemies. That makes it very personal. I walk into a situation like yesterday, a man points a gun at me and I know he will kill me if I don't kill him. So, I kill him, which is what I did to Ramirez.

I get no satisfaction from ending someone's life. But sitting out there in the sandpit with a bunch of your fellow soldiers, the inevitable banter starts as the realisation kicks in that you've managed to survive again, you're still alive and one of the ways for most special ops guys to cope with that is humour. You make light of it. If you don't, it would start to mess with your head, because you're still in the land of the living and maybe some of your mates are coming back in body-bags.

I got no pleasure out of killing Ramirez, Anita, because I didn't even have to think about it. Instinct kicks in. If it didn't, I'd be dead."

"And his friend would have killed me as well."

"Anita, if that instinct wasn't there, I'd have been killed years ago, Ramirez would have been too late." Brodie smiled at Malik as she started to understand his logic.

"Anyway, I need a shower and we need to get going. It's about a three and a half to four hour drive to Puerto Banús."

Brodie walked through to the ensuite shower-room, undressed, leaving his running clothes in a heap on the floor, ready to put into the wash. He stepped into the shower and stood under the deluge of warm water, showered, dried himself and then stepped out into the bedroom to find some clothes.

He sensed, rather than heard a presence behind him and looked over his shoulder to see Malik, without her towel or coffee, looking up at him.

"Can I have a hug, Alan?"

"Sure, 'course you can." Brodie held out his arms and pulled Malik to him.

She wrapped her arms round him and began to cry softly into his chest.

"All night, I have been thinking about my colleagues who were killed in Algeciras, Alan. They were my friends, I found them lying dead and I can't stop thinking that could have been me last night, if you hadn't come up when you did. I'm sorry, you must think I am stupid and weak." Malik sobbed.

"Hey, nobody thinks you are stupid or weak. You came very close to being killed last night, but you weren't and from where I was standing you did a very brave thing. Instead of running away from the guy, you stood your ground and retaliated. I was actually very proud of the way you reacted last night."

"Really?" Malik looked up at him.

"Really," Brodie smiled back at her, "although, I still think you should trial for Real Madrid when you get back."

Surprisingly, Malik laughed.

"Thank you, Alan," she said as she pulled him close, then kissed him. "Hold me tight, Alan."

Chapter 38

THE AP-7 *AUTOPISTA DEL MEDITERRÁNEO* RUNS FROM LA Jonquera near the French border with Spain to Algeciras in the south and at thirteen hundred kilometres, is the longest motorway in Europe. On this particular day it was taking Brodie and Malik from Vera to Puerto Banús, a distance of three hundred and sixty six kilometres, which the Mustang's sat-nav said would take three hours and forty four minutes, if they kept to the toll sections of the road, the AP7.

The next morning, traffic was reasonably light for most of the journey and Brodie switched on the cruise control once on the AP-7.

The soft-top was still in place as the big Mustang ate up the miles effortlessly and Brodie had relaxed into the journey, using the Bluetooth facility in the car to listen to a playlist from his phone.

He and Malik remained quiet for the first hour or so of the journey and they had just passed Almeria when Malik looked over at Brodie.

"I am sorry for this morning. You must think I am very weak, crying on your shoulder."

"No, Anita. I don't. The problem starts when you bottle up your emotions. You must have thought that guy was going to end your life last night, and contemplating your death is not a good feeling. It's even worse later when you start to think about it and you reflect back to the colleagues you've lost, which is what you were doing this morning.

You said yourself, you've never been so close to death, and it's frightening the first time, but eventually, as you survive other near misses, the feeling gets easier. You never get used to it, but you learn to cope with the emotional side of it. Strangely enough, having been almost killed, you'll be more determined not to let it happen again."

"And not think, before I kill a man who points a gun at me."

"Exactly."

Malik was quiet for a few minutes, mulling over the discussion.

"I still think you should talk to Real Madrid when you get back, the way you kicked that guy...."

Malik thumped Brodie's arm and laughed.

"Ouch, that's police brutality."

The mood in the car was lighter for the remainder of the journey, with Malik giving Brodie more of an insight into her family history and talking about her ambitions for the future. She asked Brodie about his past in the armed forces and the security work he had undertaken since leaving the armed forces. He told her some of his military past but very little of his involvement with Special Forces, as much of that was covered by the Official Secrets Act. He did, however, tell her about much of the security work he had undertaken in recent years and explained his past relationship with Alexander Salenko.

"I did some security set-up work for a Russian diplomat in Amsterdam. He introduced me to Salenko, who wanted to review the security system in his house in London. Then he brought me out here to do the same in his villa in Malaga. I stepped in when he was accosted by a guy who had had too much to drink one night in a club in Puerto Banús, while we were doing his villa; he started to use me as close protection for him and his family if they were travelling.

Had some decent holidays out of that, to be fair. One day he basically asked me to kill some guy who was pissing him off, I said no. He fell out with me, went off in a strop. He stopped using my services for a while, but came back to me about three months ago to look after his wife on a trip to Ukraine. She's Ukrainian and her father had just died. Alexander was committed and couldn't go with her."

"He must trust you, sending you away with his wife."

"He does and I'm about to play on that, because I think he is up to his ears in this drug cartel and if he is, I'm going to take him down with the rest of them."

"You think he's involved?"

"I think he's more than involved, Anita. I think he's Romanov's boss. I'm convinced he's the head honcho here."

"Really! Why? What makes you think that?"

"Every time I hear this weekend being discussed, his name crops up somewhere in the conversation. Romanov refers to him as his friend, but Salenko is in a different league to Romanov, he's intelligent, educated and to cap it all, he could buy and sell Romanov. I've met some of Salenko's friends. They would have nothing in common with Romanov. He's Salenko's lackey, I'm sure of it."

Just then, Brodie's phone rang.

"Alexei, good to hear from you. I trust you are well."

"I have been better. Where are you? We need to talk."

"I'm about half an hour from Puerto Banús."

"I am in Puerto Banús. Where are you staying?"

"Not sure yet. There's an Argentinian grill at the far end of the marina. Meet me there at seven o'clock. It'll be quiet then. You book a table for two in your name."

"OK, is Anita Malik with you?"

"Yep and listening to every word, you're on hands-free."

"She is not joining us for dinner?"

"No, she's going to find somewhere to stay."

"OK, I will see you at seven."

Markov cut the call.

"You don't want me at dinner tonight?" Malik asked.

"I don't want Markov or anyone else knowing where we are staying, but I would rather say 'I don't know' than 'I'm not telling you', hence you can be looking for somewhere when I meet Markov.

"You don't trust Markov?"

"I don't trust anyone in this scenario, Anita. It's messy. Too many people involved who may not be what they seem."

"What do you mean?"

"We had these two guys, Ramirez and Gonzales from Europol, but feeding info to the cartel. We have Markov, a professional hitman, planted in the cartel, but supposedly working for Europol, which the gruesome twosome didn't know about. On top of that, the cartel appear not to know that Markov is a plant, despite the best efforts of Ramirez and Gonzales, but Romanov knew that you were a police officer and managed to get your Europol file. All these interfaces.... and every one of them presents a possible risk to you and me."

"And Moreno?"

"I reckon Moreno's OK. I'm usually a good judge of character and I think Moreno is exactly what he appears to be; a straight up policeman. Bear in mind it was Moreno who asked Madrid for support to bring these guys down and he pulled me in. He didn't need to do that. Also he'd done his homework on me, he knew I'd hit this like a wrecking ball. Plus, he's been a good support to us all along. He's let us do things as we saw it."

"Do you know where this meeting is being held on Saturday?"

"No, Markov is going to give me details on that tonight."

"You want me to find a hotel for us for two nights?"

"No, there's not many hotels that overlook the marina, but there are plenty of apartments. We'll be harder to find in one of those if anyone's looking. Find us a decent one with a good view over the marina."

"OK, I'm on it."

Chapter 39

As Brodie drove the last few kilometres into a bustling Puerto Banús,, Malik took to the internet on her phone and chose four likely apartments, all of which overlooked the marina. She would check their availability for the two nights, then visit any that were available to make sure they were suitable. Brodie left her to it, parked the Mustang in the underground carpark of one of the nearby hotels. He went upstairs to the reception desk and booked a room for two nights. He smiled as he walked down to the marina, a little deception never hurt anyone.

He was dressed casually in a white branded polo shirt, a pair of denim jeans, and navy Geox moccasins, with a navy baseball cap which he kept in the glovebox of the Mustang. Brodie found the cap not only stopped people from instantly recognising him, but acted as an effective shield to hide his face from CCTV cameras. He did not want anyone to recognise him and report the sighting back to the cartel when he was doing his reconnaissance of the marina. Something about this meeting was unsettling Brodie; he couldn't put his finger on it, but alarm bells were ringing.

He walked round the moorings, looking for Alexander Salenko's yacht, and eventually found it, moored, stern first, near the top end of the marina with a short gangway from its stern giving access to dry land. *"Nijinsky"*, had been built six years ago in Italy, was just over sixty metres long, with accommodation for thirteen guests and had a price tag of thirty-five million euros. Salenko took great pleasure in sailing her, he loved the feeling of power he experienced from owning and sailing this magnificent vessel. He knew that on leaving the military, Brodie had spent a year in the Caribbean and had achieved his Yacht Master's ticket, so he had allowed him to take the helm on one or two occasions.

He dropped his head to hide his face from the security cameras that he had had installed on the vessel when Salenko bought it. He walked past the yacht, continued along the marina, crossed the road and walked back in the direction of the main shopping area. It was getting dark and he was due to meet Markov in the Argentinian grill in fifteen minutes. He walked briskly in that general direction, stopping every so often, looking in shop windows, occasionally entering a shop, sometimes admiring the yachts berthed in the marina and every time he stopped, he looked around to see if anyone was following him. He couldn't dispel his general feeling of unease.

At seven o'clock exactly he walked into the Argentinian grill and was met at the door by a young lady.

"Mr Markov has booked a table." Brodie informed her.

The young lady checked the bookings then asked him to follow her

"Your friend is already here, sir."

Brodie nodded and followed her into the restaurant.

As they approached the table, situated in a small alcove near the rear of the restaurant, Alexander Salenko stood to greet him.

"Alan, how good to see you. You look well. Life in Spain must suit you."

Salenko held out a hand to Brodie, who shook hands with his ex-client.

"Alexander, this is a surprise. Not an unpleasant one I hasten to add, but I was expecting to meet Alexei Markov," Brodie said as Salenko motioned him to sit down.

"Yes, I am sorry, Alexei should have called you. He has been unavoidably detained, Alan, but he was only going to give information about the meeting on Saturday, which I gave to him. We are cutting out the middle man, if you like." Salenko smiled.

"It is a long time since we sat down together to share a good dinner. We should take this opportunity to have a catch-up. Let us enjoy our meal and some good wine before we get down to business. I like this restaurant, we have been here before, you and I, do you remember?"

"Yes, I do. We've been here a couple of times, I think. That's why I suggested it to Alexei."

The two men studied the menu in silence for a few moments, before Salenko signalled to a hovering waiter. They ordered their food. Both men bypassed the starters, selecting large medium rare steaks.

Brodie had always appreciated Salenko's taste in wine and was happy to allow the Russian to select an Achaval-Ferrer 2015 from the Mendoza region of Argentina. The waiter indicated his approval of Salenko's choice and made his way to the kitchen with the food order. He returned a few moments later with the wine, which he allowed Salenko to taste and approve, then left the two men to themselves.

Salenko lifted his glass, *"Za tibjá"*

"Cheers," Brodie replied.

"I hear you have bought your own bar here in Spain. I never

saw you as a barman, Alan, I think of you and I think, security, close protection, not as a bar owner."

"I've had enough of security and the like, Alexander. I survived the military and now private security work, but sooner or later, my luck would have run out. I didn't want to end my life that way, so I started to look for something else. I bought the villa in Puerto Ricos, as you know. We talked about it at the time."

"Yes, I remember."

"I love the pace of life in Spain, the social atmosphere, just the general ambiance, you know what I mean. You love Puerto Banús,."

"Yes, I do."

"I got to know El Puerto as my local and made friends with the Spanish couple who owned it. I saw the 'For Sale' sign on the building and as I was looking to buy something, it just seemed too good an opportunity to miss. Not long after that, I was introduced to Ivan and we agreed to do a bit of occasional business. He knows my background, so a few days ago, he asked me to act as his security consultant for this weekend, which is why I'm here."

"Yes, I know all this. Ivan and I talk regularly and I told him to ask you to look after security this weekend. I know you will do a good job."

"I'll do my best, but you know me, it'll be my way or not at all. I have spoken to Ivan about this. I don't think he is too happy to take instruction, but if things are not done as I ask, I can't be responsible for everyone's safety. If things go wrong, it's my reputation that's on the line."

"I understand. Leave Ivan to me."

A waiter appeared at Brodie's shoulder with two large steaks, medium rare, a second brought a selection of lightly cooked vegetables

"*Buen apetito,*" the waiter wished the two men, leaving them to their meal.

The conversation during the meal was basically small talk, which skirted around the subject of the meeting, frequently interrupted by the enjoyment of their food.

As they finished the steaks, Salenko poured another glass of the excellent Malbec and sat back in his chair.

"So, Alan, we have business to do on Saturday and I haven't made up my mind where to conduct the business. Do we meet at my villa or do we pick a neutral venue, a hotel perhaps?"

"Can I make a suggestion? The hotel is not a good idea from a security point of view. Too many people with access to the building or the area around it. Your villa is a better option.... but again more than one way to get access for intruders, so not ideal. Your yacht on the other hand, is secure. We only allow those on board that we want at the meeting, we sail her out into open water, anchor and take the crew off by tender while we meet in total privacy, then we bring them back when we need them to return us to the marina. Plus, let's be honest, Alexander. If you want to impress anyone, how better to do that than take them out to '*Nijinsky*', the sign of a very successful man."

Salenko, looked at Brodie for a few seconds, then smiled.

"Yes, Alan, I like it. We can have a meeting that way in total privacy. Security will be tight and I would get to show "*Nijinsky*" to my suppliers and those that I supply. It is as you say, 'thinking out of the box'. How do we organise the security, getting people on the yacht?"

"Send out a confirmation of the venue about an hour before the meeting. Sail out of the marina and drop anchor out in the bay. When your guests are ready to come out to "*Nijinsky*", light her up like a Christmas tree to make an impression. Use a tender to bring the guests on board, let them see the crew and have them do a tour of the yacht. Once they do that, use the tender to take the crew ashore before the meeting starts, to maximise security"

"We are thinking out of the same box, Alan," Salenko smiled. "I will arrange that. You will be at the gangplank?"

"Yes, with Anita Malik. She is here with me."

"The ex-police officer. Ivan told me about her. Are you sure you can trust her."

"Yes, with my life."

"OK. What about Alexei Markov?"

"He is one of Romanov's men. Better that you ask him, but he seems OK from what I have seen."

"What about the security people some of the others will have with them?"

"They don't come on to *"Nijinsky."*

"I will arrange that. You think of everything."

"That's why you and I are still both alive, Alexander. I get paid to think of everything." Brodie laughed.

Salenko smiled in agreement and once they had confirmed a few more details, he said his goodbyes and left. Brodie gave him a couple of minutes then followed him out of the restaurant.

Brodie walked back towards the centre of the town, now bustling with the noise of music and the buzz of people out for an enjoyable evening of food, drink and entertainment in the many bars and restaurants that overlooked the brightly lit marina. As he walked, he stopped to look at menus posted outside various eateries and expensive designer clothes on display in the upmarket boutiques that were dotted around the marina area. But despite popping into a few of the shops, Brodie was not shopping, nor was he in need of a meal. He was looking for anyone who was tailing him and eventually he spotted them, ensuring by his own movements that they were actually following him.

Two men dressed in dark clothing, walked along the

marina side of the road, away from the bright lights of the shops and restaurants, watching from a distance but still very visible to someone of Brodie's background. By looking into shop windows, Brodie could see the reflection of the two men, He stopped, they stopped. He walked, they followed. He stopped to browse, they stopped, one to watch Brodie, one to admire yachts.

Brodie smiled. Time for some fun. These two were just a nuisance, nothing more. Brodie could lose them easily, if need be by killing them, but two murders in Puerto Banús, would bring a heavy police presence into the town; Brodie didn't want that on the eve of the cartel's meeting. He had a plan.

He crossed the road and walked directly toward the two men, who taken totally by surprise, began to panic, unsure of how to react. One walked away, moving to Brodie's left, the other stood still at the edge of the harbour, turning to face the large luxury yacht moored nearest him and pretended to admire the vessel as Brodie approached.

As he passed the man, Brodie barged into him, knocking him off balance and sending him over the edge of the harbour, hitting the water with a loud splash.

Brodie peered over the edge.

"Oh, no! No! Are you OK mate, can you swim?" He shouted down at the man floundering in the water below.

Turning to his accomplice, Brodie pointed down to the water.

"Can he swim? He can swim, can't he? No, no he can't, can he? He can't swim."

The second man ran back to peer over the edge of the wall at his beleaguered colleague. And as he stood there, Brodie seized the opportunity, aimed a vicious kick at the man, hitting him with force in the middle of his back, and sending him over the edge into the water, to land on top of his partner.

Brodie turned to see if anyone had witnessed what had just

happened. No one appeared to have noticed. Two people had just emerged from a bar and as they looked over at Brodie, he shouted to them.

"Someone's in the water. Can you get help?"

"We'll alert the bar staff. They'll know what to do," and they both disappeared back inside.

Brodie didn't wait for their return. He quickly made his way further down the marina disappearing into a crowd. He called Malik.

"Anita, where are you?"

"I'm in our apartment"

"You got us one? Overlooking the marina?"

"Yes, almost exactly where you wanted it."

"OK, that's good. Text me the address and I'll grab my bag and head over to you."

"How did your meeting with Markov go?"

"It didn't. It was with Alexander Salenko. Markov was unavoidably detained he said. I'll fill you in when I see you. Text me that address."

Brodie took some back streets, sometimes walking, sometimes running, occasionally doubling back on himself to ensure he didn't have any unwanted company. He made his way back to the hotel car park to retrieve his bag from the Mustang, having left an almost empty bag as a decoy in the hotel room. Once he received the text message from Malik, he made his way over to the apartment she had rented, checking as he went that he had not picked up another tail.

Chapter 40

HE FOUND THE APARTMENT EASILY, DID A QUICK SURVEY OF THE immediate area to confirm no one had followed Malik, and was now watching the apartment. Having satisfied himself that it was safe, he approached the door to the building, encountering a door entry system. Rather than use the call button, Brodie called Malik on his phone to announce his arrival.

The apartment Malik had rented was bright and spacious, having obviously been recently refurbished, redecorated, and furnished with a modern theme. It comprised a lounge/dining/kitchen area, two bedrooms, one of them en-suite, and a separate bathroom. The lounge area had a large balcony which, as Malik had promised, overlooked the entrance to the marina.

"They just started to advertise it again after a big refurbishment. That's the only reason it was available at such short notice," Malik explained as Brodie looked around, nodding his head and making noises of appreciation as he went.

"It's a bit better than I'm used to as a base for surveillance, but hey, I'm not complaining."

The owners of the apartment were locals who owned a mini-market not far from the flat. Because of the short notice, they had asked Malik to collect the keys and pay for the apartment in person. She had picked up some food and drinks when in the shop. They sat on the balcony with a complimentary bottle of Rioja, while Brodie brought Malik up to date with the conversations and events of the evening.

Malik gasped when Brodie described how he had unceremoniously dumped the two men following him into the marina.

"You just pushed them into the water?" she exclaimed.

"Yeah, well, I didn't want to leave bodies lying about the place the night before the meeting. We'd have the place swarming with police and we could do without that, so it seemed like a good way of getting them off my case. I did get them some help; the guys from the bar will fish them out."

"You're unbelievable, Alan Brodie!" Malik laughed, almost spilling her wine.

"All joking aside, I'm still not happy with this whole set-up. Something isn't right. I feel it in my bones. Too many people might or might not be who they seem. Is Alexei Markov really working for Europol. Or is he out to line his own pocket? Man like him is capable of disappearing off the grid any time he wants to. South America, Far East, Africa, take your pick. Have they got a police informant in Mojácar or in Madrid for that matter, leaking information to these guys?" If so are they setting us up? Are we walking into a trap tomorrow? I just don't know, Anita, and I don't like it."

"I understand. So, what can you do about it? What can I do?"

"I'll try to mitigate any risk I can. I'll find out as much as I can tomorrow and try to work round anything I'm not happy with."

"You know you can pull out of this if you want?"

"I can't, Anita, not now. If I did, they would come after me and I'd be constantly looking over my shoulder. I need to do this, for me as well as Manuel and his family. Add to that the time, effort and resource Europol and you guys at Mojácar police have invested in this operation, there's no way I can pull out now. We just have to cut down the risks as much as possible."

Brodie drank the last of his wine and stood up, "OK, I'm going to grab a shower and head for bed."

Malik followed Brodie in from the balcony and slid the doors shut as he made his way through the bedroom to the en-suite shower room.

He stripped off his clothes and switched on the shower, letting it come up to temperature before stepping under the warm torrent. He stood, letting the water cascade over him, eyes closed, his mind full of thoughts.

Chapter 41

BRODIE WOKE EARLY AS HE FELT MALIK SNUGGLE INTO HIM, HER body mirroring the profile of his own. They gradually found each other once again, making love slowly as they gradually woke to the dawn breaking. Afterwards, they lay in each other's arms, from time to time drifting in and out of sleep, till they could no longer put off the new day.

While they were both apprehensive about the coming days, they were also aware that irrespective of the outcome, they would have very little more time together as the operation neared its conclusion. Either Malik would return to her career in Madrid and Brodie to his bar in Puerto Ricos or the evening would end badly for one or both of them.

"I feel like a condemned man having his last meal," Brodie murmured in her ear.

She turned to face him, tears in her eyes, "Don't say that Alan, it is not true."

"No, you're right Anita, I'm like Oliver Twist, asking 'can I have some more please'" he replied.

"What is Oliver Twist?" Malik frowned.

"It's a book by Charles Dickens, in it the little boy, Oliver, comes back after he has been given his daily food ration and asks for more," Brodie explained, pulling Malik closer and kissing her lightly. 'Can I have some more, please,'" he mimicked.

Malik laughed and rolled on top of him.

Eventually, Malik rose and without a word, padded across the bedroom, her dark skin glistening with perspiration and disappeared into the bathroom. After a few moments, Brodie heard the sound of cascading water as Malik stepped into the shower.

Later, they sat at the dining table and ate a breakfast of ham, eggs and crusty bread, accompanied by Malik's signature, strong coffee.

"What do you need me to do today?" she asked eventually.

"Just what we discussed. You stay here and watch the marina. If anything unusual or unplanned happens let me know. I've suggested that Salenko takes 'Nijinsky' out of the marina and moors her out in the bay, then uses a tender to ferry his guests out for the meeting. He probably won't do that until tomorrow. If I don't answer my phone just leave a message asking me to call you back, but don't say anything else, don't say why."

"What are you going to do?"

"I need to pick up some stuff from my car, then I'm going to 'Nijinsky' to check out the security and make sure everyone knows what they are doing. After that I'll come back here and get changed. You can get to wear that dress of yours then we head out on the town."

Brodie stood to leave but turned back to Malik, "Have you heard from Moreno?"

"Not since two days ago, why?"

"Nothing. Just wondered." He picked up his phone, keys and cap. "Must go, try to keep out of sight when you are watching what's going on."

"I will. Be careful, Alan."

Brodie stopped, turned and kissed her softly before he left, closing the door to the apartment behind him.

He stood in the shadow of the entrance looking for anyone who may be watching, but seeing no one, he walked away, heading for the hotel garage to retrieve his equipment bag from the boot of his car.

On the way down to the hotel, he constantly watched and checked he was not being followed and arriving at the garage, he entered carefully and sat in the Mustang for almost twenty minutes before he decided it was safe to collect his equipment.

He lifted the boot lid and peering into the near empty space, took out a small package from beneath the floor covering and placed it in his rucksack, which he slung over his shoulder as he closed the boot-lid. He locked the car and left the garage.

Brodie was unsure as to whether 'Nijinsky' would still be moored at the quayside; but she sat where she had been when he last looked for her. By the gangway stood Ivan Romanov, who was in conversation with one of the crew.

He noticed Brodie approach.

"Alan, I wondered when you would come down, I thought you would be here earlier to familiarise yourself with the boat."

Brodie laughed, "Ivan, I know 'Nijinsky' almost as well as Alexander. I designed the security systems on board when he bought her, spent months pouring over the plans and then weeks supervising the installation of the equipment. I just need to make sure everything is as it was and talk to the security guys. We only need a couple of people on board. The others should concentrate on the tender and boarding to make sure that we only have the people on board that we want. Too much security on board will only spook the guests. A couple of guys will be enough to look after anyone who drinks a little too much and gets troublesome."

"I'd better confirm that with Alexander."

"No need, I already have. Remember, Alexander put me in charge of security, so I've told him what we need." Brodie stepped onto the yacht as he spoke. "Better get on, Ivan. When is she leaving her mooring?"

"Three o'clock tomorrow afternoon. That's what I was telling the crew when you arrived."

"That's good. Best not to leave too early." He walked up the deck of the vessel, waving at Romanov over his shoulder as he went.

Brodie had not being exaggerating when he had told Romanov that he knew his way round "Nijinsky". He had personally, designed the security systems on the vessel, supervised the installation of the cameras and sensors and tested the completed system. He needed to check that nothing had been changed, no hardware changes, no software upgrades, nothing that would catch him out.

He headed up a set of steps on to the bridge and proceeded to check the mimic diagram of the security sensors and cameras on a large computer monitor which was built into the main control panel of the vessel. He then used a few clicks of a mouse and strokes of a keyboard, to bring up a separate window on the screen that displayed the details of the system. It showed Brodie the version and revision of the software he was looking at and the date of the last amendments. Armed with this information, Brodie knew that everything was as he had last seen it, no updates or alterations had been made since he had commissioned the system.

Brodie shouldered his rucksack and headed down into the reception and accommodation areas of the vessel, checked out all the rooms then went down to the technical area where the main engines were housed along with the fuel tanks, a small cabin for the engineers and other assorted storage areas. As he reached the main fuel lines from the tanks to the engine, Brodie delved into the bottom of his rucksack and lifted out a false bottom from the bag. He took two small packages from the bag, climbed over a safety rail to allow him access to the fuel lines and attached the larger of the two packages to the main fuel feed using three cable ties. He climbed back out on to the walkway and examined the area to ensure that the package could not be seen by anyone walking or working in the area.

Satisfied with his handiwork, he continued his tour of the vessel and having completed his recce he returned to the bridge. A few keystrokes and mouse clicks later, Brodie had reactivated the camera feeds on the security system, so that the pause he had introduced into the system was virtually undetectable. He checked that all the cameras were again working properly, and climbed down to the main deck.

"All good, Ivan. All the cameras appear to be working as they should, and the fire alarm system is set properly."

"Good. Now, tonight we are going to the Argentinian restaurant you and Alexander met in, then we are going to a vodka bar called Vlad's, it's in town."

Yeah, I know where it is. I've been there with Alexander a couple of times."

"Good, we need you at the restaurant and at Vlad's to make sure nobody bothers us."

"We? Which 'we' would that be Ivan?"

"Myself and Illy. Maybe a couple of others."

"OK, when is your table booked for?"

"Eight o'clock, in my name."

"Right, we'll meet you there."

"We?"

"Yeah, Anita and me."

"Anita?"

"Malik, she's an ex-police officer, she'll be there to look after me. Always good to have someone covering your back, Ivan."

"No one agreed to that...."

"Ivan, Ivan, like I said at yours, my way or the highway. We do this thing my way or not at all, remember? Alexander knows what I am doing with Malik. Yeah?"

"Sure, OK, this time."

"Good, I'm glad we understand each other...."

"Got your bow tie looked out for tomorrow tonight, I hope," Brodie joked as he lightly punched Romanov's shoulder with a broad grin and stepped on to the quayside.

"Sure. You too, my friend," Romanov returned Brodie's grin and raised a hand to wave at Brodie as he walked off.

Chapter 42

BRODIE DROPPED HIS RUCKSACK INTO THE SPARE WHEEL RECESS IN the Mustang's boot and made his way back to the apartment, taking care as always, to ensure that he was not being followed.

The day had passed quickly. Having checked out the yacht then taken his bag back to his car, Brodie went for lunch in one of the many little bars dotted along the quayside. He had picked one that afforded him a view of 'Nijinsky', without putting him in clear sight from the yacht. He ate slowly and took his time over a glass of Rioja, using his phone to take occasional photographs of people coming and going from the vessel.

Later, he took a long slow walk round the marina, noting the police boats moored in a quiet corner of the harbour at the side of a steep ramp that angled down into the water.

He buzzed up to the apartment when he arrived back. Malik answered immediately.

"Anita, it's me," Brodie announced, Malik pressed the door release.

She met him at the door and threw her arms round his

neck. "Thank goodness you're back, I was beginning to worry that something had gone wrong."

"No, all good. I've checked out the security systems that I had installed on 'Nijinsky' for Salenko and it's all as was, so no surprises there."

"You were gone longer than you said, I was worried."

"I didn't know you cared," Brodie smiled, slipping his arms round Malik's waist as he spoke.

"Of course I care you big ox," Malik returned his smile, pulling him closer.

They stood holding each other, saying nothing, for a few minutes.

"What now?" Malik eventually looked up at him.

"Ivan wants me at the restaurant he has booked for eight o'clock and then at a vodka bar called Vlad's, so I told him he will get both of us. He was a bit miffed at first but I made it clear that security was my way or not at all, he eventually agreed. We've got a bit of time, it's nearly four o'clock and we don't need to be down at the restaurant till half seven, quarter to eight, so any ideas on what we can do till then?"

"Oh yes!" Malik smiled and kissed Brodie.

It was almost half past five when Brodie stepped out of the shower and began to get dressed. He walked through to the open plan area where Malik, dressed in a short silk robe, was working in the kitchen

"I put out some cold meats and cheeses, if you want, you could make us some coffee."

The two sat quietly at the breakfast bar eating their food, contemplating the probable events of the next two nights, conscious that one slip-up could ruin the plan and end the whole scenario with a very tragic outcome.

Eventually Brodie stood, collecting their plates and cutlery.

"We should get ready. We need to get to the restaurant before Romanov and check it out. You need to get yourself ready, then put on that posh frock, so that you don't look out of place in Vlad's."

"Ooh, I get to wear my posh frock, do I?"

"Yeah, just try not to get any blood on it."

"Alan, I will not even spill water on that dress."

Brodie finished clearing the kitchen and checked his email then looked at his watch to confirm the time when he heard a noise behind him and turned round to find Malik standing in the doorway, wearing her new blue dress, with matching shoes and bag.

He sat and stared at her. "What? What's wrong? You don't like the dress? Is it too tight? Say something, Alan"

"Malik, you look beautiful. Even in a police uniform you are a beautiful woman but in that dress, you look absolutely stunning. The blue colour of the dress really compliments the colour of your skin and it fits you perfectly."

"Thank you. I don't often get compliments from you, so I appreciate them when I get them."

"I don't do compliments without good cause and I mean it when I say you look beautiful."

"Now, I assume you're ready to go, so just let me grab a jacket."

The two walked down to the Argentinian Churrascaria, which was only a few minutes' walk from the apartment, arriving at twenty to eight.

Brodie left Malik at the door, watching who was coming in and having explained to the owner why he was there, went to check the rear exit and where it led to. He checked that no one was skulking in the toilets and having satisfied himself that all was as it should be, he returned to the front of house. Malik had been observing a few other patrons as they had arrived and with the front of house manager was now looking at the booking system to see who else was expected that evening. The two women chatted and smiled as they went through the bookings.

At ten minutes past eight, a large Audi pulled up at the front of the restaurant and two big men got out of the car. One of them opened the car door to allow Romanov and a woman Brodie knew only as Illy get out of the car. The second minder opened the restaurant door standing aside as Ivan Romanov and his female companion, who was wearing a short, emerald green dress entered. The two men returned to the Audi and drove off at speed.

Brodie approached the couple as they were shown to their table in a quiet spot at the rear of the restaurant which Brodie had requested for them prior to their arrival.

"Good evening, Alan. You remember Illy I assume," Romanov said as he put his arm round the woman,

"Yes, I do. Good evening. Good to meet you again."

"Señor Brodie, my pleasure."

"And you must be Sergeant Malik?"

"Please, call me Anita. In the wrong company 'Sergeant Malik' could get me shot, Señor Romanov."

"How true, Miss Malik, how true and you must call me Ivan."

"Ivan, please make yourselves comfortable, Anita and I will be by the door, looking out for anyone who might be troublesome."

"Thank you, Alan."

Brodie and Malik sat at a small, out of the way table near the entrance, which gave them a good view of the pavement immediately outside and the doorway itself, as well as allowing them sight of Romanov and Illy as they ordered their meal.

The restaurant had a steady flow of customers over the next hour as Brodie and Malik watched and waited as the Russian couple enjoyed their dinner. The time passed without incident and at nine o'clock the Audi which had dropped off Romanov, returned to pick up the couple, accompanied by a second car. The two large men who had ushered the couple into the restaurant stood outside waiting for them to leave.

Brodie stood, motioning to Malik to stay where she was, and walked outside. He crossed the road for a more in-depth view of the nearest doorways that could house possible dangers and having satisfied himself that they were clear, re-crossed the road, just as Romanov and his companion exited the restaurant with Malik in tow.

"Alan, we will not all get into one car, so I arranged for two."

"OK, I'll ride with you and Illy, the others in the second car."

"Very well," Romanov replied, then had a brief exchange with his Russian heavies, who nodded and went to the cars as Brodie had instructed. They opened the doors for Romanov and Illy in the lead vehicle with Malik in the second waiting for them to get seated before closing the doors and getting into the cars. Brodie sat in the front passenger seat and signalled the driver to move off.

Chapter 43

VLAD'S WAS HARD TO MISS FOR ANYONE PASSING BY. IT WAS BIG, garishly decorated with red, white and blue neon signage with the name of the establishment prominently displayed. The thumping bass of the music from inside could be heard the minute the cars pulled up at the entrance to the club.

There was always a substantial Russian presence in and around Puerto Banús,, with many of the larger villas and luxury yachts in the ownership of Russian oligarchs, who with their entourages and employees, ensured that Vlad's was rarely a quiet spot. It seemed that night was no exception.

There were two tall, muscular doormen in attendance. They greeted Romanov politely then picked up wands to scan Brodie and Malik while the others stood back on the pavement.

Brodie held out his arm to stop the scan, "Ivan, tell him no scan. I can't fully protect you if I'm not armed."

Romanov, stopped and gestured to the doormen, saying something in Russian. The doorman looked at Brodie then stepped back and waved the party in.

The noise inside made conversation difficult but there was a short flight of stairs at the back of the club that led up to a mezzanine area. This area was for members only and was much quieter than the main floor. A large Russian opened a silk rope barrier at the bottom of the stairway to allow them entry. Brodie and Malik followed Romanov and Illy up to the member area, where a hostess showed them to a table at the back of the mezzanine. Romanov and his companion sat, while Malik stood behind them and Brodie went for a slow walk around the other tables, half of which were unoccupied. The members' area was surrounded by a glass barrier which ran along the front of the mezzanine and Brodie took time to examine it as he walked round.

As he walked back to the table, the hostess was delivering a bottle of Krug champagne to the table along with two bottles of sparkling water.

"Sit, both of you, please. Anita said I should order you some sparkling water. Alexander said you would not drink alcohol while you were working."

Brodie sat and Malik did likewise, "Alexander has a good memory."

The conversation was much easier up on the mezzanine; the height and the glass barrier helped to filter out the raucous noise of the main dance floor.

There was a small dance area at the back of the mezzanine and Romanov and Illy, along with four or five other couples spent a good part of the evening dancing.

At one point Brodie and Malik watched the couple come back to the table.

"Illy wants to powder her nose, Anita, would you go with her, please." Romanov asked.

"Of course," Malik stood and the two women walked off.

"I do not know if women powder their noses any more, Alan, but it is better than telling everyone that she needs to pee, do you not think?"

"Much more refined, Ivan, as I would expect from a gentleman of your standing."

Romanov laughed. "Sometimes it is good that they need powder their noses, it gives us men time to talk.

"What did you want to talk about?"

"I wanted to ask if you had seen Alexei Markov recently."

"No, not for a few days, I was supposed to meet him here in Puerto Banús,, but Alexander met me instead. Why do you ask?"

"Alexander does not like him. He does not trust him he says."

"Alexander doesn't trust anyone."

"He trusts you, Alan."

Brodie shook his head.

A few moments later, he noticed the two women make their way towards them. As they crossed to the stairs up to the VIP area, Brodie watched as Illy's arm was grasped by a man she was trying to pass. He was a big athletically built man, who was with a few others standing at the bottom of the stairs. He looked to be more than a little drunk.

Romanov saw the situation developing and grasped Brodie's arm.

"Alan, Alan, do something, he shouted."

"It's OK, not yet. If he's not careful, Malik's going to play football with him." Brodie held Romanov back and smiled.

Malik spoke to the man but neither Brodie nor Romanov could hear over the noisy music. She twisted the man's thumb to loosen his grip on Illy's arm and he turned to face her, a look of fury in his eyes, having as he saw it, been humiliated by a women, Malik struck out and buried her right knuckle directly into the man's left eye socket, bringing a howl of pain which could even be heard from the mezzanine area.

"Wait for it Ivan," Brodie grinned, "Step back, girl. Swing with the left."

Both men watched in awe as Malik lifted the hem of her dress, stepped back, and buried the pointed toe of her left shoe deep into the man groin. He stood for a moment then crumpled slowly into a coital ball on the floor. His friends, who had been transfixed by this, began to move toward Malik.

"OK, my time now," Brodie shouted as he launched himself down the stairs towards the group of men. Arriving at the bottom of the stairs he slid his arm round Malik's waist and stared at the three remaining men as they approached.

"Back off guys. You really don't want to do this."

One of the men held out his arm, a large knife in his hand.

"I could take your guts out with this, so why don't you just let her come with us?"

Brodie looked at Malik. "Do you want to go with him?"

"No Brodie, I do not want to go with him."

"She doesn't want to go with you."

"In that case, I will take your guts out with this."

"I bet you couldn't before I put a bullet in your head. What do you reckon, One hundred dollars says I can put a bullet in your head before you get near me with that knife and I can tell, you're going to be nothing like fast enough. I've done this knife/bullet thing before and, hey, I'm still here, but if you think you're faster than everyone else, go ahead. I'll tell you what, I can see you're swithering, let's make it two hundred. That what you think your life's worth, two hundred dollars?"

"Friedrich," a voice said from behind the man, "Let's go. It's not worth it, guy's crazy."

The man stood for a few more seconds, shrugged his friend's hand off and put the knife in his pocket. He stared at Brodie for a time then allowed himself to be shepherded away by his friends.

Romanov was standing behind Malik and Brodie with Illy.

"He's right, you are crazy."

"No Ivan. Firing off 9mm rounds in a crowded room like this is crazy."

"I think maybe we should go home, Ivan," Illy suggested.

"Yes let me call the cars," Romanov signalled to a man hovering just behind them," Sergei, my cars and make sure these scum are still not around when we leave."

"Mister Romanov, they are already being dealt with, they will not be a problem."

They waited until Sergei, the club manager, informed them that the two cars were waiting for them, then Brodie and Malik went outside to check that the area was secure before letting Romanov and Illy get seated in the cars as before. True to his word, the four troublesome men had disappeared as Sergei had promised and the party left without further incident.

On arriving at their hotel, Romanov and Illy allowed themselves to be shepherded into the foyer and from there to one of the lifts.

As the lift rose to the top floor of the hotel, Romanov, stared across at Brodie for a moment.

"What is it, Ivan. You're staring at me?"

"Sorry, I didn't mean to stare, but you said to that man with the knife that you have done this…. knife/bullet thing many times before and you have always won. Is that true?"

"I might be embellishing the truth a little. I've done it twice before. I won once and the other time was a draw."

"A draw? How can something like that be a draw?" Illy asked.

"Well, let's just say that I got a small scar in my side."

"And him?"

"Oh, he got an unmarked grave with amazing views."

Malik shook her head. "Brodie, you're unbelievable."

As the lift doors opened, they walked along the hallway to Romanov's room. Malik stood out in the hall with Romanov and Illy while Brodie checked the room to ensure that Romanov and Illy were alone.

As they turned to leave, Illy touched Malik's arm.

"Thank you for what you did tonight, I could never have done that."

"Don't mention it. It's what I do. I am sure you possess other talents that I do not have."

Brodie and Malik retreated along the hall to the lift then left the hotel to go back to the apartment.

They walked through the lively centre of Puerto Banús,, the air filled with the beat of music and the noises of innocent people enjoying themselves. As they walked they constantly checked their surroundings for anyone who may be less innocent.

"I like Illy. She is a nice lady. Why do women like that get involved with scum like Romanov," Malik said as they strode between the crowds.

"Eh, excuse me... she threatened to kill me, Malik."

"Ah, I'd forgotten about that. Anyway, I'm sure she didn't mean it."

Chapter 44

THE NEXT MORNING, BRODIE WOKE WITH THE SUN STREAMING IN through the bedroom window, they had not closed the shutters the previous night when they got back after completing their nights work. Brodie opened his eyes slowly, savouring his memory of Malik as they had made love slowly and tenderly, falling asleep afterwards in each other's arms.

Malik was lying, facing him, her head propped up in her hand, smiling.

"What's wrong?" Brodie asked.

"Nothing, you looked so peaceful lying there, I didn't want to wake you."

"You been awake for long?"

"No, only a little while, and it is still early."

Brodie looked at his watch, ten minutes to seven.

"Are you going for a run this morning?"

"Mm, yeah."

"Maybe later?" Malik rolled over and kissed him then sat astride him, smiling down at him.

"Maybe some warm up exercise before you go?"

An hour later Brodie was running at a steady pace round a

grassy knoll at the far end of the marina, feeling the warmth of the sun developing, even at that time of the morning. He enjoyed his early morning runs, quiet beaches with only the odd local fisherman setting up his rods at the water's edge. The temperature would be starting to climb but, except for the hot summer months, it was still cool enough to be enjoyable. As he ran, he continuously checked his surroundings, ensuring he did not have any unwanted company He managed to find a circular route on his phone, which would avoid taking him into any quiet areas where he might be vulnerable to unwanted attention.

Having run for just over an hour, he found himself back at the apartment.

Malik prepared some breakfast and coffee while Brodie showered and dressed for the day in shorts and a white polo shirt. They sat on the balcony overlooking the marina as they ate, Brodie checking his phone for messages and answering a few as he finished his coffee.

"So, what do we do today?" Malik asked.

"We wait till Romanov calls us to go keep him out of harm's way."

"And if he doesn't call?"

"Then I'll go and check on him later, just in case there's a problem. We'd look very silly if we were waiting up here for him to phone and room service found him dead in his bed.

I want us to go over everything again today, I want to go over the plan, look for flaws or loopholes, figure out any what ifs, just to make sure we're water tight."

Over the next few hours, Brodie and Malik sat at the apartment's breakfast bar, pouring over their plans, looking at all the possible scenarios and investigating a range of potential outcomes. When they were happy that they were in good shape, Brodie suggested they go out for some lunch.

They walked along the road at the side of the marina until

Brodie saw a bar where they could keep a watch on 'Nijinsky' without being easily seen by anyone either on board or coming and going from the vessel. They ordered a selection of tapas and a large bottle of sparkling water, taking their time over the food whilst keeping a watchful eye on the activity on and around Salenko's yacht.

Brodie appeared relaxed and in control. This was his profession, it was what he did. He had kept clients safe all over the world. He was good at it and had never yet lost a paying customer. That was going to change before the day was done.

Malik, on the other hand, was visibly on edge as she ordered a double espresso.

"Do you want a coffee, Allan?"

"Nah, coffee at lunchtime, I'd be awake all night."

"I don't get you, Brodie." Malik shook her head as she spoke. "You know what we are going to do tonight but you can still sit there and make jokes."

"It's *because* I know what we're going to do tonight that I can make light of it." Brodie hesitated.

"You look edgy Malik. Something bothering you? Maybe something you want to tell me?"

"No, I'm just impatient. I want to get started. The sooner we get going the sooner we get finished."

"Understandable, but one step at a time. Why don't you head back to the apartment, get things ready for tonight? I'm going to head round to Romanov's hotel and touch base with him, see what he's up to."

Once Malik had finished her coffee, Brodie paid the bill and they both left, Malik walking back the way they had come and Brodie heading in the opposite direction, to see Romanov, having first checked that no one was tailing Malik.

The walk to Romanov's hotel took just over five minutes. Brodie was not worried as to whether or not he was being followed.

They would know soon enough where he was when he knocked on Romanov's door. He took the lift straight to the top floor and stepped out into the hallway to be confronted by two of Romanov's minders, one of them pointing a nine millimetre pistol at him.

"Afternoon gentlemen," Brodie said with a smile.

"Hands above your head and turn round," the tall Russian snarled.

"What? You're going to frisk me to see if I'm carrying? I don't think so. I can tell you now I'm armed and you're not going to change that. You know I'm here to see Ivan, so just get out of my way."

As Brodie strode past the gunman to knock on Romanov's door, the second Russian pushed him into the wall face first and leaned heavily on him.

"You cause trouble here and hurt my friends. Maybe it's time for some payback while there is nobody here to help you." The Russian punched Brodie hard in the kidney, but was standing too close to his target to get any real power into the blow.

As he was about to deliver another blow, Brodie reached between their two bodies and grabbed a handful of the man's testicles, squeezing hard. The man howled in pain and tried to stand back but Brodie kept his tight hold on the man, so the more he pulled away, the more pain he suffered. As Brodie pushed back from the wall he delivered a reverse head butt, smashing the back of his head into the Russians face then drove his elbow into the man's solar plexus, driving the wind from him. By this time, the Russian was totally disorientated and Brodie had no trouble manoeuvring behind him, his arm round the man's neck. He pulled his Glock from his waistband and held it to his assailant's ear, making sure that the man's body was between him and the other Russian who was still pointing his gun in Brodie's direction.

"Put the gun down or I'll blow your friend's brain cell out through his left ear."

The Russian gunman stood his ground, staring at Brodie, his gun still pointing at him.

Just then the lift doors opened and Ivan Romanov and Illy stepped into the hallway accompanied by the two minders who had been with them at the club the previous night.

"What the hell is going on here?" Romanov demanded.

"Oh, your two monkey's said that I had hurt some of their friends and they wanted some payback."

"Put that gun down, idiot. Do you hear me?"

"Yes, I hear you," the Russian replied as he slowly lowered his weapon.

"Now, get out of here, before I shoot you myself."

Brodie released his hold on his attacker and replaced his Glock in his waistband, as the man stumbled away and followed his friend into a room further down the hall.

"Come," Romanov said as he grabbed Illy's hand and walked her to their room door. As he opened the door to the room, he looked across at Brodie.

Brodie closed the room door as he entered.

"I am sorry, Alan. Sometimes my people get, how do you say, overly enthusiastic. They should not have done that. I am glad that I came here when I did, we were downstairs in the restaurant having some lunch. I saw you come in so we came up to see what you wanted"

"You just saved yourself the trouble of having to explain to the police why there were two dead Russians lying in the hallway outside your room. They might even want to know why you are here in Puerto Banús. Alexander *would* be pleased."

"Maybe we should not tell him. He has enough on his mind at the moment. Anyway, why are you here?"

"I just came to make sure you were OK. I hadn't heard from you today."

Romanov looked at Illy. "We are both OK. No after effects from last night, thanks to your Sergeant Malik."

"Ivan, please stop with the Sergeant. She is not a police officer any more, but it might spook some of Alexander's business associates to hear her referred to as Sergeant."

"Yes, yes, I understand. Now, Illy and I have some unfinished business, if you follow me. We won't be going out until tonight."

"OK, I understand," Brodie said as he made for the door.

"Be gentle with him Illy. He's not getting any younger." He laughed as he closed the door behind him and made his way back to the front door.

He looked around to check for anyone following him and satisfied there was nobody following him, he walked slowly past Salenko's yacht to check the activity around and on board the vessel. There was nothing untoward happening or activities that would have looked out of the ordinary to anyone passing by, so he continued back to the apartment, stopping off at his car to pick up something he might need later.

It was late afternoon by the time Brodie got back to the apartment and Malik was busy in the kitchen as he arrived.

"Hi, how did you get on with Romanov. Everything OK?"

"Yep, all good. What you up to?"

"I thought we would be better to have something to eat before we went out tonight, so I'm just putting a few bits and pieces together for us."

"Sounds good, I'll make us some coffee."

They sat at the breakfast bar and ate the cold meat, cheese and bread that Malik had arranged and Brodie brought her up to date with his afternoon.

Eventually, as they cleared up, Brodie asked, "Have you spoken to Moreno today?"

"Yes, I went over the plan with him. He knows that we will be on "Nijinsky" and that he should wait for the signal from you, then approach the yacht on the Police patrol boat to make the arrests."

"Good. He sounded happy with that?

"Maybe a little nervous that we are taking a big risk to get all of these people in one place."

"I agree, but I think we have done all we can to manage the risks. I'm going to head for the shower and get changed. You need to get changed too. I won't be long." Brodie called back over his shoulder as he made his way to the shower.

He showered quickly, stepped into a pair of black boxer shorts and walked out into the bedroom where he found Malik, also in her underwear, laying out a black trouser suit and white top on the bed. She turned as he entered room and smiled at him.

"After people I loved were killed in Algeciras, I swore I would never mix work and pleasure again, Alan, but with you I have, and I could not stand to lose you the way I lost them."

"Enough," Brodie interrupted, stepping forward to wrap his arms around her and pull her towards him. "What we do for a living is uncertain and dangerous, we both know that. We could be hurt or killed at any time but we need to think positively because if we start to doubt ourselves, we will hesitate and that hesitation might be fatal. So stay positive. We are going to come out of tonight and carry on our lives afterwards. You'll head back to Madrid and I'll go back to doing what I do. We always knew that would be the probable outcome, but you'll always be very special to me."

"Why do you always make me feel a confidence that sometimes in the past has been lacking in me?"

"Because you're good at what you do. You just don't know how good you are. Moreno does. He has told me more than once, so don't doubt that we are going to get a result tonight. Just think about what we are going to do afterwards."

"Mm, now I'm interested."

"Good, now get dressed. Work first, then pleasure."

They kissed each other then turned to their clothing to get ready for the task at hand. They both dressed in black trousers and jackets, set off by white shirts and each wore a handgun in underarm holsters.

At six-fifteen, they left the apartment and started toward the marina and *'Nijinsky'*

Chapter 45

ALEXEI MARKOV WAS STANDING AT THE QUAYSIDE, ACCOMPANIED by one of Romanov's heavies when Brodie and Malik arrived.

"Señor Brodie, I thought you had forgotten your duties for tonight, Vladimir and I have been here for almost thirty minutes," Markov scowled.

"As if, Alexei. I know exactly what is expected of Malik and me tonight. I've already checked out the security on board and I know that the guests will arrive between six forty five and seven o'clock, so no need for me to be here any earlier."

"I've told Salenko I only want two of your security people on board tonight, so I hope that you and Vladimir there are all that are on board. Alexander wants everyone relaxed tonight. That won't happen if the boat is swarming with Russian heavies wandering around with guns."

"I know what you told Salenko, he called me and has given his instructions," Markov grunted and motioned for his colleague to follow him as he stepped onto the tender Salenko had hired for the night, rather than use the smaller one from 'Nijinsky'.

At just after six forty-five, the first of Salenko's guests

arrived in a black Mercedes. Malik took his name and ticked him off the list of invitees she had been given by Brodie. He quickly and efficiently swept the man with a metal detecting wand, just as Salenko arrived In a similar car to greet his guest.

Having seen his guest onto the tender and passed him to a crew member, dressed in black trousers and a white shirt with the work 'Nijinsky' embroidered on the front, Salenko approached Brodie and Malik.

"Alan, Markov told me you had arrived.... and you must be Señorita Malik," he said, turning to smile at Malik, "Alan speaks very highly of you, my darling, I hope his opinion of your abilities are not coloured by your more obvious attributes, if you will excuse the pun."

"I did not get to where I am by simply being eye candy for lecherous old men, Señor Salenko. I happen to be very good at my job."

"I'm very pleased to hear it, Señorita Malik, because your future may well depend on how you do your job tonight, yours and Alan's. But, hey, let us all relax tonight. There is no reason anything should go wrong and, I hope maybe you will both join me at my villa later for a small celebration of a successful gathering here."

"Ah, another guest." Salenko waved as another black Mercedes arrived alongside and he moved to greet the passenger as he alighted.

"Excuse us, Alexander," Brodie said as he approached the new arrival and as before, quickly but efficiently swept the man with his metal detecting wand, while Malik took his name and ticked him off her list of attendees.

Salenko ushered his guest on board and walked with him into the main cabin of the tender. As they disappeared from view, Alexei Markov and his associate stepped out of the tender and stood on the quay behind Brodie and Malik.

As they waited for more of the ten expected guests to arrive,

Markov gestured to Brodie and walked forward, leaving the other Russian at the cabin door.

"Alan, you have a list of names of all expected guests for tonight. Alexander has given you information which will be very valuable to Europol. Put it in your pocket later and make sure you keep it safe."

"I'll do my best, but Alexander isn't stupid, he's going to want it back."

"No, he trusts you. He will not ask for it." Markov turned to re-join the other Russian as another Mercedes pulled up beside the yacht.

A large, heavily built man struggled out of the front passenger seat and opened the rear passenger door. Another man stepped out onto the quayside.

"Good evening, sir," Malik greeted him, "may I have your name."

The man stopped and stared at her with disdain then brushed past her to board the yacht. Brodie stepped in front of him.

"Excuse me, sir, my colleague and I need to know your name for security reasons."

"I do not give my name to women. Alexander Salenko knows who I am, that is all that is necessary."

"I'm afraid that is not the case. Our instructions from Alexander are that we must have the names of everyone as they board. This is to help us to keep you safe and secure, as well the others on board."

"Daniel," Salenko's guest snapped and the big man behind him stepped forward opening his jacket to display a holstered Glock under his arm.

"That's very unfortunate, sir, because even if your friend manages to pull that Glock out before I reach mine," Brodie smiled, pulling out his own jacket to show the two men that he was also armed, "He is not going to be able to shoot me and then shoot my colleague behind him before she kills him with the handgun she has aimed at the back of his head."

The men turned slowly to look at Malik, who was holding a Glock pistol in her two hands, pointing it at the large man's head.

"Gentlemen, there is no need for this aggression. Tonight we are all here to relax and enjoy ourselves, but we do need to stay safe and that means we have to observe certain simple security protocols. So please give your name to my associate. She'll put her gun away, mark you off her list and I'll give you a quick scan. After that you can go on-board and your friend here can go back to your hotel."

"I am Tomas Žutautas and my companion comes with me."

"I'm sorry, my instructions are guests only tonight, just to keep it friendly," Brodie replied.

Žutautas looked as if he was going to respond but Markov intervened, "Mr Žutautas, my colleague is correct, Mr Salenko has requested no additional people, guests only, I am afraid."

Žutautas turned and spoke to his companion in what Brodie thought was Lithuanian or maybe Latvian. The big man stared at Malik, then Brodie before grunting something in response and returning to the car, while Markov escorted the Lithuanian onto the tender

The rest of the arrivals went without further incident and by five minutes past seven the fleet of Mercedes limousines had delivered all twelve of Salenko's business associates. Malik marked them off her guest list as they arrived and Brodie scanned them with his metal detecting wand. Shortly after the last guest arrived, the crew made ready to take the tender out to *'Nijinsky'* moored out in the bay; a manoeuvre which took twenty-five minutes, including tethering the tender to the larger yacht, to secure the vessel for the short time she would be there. Having completed the tours of *'Nijinsky'* the crew were taken ashore on the tender, leaving Malik and Brodie with only those guests involved in the meeting, as well as Salenko, Markov, and his other security guard.

Chapter 46

SALENKO HAD ASSEMBLED HIS TWELVE GUESTS IN THE SPACIOUS, enclosed saloon on the opulent owner's deck of the vessel, which had been refurbished in a lavish Art Deco style during a recent refit. Markov was offering the guests pre-prepared drinks. They appeared to be in good spirits and were enjoying the VIP treatment being afforded them on the luxury yacht. As the drinks were steadily consumed, the noise level in the room rose as the men chatted animatedly.... until Salenko tapped his ice hammer against the bar grill.

"Gentlemen. Gentlemen, thank you. May I have your attention, please? Just for a few moments, if I may." Salenko waited for silence and the full attention of the room, before continuing.

"Thank you, gentlemen. I want to say a few words of welcome to you all and then I have a short demonstration which I think you will enjoy.

You do not need me to tell you that we have enjoyed a year of substantial business growth; your bank balances will tell you that and our plans for the future will see your earnings continue to rise. We have built an efficient network, which works well for all of us and in which I have every trust.

That trust is important in our business, as I am sure you understand. This is the first time we have all met together and I felt that it gave me a good opportunity to demonstrate just how important that trust is. I have a special guest whom I would like to introduce to you. He is downstairs in one of the cabins with his family, one of my associates has just gone down to bring him here to meet you."

Brodie felt a chill down his spine as he sensed something was wrong, all of Salenko's people who had been agreed to with the Russian were already in the room.

Salenko smiled across at Malik and Brodie, "Alexei, open the door for our special guest, he will be no stranger to some of us," he continued to smile at Malik and Brodie.

Markov, looked across at Salenko, then at Brodie, a look of confusion on his face.

"Alexei, please," Salenko gestured.

Markov did as instructed and as the door opened, a tall, slim man wearing a light grey suit was pushed into the room by two armed men who Brodie had never seen before. Police Comisario Xavier Moreno stood in the centre of the room, like a rabbit caught in a set of bright headlights. His suit was crumpled, the collar stained with blood which was seeping from a gash in his head.

Malik looked over at Brodie, a shocked look on her face.

"Alexander, what is this?" Brodie asked the smiling Russian.

"This is the start of my little demonstration, Alan. I want to show everyone in this room what happens to people who try to cheat on us or who stand in our way. People who break our trust. This man," he gestured at Moreno, "is a policeman who has been fighting to destroy our little network, bring it to justice, he says, while you and officer Malik here have been trying to cheat your way into our network on false pretences.

You are working with this man to kill our business, but tonight our business is going to kill you as an example of what happens to such people."

Salenko's two minders drew pistols from under their jackets and pointed them at Malik and Brodie.

"Both of you, throw your guns on the floor. We know you are armed."

Slowly, Malik and Brodie took out their weapons and dropped them to the floor.

"Hands above your heads where I can see them," Ivan Romanov snarled as he stepped forward.

"Alexei, your gun," Romanov demanded, holding out his hand to Markov, who looked at him in disbelief. "Sorry, maybe if I call you Yuri, you will understand.... Señor Kuznetsov."

Markov, stood transfixed as the reality of his situation dawned on him. He pulled out his weapon as one of the two Russians covered him, handing the weapon to Romanov.

Salenko shook his head at Markov. "You think we are stupid, Kuznetsov?. We did not know you were working for Europol? Europol has too many arms and legs, many of them will give information to anyone who will pay them for it. That is how we knew about Comisario Moreno's little plot with Brodie and the delectable Officer Malik, so we invited his family to be with us, as an incentive for him to join us. So now we have all the players in one room and once you all die and we feed you to the fishes – what a good idea of yours to sail 'Nijinsky' out here, Alan. We will be able to continue to grow in peace. Now, I must leave you in the very capable hands of my colleagues, gentlemen, I have other matters to attend to. Goodbye, Alan. It has been good working with you over the years, what a shame it ends this way. How could you be so stupid?" Salenko smiled as he patted Brodie on the cheek, brushed past him and signalled two of his minders to follow.

Brodie's mind raced as he took in the room trying to collect his thoughts on the dilemma now facing them. Salenko's guests were huddled together in one corner of the saloon, Moreno was standing by the door and Malik, Markov and Brodie were faced with Romanov and the two Russians, all of them armed and pointing their weapons at the three. Markov and Malik both looked alert and ready, Moreno was not a man of action and appeared to be grossly out of his depth.

Brodie, standing with his hands behind his head, smiled at Romanov. "Should have killed you when I had the chance, Ivan. Would have been easier than killing you now. What'd you reckon, Alexei?"

Romanov laughed at the two men, then grabbed the front of Markov's shirt, pulled him in front of Brodie and pushed his Glock handgun into Markov's mouth.

"Him first," he laughed, "then you, Brodie. We may leave your delectable friend here till we have had some fun with her."

As Brodie and Malik watched in horror, as Markov tried to struggle free. Romanov pulled the trigger and his victim fell to the ground.

"Whoa! Wait a minute Ivan. No need to get personal. You do know that this woman could have been playing for Real Madrid right now, yeah?"

A second later, Malik registered Brodie's intention and lashed out with her right leg, delivering a crippling blow to the groin of one of the Russians at the same time rolling across the floor to retrieve her gun, only to see the other Russian aim for her head and as a gunshot rang out, Brodie pulled his concealed KA-BAR knife out of a pouch hanging down the back of his neck and slashed it across the throat of a still static Romanov. The lethal seven inch blade opened his throat from ear to ear, severing both arteries and windpipe.

All this happened so quickly that Romanov was still smiling when he dropped to the floor like a puppet having had its strings cut. Malik quickly realised that she had not been shot but the second Russian was sliding down the wall with an ever growing blood red bloom on the front of his shirt. She spun round to see Markov, a large exit wound on his right cheek, push a Glock across the floor in her direction.

She grabbed the gun and turned to the Russian she had kicked so brutally and fired at him just as he raised his weapon. Malik's bullet hit him high on his forehead, a second shot took out his left eye.

"That's for my sister," Malik whispered as she lowered the gun.

Brodie surveyed the room once again, Salenko's guests were still cowering in the far corner of the room. None had been able to get to an exit and all of them now in fear for their lives. Both Russian minders were dead, and Romanov lay dead at his feet. Brodie prised the Glock out of his hand. Markov lay wounded on the floor of the saloon, alive but obviously in severe pain as blood seeped from the exit wound on his face.

"Malik, you OK?" Brodie enquired, looking at her as she sat on the floor, still holding the Glock in a two handed grip.

"Never better," she replied, "never better."

"Try to look like you mean that, Malik."

She, turned to face Brodie, a slight smile crossed her face in contradiction to the tears in her eyes. "No, really, I'm fine, Alan."

"OK, Can you see to Alexei?"

"Xavier, where is your family?"

"My wife, she is down stairs. Alan, sorry, I just froze there. I thought we were all going to die."

"Well some did, thankfully all the right ones and none of us good guys," Brodie approached Moreno and using his combat knife, slashed through the plastic tie which bound his wrists.

"OK, Xavier, go and get your wife. Bring her up here. As the shepherd said to his dog, we need to get the flock out of here."

As Moreno disappeared, Malik and Brodie managed to get Markov onto his feet and sat him on a padded seat.

"Stay with him Malik and watch this lot," he gestured at Salenko's guests, "I'll be back in a couple of minutes," Brodie said as he ducked out of the saloon, returning a few minutes later with the small backpack he had secreted earlier in the engine room area.

He pulled out a handful of black cable ties, "All of you," he addressed Salenko's guests, "Tie these tightly round your ankles and I mean tightly, I will check and anyone whose ties are not tight, I'll put a bullet through your kneecap. Do I make myself clear?"

Without waiting for a response from the group, he tossed some of the ties over to the frightened men and watched as they sat on the floor or the padded seats in the saloon and wrapped them tightly round their legs. Brodie watched, and as they finished, checked the cable ties were tight then added others round their wrists.

He turned as Moreno came into the saloon with his wife, who was obviously very frightened and could easily be tipped over the edge if not treated properly.

Brodie ushered them out onto the deck, away from the blood and the bodies.

"Xavier, can you operate that small tender at the back of the ship?"

"Yes, certainly. I have a small boat in the marina at Puerto Ricos."

"Good. Can you launch it, start the engine, get you and your wife into it, and wait for Malik and Markov. We need to get out of here."

Brodie returned to the main saloon and checked on the captive guests, before turning his attention to Markov and Malik.

"How is he?"

"He'll be OK. He has lost a good deal of blood and he is in shock, but the bleeding seems to have all but stopped. He was very lucky. Must have turned his head as Romanov pulled the trigger and the bullet went out through his cheek instead of blowing his brains all over the cabin roof.

Brodie turned Markov's head round gently to examine the wound, "Lucky man indeed. We need to get that dressed as soon as we get ashore. Only air kisses for you from now on Alexei."

"Let's get him to the tender with Xavier and his wife."

Brodie and Malik helped Markov down to the small tender, where Moreno and his wife were waiting.

"Anita, wait for me in the boat, I'll be back soon."

Before either Malik or Moreno could reply, Brodie untied the tender from the back of the yacht, ran back up to the main deck and disappeared from sight.

Chapter 47

FOR A FEW MOMENTS, THE LITTLE TENDER BOBBED AROUND IN THE water, its powerful outboard engine burbling in the background as Moreno held it close to the larger vessel, awaiting Brodie's return. Moreno and Malik looked at each other in astonishment as *'Nijinsky's'* engines started. Seconds later the big yacht began to move forward.

"What is happening? What the hell is he doing?" Moreno shouted to Malik, above the engine noise."

"I don't know, sir," Malik answered. "I'll go and find out. take us in close."

Moreno eased the throttle open on the little tender and nudged the back of the yacht as Malik leapt across to the vessel's rear deck and followed the same direction as Brodie had taken earlier.

Just then, the engine noise from *'Nijinsky'* changed as the throttles of the larger yacht were opened to provide maximum power from the two 1850 horsepower engines, which would take her to a maximum speed of 15 knots. The yacht began to move forward changing direction slightly. Malik began to shout for Brodie as she ran into the saloon.

The prisoners were all still there, although trying vainly to break the plastic ties which held their ankles and wrists, but no sign of Brodie. She left the saloon and bounded up the steps to the bridge, still no sign of Brodie.

Malik was on her way back to the main deck, feeling 'Nijinsky' begin to pick up speed, when she literally bumped into Brodie coming up from below.

"Where have you been? What are you doing?" she demanded.

"Malik, what are you doing? You should be with Xavier in the tender!"

"I was looking for you."

"Never mind that now. We need to get out of here. There's fuel leaking all over the engine room. Looks like a big leak and I'm sure it's deliberate. It could go up any minute. Move, now!" Brodie shouted, pulling Malik behind him as he made for the stern rail of the yacht.

"The prisoners, Alan!"

"No time. Get out of here, now!"

Malik finally relented and climbed over the rail ready to jump into the water, Brodie followed just behind, giving her a final push. As they jumped, they were hit by the blast of an explosion and hurled head over heels into the sea when the leaking fuel combusted.

Brodie hit the water hard and began to sink into the dark depths, disorientated at first, he quickly got his bearings and struck out for the surface. As he broke the surface he looked round but could not see Malik anywhere. He looked round again to try to find her, then caught sight of her floating face down in the water about ten metres to his right.

"Malik," he called out as he swam quickly over to her.

"Malik?" He pulled her round so that her face was no longer in the water, but she was totally unresponsive. Just then Moreno pulled the tender alongside them and leaned over to help pull the still unconscious woman into the tender, Brodie pulling himself into the boat.

"Get out of here, Xavier! That yacht is going to blow, big time. With the amount of fuel she has on board, it'll be a catastrophic explosion. Go! Go!"

Moreno opened the throttle hard and swung the rigid inflatable boat round in a tight turn and headed at speed towards the safety of the marina. His wife, who had now recovered some of her senses, was trying to revive Malik as best she could in the tight confines of the crowded tender.

Like most rigid inflatables, the little boat was capable of relatively high speeds and it sped across the water heading for the marina. Just as they reached the entrance, the sky around 'Nijinsky' lit up with a flash, followed by a mighty explosion and a thirty-five million euro fire bomb erupted into the night sky as the luxury yacht was ripped apart, blown to pieces in a hail of fire and debris. As the wake of the explosion reached the shore, the super yacht was fast disappearing under the waters of the Mediterranean, to be replaced by a blanket of debris and burning fuel.

Malik coughed, spluttered, and vomited sea water into the bottom of the tender as Moreno shut down the throttle to idle and looked back in horror and disbelief at the scene of devastation.

"What the hell just happened there, Brodie?" he called above the noise and the ringing in his ears.

Brodie, however, was more intent on helping Moreno's wife revive Malik, who was still coughing up seawater in the bottom of the tender.

"Malik, are you OK?"

Malik squinted up at him. "Do I look OK?" she coughed.

"To be fair, you look like shit but you sound OK. Had me worried for a bit, though."

"What was that explosion I heard?"

"That was the sound of a two hundred foot super yacht self-destructing."

"What!" Malik sat up unsteadily in the bottom of the tender, her hand raised to the back of her head and looked out into the bay. She swayed slightly and fell back onto the floor of the small boat with a groan. She pulled her hand away from her head to find it covered in her own blood.

Brodie looked at the back of her head and saw that she had a deep wound, bleeding freely, just behind her right ear.

"Xavier, take us in. Malik and Alexei are going to need some medical attention to their wounds, soon as we can."

Moreno signalled his understanding and took the tender quickly to a ramp in the marina where emergency vehicles were already beginning to congregate, flashing red and blue lights announcing their presence.

"Xavier, you'll be the senior officer with the authority here. You'll need to deal with these guys. Get a quick reaction from them to have these two transferred to hospital."

"No problem," Moreno called back as he nudged the tender into the ramp and was met by three pistol wielding Garda officers.

"I'm Comisario Xavier Moreno. Who is in charge here?"

"I am," a young sergeant replied approaching Moreno

"Good, we need medical attention for our colleagues. Quickly sergeant and find Comisario Gutiérrez for me. He is aware of our operation."

"*Médicos,*" the sergeant called back up the ramp then watched one of the paramedic crews approach the waterline as Moreno and Brodie helped a still very much disorientated Malik out of the boat and sat her gently on the ramp.

While the paramedics attended to Malik and Markov, getting them ready for transporting to the hospital for treatment, young Sergeant Gomes, who appeared very self-assured and able, insisted that another paramedic crew examined

Moreno's head wound and checked that his wife had no ill effects from her time being held captive on 'Nijinsky'.

Gomes orchestrated a call with Comisario Gutiérrez; as a result, police officers were dispatched to Salenko's villa to arrest him and bring him back to the police station in Puerto Banús. Moreno and Brodie were taken to the police station to wait for him there.

Chapter 48

Brodie paced up and down Comisario Gutiérrez's office as the police officer asked questions about the events of the evening, with both Brodie and Comisario Moreno giving him almost monosyllabic answers as they had been instructed by Europol to give as little detail about the whole operation as possible. Gutiérrez was becoming more and more irritated by this lack of information; Brodie was relieved when the senior officer's phone rang.

"*Gutiérrez, dígame.*" The voice at the other end spoke for some time before Gutiérrez slammed the handset down on its cradle.

"He is not there. His wife says he has gone to London on a private flight from Malaga. She has been put under arrest and is being brought here."

"London? Why would he go to London?" Moreno asked.

"He has his main residence in London. It's where his wife normally lives when she is not out here.

Gutiérrez's phone rang, "Gutiérrez!" He was quiet for a minute before he ended the call and replaced the handset.

"That was my boss, he said Europol has been in contact

with him and has asked that we give you gentlemen every co-operation and leave you free to conduct your enquiries, as much of your operation is very sensitive."

"Thank you Comisario," Brodie replied, "I know that is not an easy thing for you to accept, so thank you for your understanding. I would like to talk to Señora Salenko when she gets here. I know her quite well from my time providing close protection for them, so she may talk to me."

"Very well, Señor Brodie. They are on their way now, so they should be here in about fifteen minutes. Allow another fifteen minutes to get her into custody, then we will take you down."

"OK, if you don't mind, Xavier, I'm going to nip across to my hotel and change out of these damp clothes. It's just round the corner so I shouldn't be long."

"Sure, Alan, please do. We will wait for you."

Brodie walked out of the police station and turned toward the apartment Malik had rented and jogged along the side streets and down on to the quay front to the entrance. He retrieved a key from the keysafe by the front door and ran up the stairs to the apartment. He went straight through to the bedroom, showered quickly, dressed in fresh clothes and made his way through to the kitchen. He felt into the back of one of the kitchen cabinets and found his and Malik's mobile phones in the plastic bag together with their keys where he had hidden them for safe keeping, choosing only to take cheap burner phones with them on board 'Nijinsky'. He picked up both phones, pocketed them and headed back to the police station.

He arrived at the front steps as Moreno and Gutiérrez were finishing their cigarettes under the front door canopy.

"Ah, well timed, Señor Brodie. We have just finished processing the detention of Señora Salenko, we can go down now and speak with her."

"Actually, Comisario, can we bring her up to one of the

offices upstairs? I want to speak to her in private and don't want the conversation recorded or overheard. One of the reasons I am here is that I can operate outside the normal framework of the investigation. I don't break the laws, Comisario, just bend them a little. If in doubt, talk to Europol. They will give consent."

Gutiérrez looked at Moreno, who nodded slightly in approval. Gutiérrez nodded in return and walked off to make arrangements.

"What are they charging Helena Salenko with, Xavier?"

"Conspiracy."

"Have they got a case, evidence?"

"No, I don't think so, but it is not my arrest."

"Call Comisario Hernandez. Tell him we might need immunity from prosecution for Helena, I don't have time to explain, but trust me on this."

"OK, I will call him."

"Don't let anyone know. Do it quietly, Xavier."

Gutiérrez reappeared at the top of the stairs.

"Señor Brodie, Señora Salenko is in the Sergeants' office. They are both out at the moment. I will show you."

"Thanks," Brodie followed the Comisario down the corridor to the office.

As Brodie stepped into the room, Helena Salenko stood. She was a beautiful woman in her mid-thirties, slim, athletic build with long fair hair tied back into a pony tail. She smiled warmly at Brodie as she held out her arms to him.

"Alan, darling!"

Brodie held up a hand to silence her and looked around the room. He then checked the corridor to make sure no one was listening from there, then shut the door.

He turned to Helena Salenko. "You look as beautiful as ever Helena," he walked across the room and kissed her lightly.

"Please, tell me Alexander has been arrested."

"Not yet, but it's just a matter of time. I take it you're still out of love with him?"

"I have been out of love with that monster for years. I have known what he does, where his money comes from for years, but he cheats on me and he hits me sometimes. You know he does. You've seen the bruises. He knew I wanted you, Alan, which is why he stopped contracting you."

"Helena, you and I were never on, I made that clear. I start messing around with clients' wives when I'm meant to be minding them and my business would go down the pan."

"But you wanted me, Alan, I know that." Helena stood and draped her arms around Brodie's neck. "You still do, I can tell."

"Now I'm not working for your husband and he is going to jail for a long time, once we find him," Brodie smiled down at her.

"Maybe he will be killed when you find him, that way I will be free."

"Free to do what, Helena?"

She reached up and kissed Brodie and he kissed her back.

"I know all of his business contacts, Alan, the ones on the yacht earlier and more. We could continue and make his business ours. I cannot do it without you and you could not succeed without me, but together, just think."

"Do you know where he is now?"

Yes, of course, he tells me everything. I am his wife and what he doesn't tell me, I hear anyway, I'm not stupid."

"Are you serious? You want Alexander dead so that you and I can take his business?"

"You know how I have always felt about you, you know I hate Alexander, but I like the life his business gives me. The house in London, villas in the Caribbean and here in Puerto Banús, fast cars, jewellery and big bank accounts, getting bigger all the time. All that can be ours, Alan, yours and mine."

"OK, so if I kill Alexander, you know his drugs contacts and other business associates, and we just carry on without him?"

"I already run most of his drugs business. He is just a figure-head because it looks better for a man to run this business. If you can get me out of here and back to the villa, I will show you."

"OK, let me see what I can do, it may not be easy." Brodie made for the door," Are you sure about this?"

"Yes, Alan, of course I am."

Brodie closed the office door behind him and walked along to the Comisario's office, where Moreno sat with a cup of coffee.

"What does she say?"

"Singing like a bird Xavier, but she needs to see that she can trust me. How did you get on with immunity from prosecution?"

"No need. They have no real evidence or basis for prosecution, so she will probably be released after questioning."

"Right, I'll take her back up to the villa, now. Can you clear that with Gutiérrez, I've got an idea."

Chapter 49

By the time Brodie outlined his plan to Moreno, Gutiérrez had cleared the paperwork, made arrangements for Helena Salenko's release and organised transport for them. It was well after midnight when they arrived at Salenko's villa, set high on the hillside to the north of Puerto Banús,.

As the police car disappeared down the drive and turned onto the Puerto Banús, road, Helena Salenko closed the front door and made her way back to the lounge where Brodie was waiting. She walked up to him, pulled him to her and kissed him; she started to unbutton his shirt.

"Sorry, Helena, there are things we need to do first. We've got the rest of our lives for that, but first we need to attend to Alexander before we lose him. Where is he now?"

"He is on his way to the house in Holland Park, London. He got a private flight from Malaga around nine o'clock this evening. When he left 'Nijinsky' he went straight to the airport by helicopter. He knew you were working with the police and wanted to get away from the area as quickly as possible, to create an alibi."

"Really, does he know what happened on 'Nijinsky' after he left?"

"What do you mean, what happened on 'Nijinsky'?"

"Nothing, it's not important."

"Alright, Alan, pour us a drink, I'm going to have a quick shower, I smell of police stations."

She left the room and padded bare foot to the master bedroom and started the shower running. Brodie could hear her moving around as he walked across the lounge to pour two drinks for them. He picked up his drink and wandered round the room looking for anything that might be useful. Eventually, he came to a door and opened it to find a moderate sized office with a wide desk and a dark brown padded chair, surrounded by shelves and storage units. He checked the few papers which were lying on the desk, looked under wall mounted paintings, photographs and plaques in a search for a safe. He found what he was looking for under an aerial photograph of Puerto Banús,.

As he looked at the dial on the front of the safe, he heard a voice behind him, "You're going to need a combination if you want in there," Helena Salenko smiled at him as she stood in the doorway, dressed in a brightly coloured robe, her long fair hair hanging wet on her shoulders.

"Sorry, just being nosey."

"Let me," she said pushing past him.

Brodie stood back and let her pass, wandering round the far side of the desk as she spun the dials on the safe door

"Found what you're looking for, Brodie?" Helena Salenko's voice sounded harsh as Brodie looked up from the desk and stood looking into the barrel of a Beretta PX4 Storm handgun.

"You think I am stupid, Brodie? You think I would just let you kill my husband and take over his place in his business and in my bed? I just spoke to Alex and he told me you blew up

'*Nijinsky*' and killed all these people he did business with and when I ask you about it... oh, it's nothing."

"What makes you think you can believe him about '*Nijinsky*' what if I were to say that it was him, not me?"

"Because I run his drugs business Brodie, I know his business better than he does. Why would he want to kill his network of clients and one of his main suppliers? Why would he do that?"

"Maybe he wanted to take over their businesses."

"Maybe I am not as stupid as you think I am, Señor Brodie."

"Well in that case, why did you let me record our conversation at the police station on a mobile phone and email it to Comisario Moreno? Why did you let me have police officers come up here before we did? So that they could hear what you had to admit to? Tell me how clever you are now, Helena. You've just talked yourself into a prison cell for quite a long time. Kill me and all you'll succeed in doing is extending that to life, so the question is, are you that stupid?"

"He's right," the voice from the doorway said.

Salenko swung her Beretta round in the direction of the voice, but Sergeant Malik hit her with two shots before she had the chance to fire at her. Salenko screamed, fell backwards and slid down the wall, grimacing in pain, blood flowing from two wounds in her leg.

"I knew you wouldn't let me down, Malik," Brodie smiled across at the police officer.

"Oh, you did, did you? The last you knew, I was in a hospital bed."

"Yeah, how did that go?

"Try to sound as if you give a shit, Brodie."

"Oh, I do Anita, believe me, I do."

Malik was quiet for a second. "Manolo, call this in and get some medical attention for Señora Salenko, before she bleeds out and saves us the trouble of a court case."

Just then Xavier Moreno stepped into the room and quickly surveyed the situation.

"Señor Brodie, Alan, please stop putting your life in danger, like that. One day you will run out of luck and I do not want to have the task of explaining to my superiors, why I let it happen. If you will not stop for you, please stop for me."

"She was never going to kill me, Xavier. I know her too well. Anyway, Malik wouldn't have let her, would you, Malik?"

Malik humphed and walked through to the lounge.

Moreno smiled, "You do like the record feature on your mobile, Alan. That's twice you used it tonight. Between your recordings and what Malik heard when we got here, Helena Salenko has more than incriminated herself. We will have no problem in getting a conviction against her."

"That's good, but we still need to get Salenko. While he's on the loose, we still have the head of the snake, ready to bite. He won't take this lying down; Alexander will want revenge."

"I have no jurisdiction in London, Alan, if that's where he has gone. I can only let Europol know that he has gone there."

"I'm not sure how much sway Europol has in the UK either, now that Britain isn't part of the EU. Having said that, I'm not a policeman, I don't need anyone's permission to go to London and I have a few strings I can pull. The sooner we finish this off the better, Alexander Salenko has the wherewithal to drop off the radar, so we can't let him do that. We need to act quickly."

"Alan, I am sorry. I cannot sanction you going to London to pursue Salenko."

"With all due respect, I don't need your permission to go anywhere. Anyway, who said I was going to London? I've got a bar to run."

"With all due respect, Alan, I don't believe a word of that."

"With all due respect, you're becoming Anglicised, my friend."

Brodie laughed and wagged his finger at Moreno, who smiled and shook his head.

"Seriously though, I need to crack on and you should get to the hospital with Helena Salenko, make sure she doesn't slip through the net. Can I have one of your guys drop me back to the hotel in Puerto Banús, to pick up my car?"

"Sure, no problem. We can talk back in Mojácar."

Brodie waited till Moreno had gone, then looked around Salenko's villa, but found nothing of interest. He went into the study and found Malik sitting in Salenko's chair, behind his desk.

"So you're off to London to get Salenko."

"You may say that, but I couldn't possibly comment."

"I'm coming with you."

"No, you're not. You have no jurisdiction over there."

"I will not be coming as a Spanish police officer, I will take leave and come as a private citizen. There are things you do not know about me, Alan. I will not come as a Police officer."

"There is very little I don't know about you Malik, but this is not the time or place to discuss that. Now, I need a lift to pick up my car. Your Comisario said that was OK."

"Alan...."

"No, Malik. Just a just a lift into town. Our job is finished here."

"Very well, if that is what you want, follow me."

Malik pushed off the chair and strode angrily out of the room.

Brodie followed.

She walked out to a waiting police vehicle, held the rear door open for Brodie before she slammed it closed and climbed into the front passenger seat instructing the driver to take them to the hotel where Brodie had left his car. They drove in silence to Puerto Banús,, Brodie sitting pensively in the back, considering his options. The police driver asked Malik a couple of questions but he was ignored so he gave up on conversation.

As they arrived outside the hotel, Brodie tried to speak but Malik pre-empted him.

"Goodbye, Señor Brodie, I wish I could say it was a pleasure."

Chapter 50

BRODIE DROVE THE MUSTANG HARD AS HE SPED UP THE AP-7 *Autopista de Mediterráneo* towards Puerto Ricos. It was a 365km drive and would take approximately four hours, plenty of time for him to gather his thoughts and plan his next move. Conscious that he could not be in two places at once, Brodie eventually decided that he needed help in locating and following Salenko. Engaging his phone via the Mustang's Bluetooth, he found the number he wanted and pressed the call button.

The phone at the other end rang for a lengthy time before a sleepy sounding Rob MacLaine, CEO of Harper MacLaine Security and an old Special Forces colleague of Brodie's, answered.

"This better be good, Brodie. You do know its half past three in the morning?"

"Sorry mate, I hadn't thought, sorry, but I need some help."

Brodie summarised the events of the past few weeks to his old friend, who listened quietly, then asked a number of questions to clarify the situation. They discussed the options and MacLaine agreed to afford Brodie the help he would need to execute a plan they had put together. MacLaine agreed to pick Brodie up at Gatwick.

Brodie parked up in his underground parking spot, feeling better that he now had a definite plan in place with Rob MacLaine. He had also booked a flight from Almeria to London Gatwick. He walked round to the apartment ran up the stairs, heading straight through to his bedroom. After taking a quick shower and stepping into fresh clothes, Brodie packed a small overnight bag, returned to the Mustang and headed for Almeria airport and the 10.40 flight to Gatwick.

Brodie arrived at Almeria International with time to spare. Having realised on the drive there that he had not eaten since the previous day, he head for the airside café, ate some breakfast, and drank some good strong coffee. As the flight was called, he made his way to the aircraft with the other passengers, texting his friend to let him know the flight was leaving on time.

By lunchtime, Brodie was striding purposely through Gatwick Airport, his backpack slung over one shoulder, through passport control, customs and from there to the arrivals hall, where he saw the tall figure of Rob MacLaine waiting by the barrier.

The two men greeted each other with the enthusiastic affection of old friends.

"Looks like married life is suiting you, Lieutenant MacLaine."

"Hey there, Captain Brodie. Great to see you. Sounds like you've got some problems."

"Just one, Alexander Salenko, and I'm here to do something about that."

Brodie filled in his friend with some more details on the recent events as they strode out to the car park and into Rob's black BMW.

"OK, let me bring you up to speed with this end. You

remember Ryan Hughes and Tom Johnson, yeah? Well, Tom's been learning all about drones, along with a couple of others, me included, and these two have got eyes on Comrade Salenko as we speak. Tom driving and Ryan piloting. I checked in with them when your flight landed and Salenko is at home, right now. He arrived back in Holland Park with a couple of heavies, about 7 o'clock this morning and hasn't moved since. As far as we can see, there are only the three of them in the house. I've told Tom to update us if there are any signs of them leaving. One of the minders smokes and comes out for a cigarette pretty regularly, but other than that, nothing other than a guy on a scooter delivering a takeaway about an hour ago. How do you want to play this?"

"I want to move on him as quickly as possible, I don't want him disappearing off to Russia. I want to take him out tonight if I can and I don't want your guys involved for any more than surveillance. I don't want a dead Russian oligarch landing on your doorstep."

"Well, actually, I got a call from my friendly neighbourhood Deputy Director at NCA, who said he was up to speed with this through a back door into Europol, to which he still has a key. Tony knows what you've been cleared to do and said he'll handle any clear up that's needed. I think he just thought, you, Salenko, London, me, two and two, all added up. He's a bright guy is Tony. What I'm saying is that there won't be any dead Russians floating around to land on doorsteps, so we're good to go."

"Good old Tony Urquhart. OK, let's figure out how we do this."

"I've booked you in at the Holland Park Mews. It's far enough away from Salenko's house but close enough to allow us to use a drone if we want and it's a pretty decent hotel."

"Thanks, Rob, but this is personal. It needs to be done face to face. I know the security system in that house, I designed it and I left a wee corridor in the garden where the cameras can't see, so I can get into the grounds. I just need to figure how to get access to the house itself."

Chapter 51

THE EXECUTIVE ROOM WHICH ROB MACLAINE HAD BOOKED IN the Holland Park Mews Hotel was large and comfortable. Rob opened his laptop on the round table and logged into the feed from the drone's camera as Brodie ordered a selection of room service food for them both.

A half an hour later, as Rob was perusing the recorded feed, the door buzzer sounded and a voice announced the arrival of the food.

"Food, Rob, lets grab it while it's hot," Brodie suggested as he sat the tray of food on the same table and poured two mugs of coffee.

Rob looked up, "Sorry, Al, that's it logged in. Oh, this looks good."

Rob swung the laptop round so that they could both see the screen and as he hit the play button, the recorded feed from the drone sprang to life.

"The camera has a motion sensor on it. It'll only record when it picks up movement, otherwise we would get hours of recording, showing us nothing and taking up memory on the system."

The feed started as one of Salenko's minders arrived and let himself into the house. The clock display in the bottom corner of the screen showed Salenko and his other minder entering the house nine minutes later.

"Not taking any chances, is he, getting his man to check the house before he enters," Rob observed.

The clock on the screen skipped an hour, as the feed showed one of the big men come out onto the front path. The drone recorded him as he stood beside the door and smoked a cigarette, then flicked the still glowing end into the garden. He stepped back into the house and within seconds, the recording stopped. Forty minutes later, a pizza delivery arrived, then nothing for almost an hour. Eventually the same man came out again to smoke another cigarette. This was repeated approximately every forty to forty-five minutes. The man would come out, stand on the front path near the door, smoke his cigarette, flick the end into the garden, stroll back into the house.

Brodie stopped, then rewound the recording, watched the man smoke his cigarette, then paused the feed.

"Look, see that. "Brodie pointed at the front door of the house as the man smoked. "He's not shut the door. He is standing there, smoking his cigarette.... and left the door open, the lazy sod. That's my way into the house."

"Well spotted. You're right."

Over the next few hours, the two men sat in Brodie's hotel room, put together a plan to get Brodie into the house undetected to do what needed to be done.

"OK, that all sounds good. Did you manage to bring me what I asked for?"

"I've brought a Glock, with a suppressor, a black tracksuit, with matching balaclava, and a couple of pairs of black nitrile gloves."

"Everything the fashion conscious assassin needs, especially the matching balaclava."

"Courtesy of Tom Johnson. Says he never goes out without one in his inside pocket."

"Why not? You never know when you might need a matching balaclava."

"Indeed."

"Changing the subject, I want to get a late flight tonight to Madrid from Heathrow, so I'll book that now. Can your guys drop me out to Heathrow later?"

"Sure, I'll take you out on my way home."

Brodie spent the next half hour on his phone, booking a British Airways flight to Madrid later that night together with an overnight hotel at Madrid airport. His passport and credit card were both in the name of Greg Palmer; payment for both went through without a hitch.

Darkness had set in by the time Brodie was finished on the phone and the two men headed down to the car park to collect Rob's car. By this time, Brodie had slipped the oversized black tracksuit over his jeans and cotton jacket. They drove the short distance to where Tom Johnson and Ryan Hughes had parked, two streets away from Salenko's house.

Brodie collected his matching balaclava from Johnson, and he and Rob brought the two men up to speed with the plan for the evening.

"I want to move early, guys, just in case Salenko decides to go out, which I doubt. Also I'm booked on a flight back to Spain tonight."

"OK, Al, no problem. Just tell us what you need and we'll go for it," Johnson replied,

"Showtime folks," Rob announced and slid out of the car. "Once you guys see the action completed, you hightail it out of here, Rob will take me on from here."

Brodie walked away, heading for Salenko's impressive house, an extensive, detached, beige painted property, set in large gardens and surrounded by two and a half metre high walls. The timber gates had a video call system to alert the occupants of any visitors.

Brodie deliberately walked in the opposite direction to avoid passing the camera at the gate, knowing that all of the other cameras pointed inwards, covering the gardens. Brodie knew the positioning of these cameras and sensors in the gardens and was about to access the gardens, knowing that there was a deliberate blind spot in one dark corner of the grounds. He looked at his watch. It was nearing the time when the big minder would most likely come out for a smoke.

Brodie pulled his balaclava over his head and scrambled over the wall, dropping noiselessly to the ground. He crouched in the bushes and waited a few minutes to see if anyone appeared or seemed aware of his presence. All looked clear. He made his way to the corner of the big house, ensuring that he remained unseen.

He reached the corner of the house, and waited for the man to come out for his nicotine top-up. Twelve minutes later, the front door opened, Brodie pulled the silenced Glock out of his waistband. He waited for the man to light his cigarette before moving away from the cover of the bushes. Suddenly, from the opposite end of the property, a firework fizzed into the sky, then burst into a blaze of glittering snow. The smoker turned to watch it, unaware of Brodie's approach.

Probably sensing rather that seeing movement behind him, he turned back to see Brodie, with the Glock pointed at his head. His hand moved to a leather underarm holster as Brodie pulled the trigger; the soft pop of the supressed Glock sent two bullets into the man's face. Brodie stepped forward to catch his victim, lowering him quietly to the ground to prevent the thud of his falling body alerting someone in the house. As he did so, a buzzer sounded from inside the house, which Brodie recognised as being from the front gate entry system.

"Mikhail?" Salenko's voice floated out to where Brodie

stood. "Mikhail, that will be our food. Ivan, go and see if that lazy bastard, is answering the gate. He is certainly not answering me.

"Sir, I am checking."

The second of Salenko's minders stepped out on to the path and looked around for Mikhail. He saw only Brodie, who without waiting for him to shout an alarm to Salenko, shot two silenced bullets into the man's upper left chest. Two large red areas of blood bloomed on his shirt as he fell to the ground. Brodie stepped over him into the house, closing the door behind him.

"Ivan, what is going on out there, where is my food, where...." Salenko stepped into the hall looking towards the closed front door, where Brodie stood, Glock in hand.

"Hello, Alexander. Long time no see. You and I have unfinished business."

"What do you want? You are being filmed. There are cameras everywhere."

"I know all about these cameras, Alexander, you may remember, I had them installed. I also know how to switch them off and wipe the memory. I hope you haven't paid for that food, by the way, 'cause you're not going to eat it."

"Hah, you will not kill me Brodie. You would not shoot an unarmed man. You are too much of the English gentleman."

Salenko raised his arms and walked slowly toward Brodie. "If you are going to shoot me Brodie, maybe you should do it before my two companions come in."

"Oh dear, that's two things you've got wrong. Firstly, the fact is that your two pals are sadly no longer in this world, and I'm not an English gentleman, I'm a Scottish gentleman and Scottish gentlemen, given the right circumstances, will shoot an unarmed man.

Brodie stepped forward and placed the suppressed Glock against Salenko's forehead.

"Goodnight, Alexander," Brodie slowly increased the pressure on the trigger and again the Glock coughed quietly.

Brodie wiped the security system memory then switched off the system, including the cameras. He pulled the bodies of both heavies into the hall, out of sight and laid them beside Salenko. He closed the front door, retraced his steps to the area where he had entered the grounds, checked that no one was around. He dropped to the ground, pulling off the balaclava as he went. Rob had parked close to the house and Brodie sat beside him as he pulled away from the kerb. He stripped off the tracksuit and gloves and put them into a plastic carrier bag along with the balaclava.

"Dump these on the back seat. I'll get rid of them later." Rob suggested as he headed for the A4 en route to Heathrow.

"Cheers, mate. Thanks for doing this, I owe you big time."

"Don't worry, it's all noted. Everything went as planned, almost. I was watching on Ryan's drone footage. The takeaway delivery could have really screwed things up but as it happened, it actually helped. I take it Salenko is now a former Russian citizen."

"Yep, gone to that great vodka bar in the sky. With him dead and his wife in prison, we've taken out the heads of the drug network and with the other major players all going up in that explosion on the yacht, the whole network has pretty much gone. Salenko's suppliers and his main dealers have all been taken out. That was what Europol wanted, unofficially, obviously."

"So, it's back to running El Puerto now, is it?"

"I've got a couple of loose ends to tie up but other than that, yeah, back to cold beers and hot snacks."

"I've got a contract coming up in September that might interest you if you want a break from the bar. Couple of weeks here in the UK babysitting a group of high level Americans on a military equipment based trade mission.... some of it pretty hush, hush."

"Yeah, sounds like a walk in the park. Keep me in mind."

"Will do."

The A4 and M4 had only light traffic at that time of night, so half an hour later, Brodie was making his way to the check-in desk for his flight to Madrid.

Chapter 52

BRODIE WOKE EARLY THE NEXT MORNING, ROSE, SHOWERED, dressed, and went down for breakfast. He ate heartily, having not eaten the previous night. He sat for a few minutes contemplating the recent events and thinking out his next moves.

After a while, he went back up to his room picked up his phone and dialled a familiar number. It was answered after three rings.

"Morning Xavier, I am in Madrid and I want to talk to Malik. We sort of fell out the other day and I want to apologise to her. Do you have her address?"

"Yes and she is at home, we have just spoken. I will text you her address, but please do not tell anyone. I would get into trouble!"

"Yes, I understand, thanks."

"No problem, good luck." Moreno ended the call.

Brodie packed his rucksack, pocketed his phone, and made his way down to the taxi rank at the front of the hotel, dropping his room key into a box at reception. He gave the taxi driver the address Moreno had given him and sat back for the thirty minute journey.

Brodie stepped out of the taxi and looked up at the block of apartments, checked the address with the message Moreno had sent him. Satisfied he was in the right place, he crossed the road and climbed the steps to the front door. There was a door entry security system, but no video facility, which was a plus for Brodie. He pressed a few buttons and eventually got a reply from one.

"Excuse me, I have a parcel for number forty one and there is no reply," Brodie managed in his best Spanish, having practiced that statement on his way over in the taxi.

The door buzzed open and Brodie pushed into the hall. The apartment he was looking for was on the top floor. The lift rose quickly and quietly, the doors sliding open noiselessly as Brodie stepped out onto the landing. He followed the numbers on the doors till he reached the corner apartment. He hesitated slightly before pressing the doorbell. He waited nervously, not knowing what response he would get from the occupant. Finally the door opened.

"Brodie!" Malik stood, wearing a white towelling robe, a white towel wrapped round her head.

"Hello, Sara. I think we need to talk."

"Sara! What... how...?"

"Did I know? Long story. We can talk about it out here if you want. We can discuss it inside, or I can just go away, seeing as I wasn't your best friend when you dumped me off in Puerto Banús."

Malik stared at him for a moment, obviously shocked by Brodie's greeting, then finally she stood back from the doorway and gestured for Brodie to enter.

"How did you know where to find me?"

"I asked the right people. You weren't too difficult to find, Sara."

"Why are you calling me Sara?"

"Because you're Sara Malik, younger twin sister of Anita

Malik, who was sadly killed in Algeciras along with two of her colleagues."

Malik's hands went to her face as she dropped into an armchair.

She gestured to the settee opposite. "Please sit down," she added gathering herself, "Would you like a coffee? You're right, we do need to talk."

"Coffee would be good."

Malik brewed two mugs of coffee, placing them on a low table which sat between the settee and her chair.

"How did you guess?"

"I didn't guess. I made it my business to find out. I was about to trust you, potentially, with my life. I wasn't prepared to put that kind of trust in someone I knew nothing about. I have a friend in the UK who I met when we were in Special Forces and we both served under a commanding officer who is now very senior in the NCA.... National Crime Agency. This guy still has good contacts and relationships with Europol. We asked him to make some discrete enquiries about Anita Malik. He was sent a file, which outlined her career in the Spanish police and her undercover work with Europol, fighting drugs cartels. This came from someone in Europol who is much more senior than Comisario Principal Alonzo in Madrid.

She showed as being a first class officer who got results, which is why she was chosen to be part of the operation to trap the cartel in Algeciras. The team were successful in breaking the cartel but sadly, as the file says, it cost Anita her life. I remembered that you had said you had a twin sister and it references you in Anita's file, so I asked for yours and bingo.... there you were. Part of a Special Operations Group of the Spanish Army, a commissioned officer with a record to match that of your sister.... and desperate to get justice for Anita, you approached Europol. They were able to tell my contact that Comisario Principal Alonzo had managed to slot you into the team in Almeria. Because you were identical twins and Anita's murder was never made public, they could pass you off to the team in Mojácar as Sergeant Anita Malik."

Brodie delved into his backpack and pulled out two large brown envelops. One had Anita Malik written on it, the other Sara Malik.

"It's all in there," Brodie pushed the two envelops across the table to Malik, who stared at them for a few seconds.

"You've known all this time and said nothing?"

"What would Moreno have done if he had found out?"

"Kicked me out, I dare say."

"Exactly and what would that have achieved? He'd have had to find a replacement to work with me and that would have taken time, which would have slowed the whole process down. Once we started that bull running, it was too late to stop it. We were committed and your file said that you were a competent and experienced officer, so why not?"

"Thank you, I needed to do that for Anita. Most of these people were not involved at Algeciras but they all came from the same mould. I could not bring my sister back, but I could carry on her work with this network of drug suppliers. There is only Salenko left to pay and he needs to be made to pay."

"Sara, he already has. Someone shot him dead in his house in London last night."

"No, it cannot be."

"Oh yes it can, believe me. I have irrefutable evidence."

"Evidence. What evidence is 'irrefutable', Brodie? Unless you were there and saw it with your own...." Malik stopped and stared at Brodie. "Oh my God! You shot Salenko. You knew where he lived. You killed him. Tell me I'm wrong."

"You may say that, I couldn't possibly comment."

"Can you tell me, categorically, that Alexander Salenko is dead?"

"Yes, Sara, he is dead."

Tears slowly tracked down Sara Malik's cheeks. She sobbed once and shook her head in disbelief, "Then it's over, Anita's death has been avenged.... the man who caused her death is now also dead." She wiped away her tears and took a sip of her coffee. She looked back at Brodie.

"What if someone investigates his shooting, sees what has happened in Puerto Banús, and sees that you were in London last night?"

"There is no record anywhere of Alan Brodie being in London last night. There is no record of me staying at the hotel at Madrid airport last night. Alan Brodie will not be on a flight from Madrid to Almeria today and I am a past master at avoiding cameras in public places." He delved once again into his backpack and retrieved a baseball cap and a pair of RayBans, which he put on.

"I've just beaten facial recognition software," he added and slipped the cap and glasses back into the bag.

"So where do we go from here, Alan?"

"I can only speak for myself but as far as I'm concerned, this operation is complete, I've had financial compensation from Europol for my efforts, which is an unexpected bonus, and I still have a bar to run in Puerto Ricos, which is what started all this off."

"You are going back today?"

"That was the plan, but it's not cast in stone. What happens with you now?"

"I will return to my unit, but I have resigned my commission giving three months' notice, which is only five weeks away. I have a few days leave right now so I'm just going to chill at home until I go back."

"Any plans for after you leave your group?"

"None yet, not definite anyway. I might look at the private sector for consultancy work. I don't know."

"Well, I wish you all the best in whatever you do. If you do want to look at the private sector, let me know. Send me your profile, I've got a load of contacts."

Brodie rose from the chair and picked up his bag.

"Well, looks like this is it, Sara."

"Is that what you want, Alan? To just pick up your bag and walk out of my life."

Brodie looked over at Malik and was taken aback when he saw tears in her eyes.

"What's the alternative?"

"Stay for a few days. I didn't think I would ever see you again and the way we parted in Puerto Banús,, I thought you would not want to see me ever again. Why don't you stay for a day or two and give us a chance to say goodbye properly?"

Malik crossed the room and put her hands on his shoulders. "Please?"

"If that's what you want, I'd love to stay for a few days."

Brodie wrapped his arms around her waist and pulled her to him as she raised her head and kissed him."

Brodie and Malik fell onto the settee and lost the next hour in lovemaking. As they lay in each other's arms, Brodie became conscious of Malik staring at him. He smiled at her.

"How could you trust me, make love to me the way you did, knowing that I was lying to you all that time... since I first met you, in fact? You knew I was living a lie, that I was not Anita."

"It's not a new situation for me. I've worked undercover in the military, worked with other people who were living under a false identity. Let me show you something."

Brodie went across to where his backpack lay on the floor, pulled his Greg Palmer passport out of a side pocket and tossed it over to Malik.

"I told you earlier that I hadn't been in London last night. I wasn't, Greg Palmer was."

Malik studied the passport for a short while, "Your Mr Palmer has been to some very interesting places."

She stood up and padded, naked across the tiled floor, handed the document back to Brodie and draped her arms round his neck. "Does that mean that I've just let a strange man make love to me?"

"Oh no, that was definitely Alan Brodie, and I can prove it."

He carried her through an open door to a bedroom, dropped her onto the unmade bed and they began once again to enjoy each other.

Later, Brodie looked down at a sleeping Sara Malik, her dark skin glistening with perspiration. Almost as if she was aware of his gaze on her, she opened her eyes and reached out to touch his face.

"So, it was not a dream. You really are here."

"No dream, but I could be your worst nightmare. How would Moreno react if he knew about your little deception?"

Malik sat up. "He would be very angry and could be responsible for a big problem on my military record, when I am just about to leave my commission. You will tell him?"

"I may need to, Sara. That's one of the reasons I came to see you. I wanted your permission to tell him. He trusts me and I did him one hell of a favour getting involved in all of this. I believe that he will eventually find out, which will make him even angrier. Plus, if he knew that I knew, it would not go down well for me, living in a town where a police Comisario has a grudge against me. He could make my life very difficult if he wanted to."

"I understand. Do you think he will listen to you?"

"He knows that I've seen some of the skeletons in his cupboard, he knows that I saw him turn a blind eye to some of the things we did in taking down that cartel, so yes, I think he will."

"If you are sure, then you are probably right, it is best that we make him aware before he finds out later. You will tell him?"

"Probably best."

"OK. You said that's one of the reasons you came to see me."

"Yeah, I was also looking for somewhere to grab a coffee. What did you put in it, by the way, whatever it was... can we have some more of it?"

Malik took a fierce swing at Brodie's head with a pillow, which he caught just before it made contact and they both laughed as they wrestled for it. Brodie eventually let go and Malik fell back onto the bed, the smile disappearing from her lips, a serious expression replacing it.

"I think I'm falling in love with you, Alan Brodie, I know I shouldn't be, but I am."

"Likewise Sara. That's why I came here, more than anything else. I just didn't think you would feel the same way, not after the way we left things in Puerto Banús. I wasn't even sure you'd let me in."

Malik laughed, "I had convinced myself that you were an arrogant, self-centred, selfish individual and that I hated you because of the way you treated me at Salenko's house, but the minute I opened the door and saw you standing there, I knew how I felt about you. I just didn't want to admit it to myself."

"You do know that complicates things?"

"I know. We would never work as a couple, Alan. We live different lives, want different things out of life"

"I know, but I don't want to lose you."

"Do you really mean that, Alan?"

"Yes, I do. Look why don't I stay in Madrid over the weekend and head back to Puerto Ricos on Monday? That gives us three days to figure out what we both want out of this and how to achieve it. You up for that?"

"Yes, of course. I just can't believe we're talking about this. I thought I had lost you and that isn't what I want either. We can still be special friends. Friends with benefits! You should stay with me, here in the apartment."

"OK, sounds good to me. I might want to pick up a few bits

and pieces, clothes, toiletries and so on. I wasn't planning on staying away from home for any more than one night."

"We can go shopping. There is a huge El Corte Inglés not far from here. We could go there."

"Does that mean we need to get dressed?"

"Yes, we cannot spend the rest of our lives, naked, Alan."

Malik jumped out of bed. "I'm going to shower. Do you want to join me?"

"Try stopping me."

Chapter 53

MALIK AND BRODIE SPENT THE WEEKEND SIGHTSEEING AS WELL AS shopping. Brodie had only been in Madrid once before, ironically, acting as close protection for Alexander Salenko, so Malik took great delight in acting as tour guide, taking Brodie round the high spots and highlights of Madrid.

In the apartment, they talked, cooked, ate, slept, made love and talked some more. By Monday morning they had agreed a way forward which suited them both and began to put arrangements into place to make it work. They mutually agreed that Brodie and Malik as a couple, living together, would be doomed to failure as they both wanted very different things out of life. Neither of them wished to walk away from the other or lose what they felt they had, a deep and special friendship and a love for each other.

They decided that Comisario Moreno needed to be told of Malik's deception before he found out from another source and made waves which would impact Malik's military record. They thought that it would be best if Malik travelled with Brodie to Puerto Ricos, but stayed in the background till Brodie had spoken to the Comisario to explain the very unusual circumstances.

Malik organised flights to Almeria which departed soon after lunchtime, and booked a taxi to take them to Madrid airport. While they waited for their flight, Brodie called Moreno and arranged to meet him at his beach house in Puerto Ricos later that afternoon. Brodie and Malik both travelled with cabin baggage only, allowing them, on arrival at Almeria to walk straight out of the terminal to the carpark, retrieve Brodie's Mustang, and head for Puerto Ricos ahead of their meeting with Moreno. The drive took an hour and the couple arrived at the beach house an hour and a half before they were due to meet Moreno.

Brodie made phone calls to let Miguel know that he was back in Puerto Ricos and to touch base with Rob MacLaine. He sent Malik upstairs out of sight, then settled down on the terrace with his laptop to catch up on email, a glass of his favourite Rioja on the table beside him. As the sun began to dip below the Sierra Cabrera mountains and the cicadas began their evening clicking and buzzing in the trees, Brodie became aware of someone stepping quietly onto the terrace to his left. He looked over as Xavier Moreno walked toward him.

"Xavier, good to see you," Brodie said offering his hand to Moreno, who took it readily.

"And you, Alan."

"How is your wife, Xavier?"

"She is much better now. Thankfully she was not injured or hurt physically, but she was much traumatised as you would imagine, but she is a strong woman. She will recover from the experience.

Brodie gestured to his bottle and the empty glass on the table, "Care to join me?"

"I am off duty for the day, so yes, why not."

Brodie poured a glass of wine for Moreno as the tall man sat down.

"Cheers."

"As you say, cheers," Moreno responded with a smile.

"You have been away, Alan?"

"Yeah, spent the weekend in Madrid, as you know, doing a bit of sightseeing."

"Not in London?"

"London? No, Madrid."

"Are you sure?"

"Check my passport, Xavier. You will see that I haven't been in London."

"Ha ha! You expect me to fall for that old one" Moreno laughed. "Of course your passport will not show a trip to London, at least not the one you would show to me, or immigration for that matter. Alan, I know you were in London but I cannot prove it. I know you shot and killed Alexander Salenko at his home, but I cannot prove that either. However, I am not a fool, so I will not waste my time trying to look for proof."

Brodie smiled at Moreno, "You're right, my friend, you're nobody's fool; on the contrary, you're a very astute and clever man who is also right about something else. Even if I did go to London, which I didn't and even if I did kill Salenko, which I couldn't have, because I wasn't in London, you would never prove it.

"Now, let's talk about Madrid, maybe we should move inside." Brodie suggested. He stood and picked up his laptop. "Can you bring the wine in, please?"

The two men moved into the house and sat down. Moreno placed the bottle of wine on a low table between them.

"This sounds serious, you haven't killed Anita Malik as well, have you?"

"Before I answer that, I want to tell you a few facts. Firstly, the woman we knew as Anita Malik, isn't Anita Malik. She's

Sara Malik, her twin sister, who belongs to a Special Forces Group in the Spanish military. Anita Malik was one of those killed by the drug cartel in Algeciras. As you can imagine, the family were devastated, Sara, with her military background, felt that she could do something to avenge her sister's murder and help to put the perpetrators where they belonged. To do just that, she convinced the powers that be that she should take her sister's place and her identity."

"Can I stop you there, Alan? I know this. Do you remember when Jose Ramirez and Diego Gonzales turned up and tried to kill her? There was some mix up when someone in Puerto Banús, was sent a copy of Malik's police file. Alfredo Suárez thought he had stopped it being sent, but apparently he hadn't. Salenko got a file that told him Malik had been killed in Algeciras. I only found out about it when I asked Suárez for a copy of what had been sent. I then checked with a senior contact I have in Europol and they confirmed that Europol had agreed to switch Sara Malik for Anita, but they were told to say nothing. By the time I received this information it was too late to stop the operation in Puerto Banús,. You were on Salenko's yacht, all of you, and he knew about Anita's murder in Algeciras. I'm sorry, I should have told you this before now, but when you said you were going to Madrid, I hoped that she would tell you herself and I am pleased that she did. I know how close you two had become."

"Well actually, she didn't tell me, I told her. It was one of the main reasons for going to see her. That and the fact, as you said, we had become extremely close."

"You knew? How, when....?"

"Pretty much from the beginning. I wasn't going to trust someone with my life, potentially, that I knew nothing about, so when you insisted that I work with Malik, I made it my business to find out exactly who Anita Malik was. I used sources of my own, to get to some very senior people in Europol, and eventually I got full dossiers on both Anita and Sara Malik. These told me Anita was dead and that I was dealing with Sara."

"Why did you not say? I would have pulled the operation if I had known."

"That's exactly why I said nothing, I knew how you would react and believe it or not, you would have had a much better chance of success with Sara than with Anita. Sara's background is much better suited to an operation like this and I felt totally safe working with her, much more so than I would have done with Anita."

"I must speak with Sara."

"Good 'cause she's upstairs."

"Sara?" Brodie called and the two men stood when they heard Malik's footsteps on the wooden staircase.

"Sara, I am so sorry. I feel that I have let you down. I almost got you killed." Moreno said as Sara Malik appeared at the bottom of the stairs.

"God's sake, Xavier, she was never going to come to any harm, she was with me. Have you no faith, man!" Brodie laughed as Malik approached Moreno.

"No, it's me who should apologise Comisario, I should have been honest with you from the start, but I was frightened that if you knew you would stop the operation and I would not get the chance to avenge my sister. I also knew that Alan would give us a better chance of success and we might not have another chance to get him on board."

"I would have pulled the operation, you're right. I have to say that you and Alan handled a very dangerous situation with great skill. I cannot find it in my heart to mourn for all the people on that yacht who were killed, they were bad people, but I would have had the blood of you or Alan on my hands for the rest of my life if I had been responsible for your deaths. We got a good result in the end, thanks to you both. Someone even went to London and killed Alexander Salenko, didn't they, Alan?"

Brodie smiled, "So I'm told, and I'm pleased to hear it."

"So what now for both of you?" Moreno asked.

"I've got El Puerto and even with a manager in place, I do need to spend some time there and I've got some other security work coming up in September, I believe, just waiting for details. Looking after an American senator and his party, be a walk in the park I'm told."

Moreno looked over at Malik, "And you, Sara?"

"My commission with the military finishes shortly so once that is over I will take some time to look at other opportunities, perhaps travel a little, maybe even a few weekends in Puerto Ricos, visiting friends." She smiled at both men.

Brodie looked over at Moreno, "What about Alexei Markov, or should I say, Yuri Kuznetsov? Have you seen anything of him in the past few days? Is he still in hospital?"

"No, I have heard nothing from him. As you will imagine, I have had much to do since Puerto Banús. The repercussions of the explosion and the deaths of so many people have had the media from all over Europe camping on our doorstep. My superiors have told me to deal with them, but give them as little detail as possible regarding the circumstances. This I have done, so I only know that Markov or Kuznetsov checked out of the hospital yesterday and had disappeared. Europol said today that he has asked for his payment to be made to a bank in Madrid and this has been done. He is now a richer man that he was yesterday."

"Sadly Alan, much as your wine is delicious, I must go and check up on my wife, find out if she is speaking to me again after her ordeal. Sara, in case I don't see you again, I hope you have closure after Anita's death. I know you will never stop grieving for her but at least now you know that those who did that to her are themselves dead, and I am sure she would want you to find happiness in your life again. Maybe this man can help you to do that."

Moreno patted Brodie's shoulder as he moved to embrace Malik.

"I am sure he will," Malik replied over Moreno's shoulder. "We will remain good friends, that I do know. I am going back to Madrid tomorrow to see my parents, but we will keep in touch. Friendship is not easy to find in this life. We will not lose each other."

Malik and Brodie stood on the terrace, his arm round her shoulder and hers around his waist, watching as Moreno got into his car and drove off.

Chapter 54

BEFORE THEY RETIRED FOR THE NIGHT, BRODIE AND MALIK enjoyed a few more glasses of wine sitting out on the terrace, their arms around each other, feet dangling into the cool water of Brodie's swimming pool, listening to the rhythmic, almost hypnotic lapping of the sea as the waves broke onto the beach. They talked about Moreno and his response to their meeting. They went over some of the detail of the operation to bring down the cartel, and talked about the future and what it held for them both.

Much of their conversation was a repeat of the discussion they had in Madrid, although a little more thought out. Just before they went to bed, Sara talked about Anita. They had been inseparable as children, with an almost telepathic under-standing between them. Their relationship had become arms-length at times because of their separate careers but the close bond between never altered. Sara had been devastated by the news of Anita's death and vowed to seek vengeance on the perpetrators.

As Sara spoke, she laughed as she reminisced about their childhood antics and teenage escapades. She cried when talking about Anita's murder and the fact that she was gone and they would never see each other again, never laugh together.

Brodie held her close as she talked, her arms around his waist, until they eventually made their way inside. It was the first night they had slept in the beach house and they made love long into the early hours of the morning, waking early, rising late, enjoying each other while they could.

They showered, dressed and walked up to El Puerto for breakfast, as Malik had wanted to say goodbye to the staff she had worked with and got to know. After breakfast, Brodie put Malik's bag into the boot of the Mustang and waited till she had finished her goodbyes.

They drove down to Almeria airport, a journey of some forty minutes, speaking little on the way and arriving in good time for Malik to check in and head for the gate to board her flight to Madrid.

As she turned to Brodie at security, she held out the keys to his apartment above the bar.

"I better give you these."

"Why? I had hoped you would need them again. These are for the beach house, by the way, I swapped them this morning while you were in the shower"

"I wasn't sure if you were serious about seeing me again. It's easy to say, harder to mean."

"I didn't ever take you as the insecure kind, Sara." Brodie smiled," Let's just say that these keys are a token of my commitment to you.... to our friendship."

"Thank you. I accept them in the spirit in which they are given. I will unlock your door with them again, but I will call you first, just to be sure you are not busy. I must go now or I will miss my flight."

They hugged and kissed while other passengers squeezed past them.

"I love you, my most special friend," Malik whispered in his ear.

"Love you too, Sara. This isn't a goodbye, it's a, see you soon."

"OK, see you soon. I must go, Alan."

Brodie watched as her bag passed through security and waved as she walked slowly out of sight.

"See you soon, my special friend," he murmured as she disappeared.

Acknowledgments

I hope you have enjoyed Malik's Revenge. Thank you for taking the time to read it.

As with my previous books, the finished article has not just been the fruit of my labour. Both my good friend Diana and my wife Val have put a great deal of time and effort into ironing out the many wrinkles in my writing, making the book a much easier and hopefully a more enjoyable read for you. Your patience and support are, once again, very much appreciated, ladies.

The Almeria region of Spain, in particular the area around Villaricos and Mojácar, holds happy memories for me and I hope I have done it justice. Times I spent there with my friends Colin and Anne, who were good friends when I needed their friendship most, will always be special to me

I have enjoyed writing Malik's Revenge and trust that you enjoyed reading it. If you have, please leave a short review on Amazon; in this very competitive market, good reviews sell books.

Thank you.

The Prodigal Son
Rob MacLaine Book 1

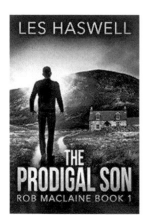

Rob MacLaine, a seasoned, battle hardened ex Special Forces operative, has just met Justine Fellows, the woman of his dreams. Then, in the middle of the night, a mysterious phone call from his past, changes his future for ever and puts his newly formed relationship with Justine in jeopardy. He is summoned back to his family home on the island of Achravie, off the west coast of Scotland.

Rob has had no contact with Achravie, or his family, since his elder brother schemed to blame him for a car accident which killed a young friend. Sent away by his father at the tender age of eighteen, Rob joined the military and progressed through various war zones, first as a regular soldier and later as a member of an elite group of Special Forces operatives.

Now Rob is back on Achravie, unrecognisable as the innocent young lad, banished by his father over twenty years earlier, back to face his past and encounter friends and enemies alike in an explosive reunion with his elder brother and his "security" people.

The explosion of violence on Achravie drives a wedge

between Rob and Justine, which Rob's friends and colleagues conspire to remove, bringing the unhappy couple back together again. With the death of his brother, Rob falls heir to the family estate and the reunited lovers put together a project to re-develop Achravie and create a profitable business on the estate.

The Good Samaritan
Rob MacLaine Book 2

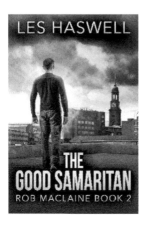

The follow-up novel, 'The Good Samaritan' - Rob MacLaine Book 2', links to the storyline of 'The Prodigal Son', but has a standalone scenario. It follows Rob and his colleagues as they are introduced to new technology and advanced surveillance techniques afforded by the use of drones, which they first use to thwart an attempt to kidnap an American Senator.

When Rob's wife asks him to help a friend to trace her sister, he agrees to help, little knowing, that this simple request would see him once again steeped in the dark world of people trafficking and modern day slavery, which he had so recently encountered on his island home of Achravie.*

Helped by his co-director, Joe Harper and Ryan Hughes, a wheelchair bound veteran of the war in Afghanistan and computer hotshot with a passion for drones, Rob goes looking for the missing girl.

Having found the last known whereabouts of the missing Magda Petric in Hamburg, the Harper MacLean team use past experiences and their new found skills in the deployment of drones to work with the National Crime Agency and Europol to track down the gang of people traffickers who appear to have taken the young woman.

The team discover links from Magda to a Europol team investigating the people traffickers as the trail leads them back to the UK, where they are joined by another ex-Special Forces colleague, Alan Brodie. Rob and his colleagues intercept the perpetrators and their cargo of trafficked girls. But the criminal gang has discovered that Magda was working with Europol and set out to take their revenge on her, triggering fast and decisive action from Rob and his colleagues who deploy the new drone based weapon to cut the head off the serpent, once and for all.

About the Author

 Les Haswell was born in Glasgow and spent his early years in Ayrshire, in South-West Scotland. Having been educated there and served an engineering apprenticeship he embarking on a world tour of Scotland, living in Ayrshire, Perthshire, Morayshire, Aberdeenshire and Stirlingshire, before ending up in Aberdeen.

Working in the offshore oil & gas industry for much of his business life, Les has travelled the world and visited places as culturally diverse as Latin America and USA, West & East Africa, the Middle & Far East.

Les now lives with his wife in Winchester in Hampshire.

———

To learn more about Les Haswell and discover more Next Chapter authors, visit our website at www.nextchapter.pub.

Printed by Amazon Italia Logistica S.r.l.
Torrazza Piemonte (TO), Italy

55748080R00165